CRAVE

THE SHADOW BRED SERIES
BOOK 4

GRACE MCGINTY

ALSO BY GRACE MCGINTY

CRAVE

For my mother, who reads all my books and is so damn supportive.
Thank you. I love you so much!
(But please don't read between pages 178-190)

PROLOGUE

SUSANNAH

Ten years ago

My breathing sounded too loud in the darkness. I was running as fast as I could in my half-form, my eyesight good enough that I didn't trip and fall over the forest debris, but not as good as it would be if I went full Beast. Quinn's hand was wrapped tightly in mine as I tugged him along, our backpacks slapping against our spines in rhythmic thuds. They were loaded down with everything we'd need. We just had to get to town before anyone worked out we were gone.

Then we could disappear.

"Susannah, we should go back," Quinn gasped, out of breath. "If your dad finds out, he'll kick your ass. If my dad finds out..." His words trailed off, but the fear in his words hung in the silence.

I stopped, my sneakers catching on a stick. My shoes were too small; I was outgrowing them too quickly for my father to keep up. If he cared to keep up, anyway. I turned, dragging Quinn closer to me. He'd had a growth spurt last year when we'd turned fifteen, leaving me nearly a foot shorter. He loved finally being able to look down at me, because I'd had an inch or two in height on him since we were three.

We'd been perfectly on par, until yesterday. Just two Betas, ignored, allowed to run wild in our childhood. Sure, there'd be problems when we turned eighteen, because Quinn's mom was a bitch. But that wasn't supposed to be a problem for another two years. We had time.

Until we didn't. Everything had changed. Time had run out.

Not letting go of his hand, I gave him my best bitch stare. It was an art I'd perfected long ago. "I don't care what your dad will do, Quinn. I can't—no, I *won't* let you go. You're mine. You're not his. Not fucking Wilkie's, no matter what your mom promised that creepy old fuck. And now... after this?" I waved a hand at his body. "You know what Wilkie will do. We can't let that happen. You don't want that, and I don't want that for you. There's a way; I know there is. We just have to get out of here. Out of Maxton. Out of fucking Montana."

Turning on my heel, I started to walk toward the lights of the town closest to Maxton, dragging Quinn along behind me. I should've known this would happen—the clues were all there. I moved faster until we were running again. There was a bus that passed through at four a.m. and I wanted to be on it. It was a long run from Maxton to town, which was how we liked it. Out of sight was truly out of mind for most humans, and we'd managed to slip under their radar for a long-ass time.

But I knew the end of our anonymity was coming. How could it not when they had computers and video cameras and satellites? No one wanted to hear about that, though. Fuck them. Let them get caught with their pants down. Quinn and me, we'd go out into the world and never come back to this shithole town.

I briefly felt bad leaving Raiden behind, but he'd be okay. He'd presented as an Omega right on schedule, though without Mom around, Dad was just raising him to be another Alpha replica of himself. That was his default. Train us hard, and we'd be too tired to get into trouble. Didn't really work for me, but whatever.

Finally, we were in the woods outside of Ol' Sam's Bar and Grill, a divey drinking establishment on the outskirts of the nearby town. We shifted back to our human form, and Quinn held me against his chest protectively, as if I didn't have a gun in my backpack and could shoot a man in the clavicle from twenty feet away. It wasn't my weapon of choice, but you couldn't fit a compound bow in your backpack next to your Doc Martens.

Quinn was still looking over his shoulder, like he expected six Legion soldiers to appear behind us at any moment to drag us home. It was possible, I guess.

A guy in a long, black coat stumbled out of the bar. He wasn't very old—probably the age of my oldest brother, Austin—but this guy was kinda hot with thick, black hair and scruffy stubble. He lifted his keys and unlocked a truck beside us.

This was our chance, and we had to take it. Dragging Quinn back into the shadows, I watched as the guy fumbled with the door, then climbed in. Moving quickly, I unlatched the tailgate while he was still trying to get his keys into the ignition. I pushed Quinn gently into the bed of the pickup, climbing in after him just as the truck lurched forward.

Quinn pulled me fully into the back and curled his body around mine. "What the fuck are we going to do if this guy lives in the woods? Or if he's some kind of crazy ax murderer?"

I rolled my eyes at him. "We're Manix. We're the original crazy ax murderers. But, you know, without the axes. We can take a human if we have to," I whispered back, ignoring his wide-eyed expression. I picked up his hand and pressed it to my cheek. "It won't come to that. He might just live on the city limits, then we can get out without leaving a trail for anyone to follow, and get the bus away from here. Maybe we'll head south. Or go to California. Wouldn't you like to see the beach?" I knew he would. I knew everything there was to know about Quinn, except the one thing that would fuck up our world forever.

Quinn fell silent, but pulled me closer. The guy in the truck cranked up the music and started singing "Y.M.C.A." by The Village People, complete with hand actions, as the car swerved from side to side on the near-empty early morning roads. Shit, maybe I should've chosen a different drunk human.

He didn't stop or slow heading out of town, but thankfully headed south, away from the mountains and Maxton. We could run to the next town if we had to. Finally, after forty minutes, he slowed the car down. The trees on the long driveway curled toward each other like spindly fingers, creating a natural arch which was probably pretty in the daytime, but was super creepy in the dark.

The driver jammed the brakes too hard, and I barely caught myself before I banged into the cab of the truck. He got out, slamming the door a little hard, whistling as he walked away. *Thank fuck.* We could climb out here and hopefully start heading toward the next town. I would've liked to have been further away, but this would have to do.

I'd barely breathed a relieved sigh when the tail-gate slammed down and a voice growled, "Who the fuck are you?" The driver appeared like he'd portalled there, and I had my knives out, sending them flying at the guy in the space of a scream. Damn, if my dad heard me scream, he'd be way more disappointed in that than me stealing Quinn and running away from home.

Quinn shifted, springing toward the man, but then it all stopped.

My knives. Quinn in mid-air. Me.

Everything stopped.

Except for the guy at the end of the truck. His arms were raised, his hands palm out, and I realized I'd been so fucking dumb. He wasn't a human. He was a goddamn witch.

"Jesus. You guys are just fucking kids. Do you know how dangerous it is to be out at night? Fuck me." He waved a hand, and Quinn floated forward. "Shifters?" He shook his head, twirling his finger and making a frozen Quinn spin like he was on a lazy Susan. "No, not a shifter. Well, not one I've ever seen." He looked at Quinn's scales, his clawed fingers, his ears. "You know what you look like? You look like Manix. I saw them in one of my Beastiology texts. But they went extinct a couple of centuries ago, I believe—better chance you're unicorn shifters." He laughed, but then his eyes switched back and forth between us. "It can't be, right? You aren't Manix?"

I didn't know what the fuck to say to this guy, but it wasn't going to be confirmation that we were Manix. So I shook my head as much as I could. "Lycanthropes."

The man made an unconvinced humming noise beneath his breath. "You two should come inside."

Damn, damn, damn. We were going to freaking die in the woods. Quinn had been right, and he was definitely going to haunt me about this from the grave.

"I think we might just be going. If you could release us, that would be awesome." I made my voice as pleasant as possible, even though I was shit-scared. I wanted to shift and run. But whatever this guy was doing, it was strong.

This must be how flies felt on sticky paper.

The guy looked at me like I was stupid. "It's three a.m. in the middle of nowhere. I'm not letting you guys wander around in the dark to be eaten by bears."

I wanted to scoff. I was Manix. I could take a bear.

"We'll be fin—"

The guy just raised an eyebrow. "It's not happening. You can leave in the morning in broad daylight, and I'll drive you wherever you need to go. Come inside. Tell me what you're running from, and the rest can wait."

I let out an exasperated sigh, and Quinn gave me a look that said *don't do it.* I was about to mouth off, and he knew it. "Look, we don't want to spend the night here with some weirdo who can hold us perfectly still. If you don't see the potential danger in that, then either you're a psycho or a dumbass. Let us go—we'll leave and never return. Everyone's happy."

The guy snorted and began to physically move us toward the house. We floated through the air, like two helium balloons on a string. "I'm neither a dumbass nor a psychopath. I just like a good mystery, and you guys? You're a *great* mystery." At the door, he stopped and looked at us both. "On my honor, with my very word to the Goddess, you're safe here. I won't harm you, and no other harm will come to you."

I'll be damned if my Beast didn't believe him too. *Trust the Beast* had been a mantra that had been drilled into my brain for as long as I could remember. Casting a quick look at Quinn, I finally sighed and nodded. It wasn't like we could have moved anyway. "Fine."

The guy nodded back and floated us into the cabin. It was a lot bigger on the inside than it had looked on the outside, which was quite a neat party trick. "Come on, we'll go to the library. I want to look at something." I had a sneaking suspicion I knew what that something would be.

The library was gorgeous, all leather-bound tomes and big comfy chairs. I wanted to live here forever. The guy walked over to the shelves, and in the soft light of the chandelier, I realized he was more handsome than

I'd thought. Even Quinn hissed out a breath. His cheekbones were carved sharply on his face, along with his jaw. His nose looked like he'd broken it once or twice, with a slight notch in the bridge. His hair was inky in the dim light and seemed to shine with an almost blue sheen.

He was beautiful. And if I'd seen him in the daylight, I never would've confused him for a drunk human. He was flicking through a book, finally stopping on a certain page. He looked up at Quinn, then back at the book, then at Quinn again.

When he finally turned to me, his eyes were alight with excitement. "You're not a Lycanthrope."

I sighed. *Dammit.* If anyone found out about this, I'd get a lot more than an ass-kicking. "No."

"Your race isn't extinct?"

"Obviously not."

He waved a hand, and we landed on the floor with a thud. Quinn didn't shift back as the guy paced around, his eyes excited.

"You can't tell anyone," I said sharply, and he looked at me with narrowed eyes.

"Why's that, little Manix?"

I groaned and buried my face in my hands. This night had all gone so, so wrong. "Because there's a *reason* we want everyone to think we're extinct. Plus, if they find out we told a witch, we'd be executed for treason."

The guy was silent until he snapped the book shut, making me jump. He stuffed it back onto the shelf and moved toward us, his expression intense. Quinn moved closer to me, his claws flexing.

The guy slowed. "I gave my word to the Goddess you'd be safe here. We don't do that lightly. You can shift back."

Quinn looked down at me, a question in his eyes, and I honestly didn't know what to do. Finally, I nodded, and he shifted back. Naked, except for his stretchy boxer shorts. The guy's eyes flicked down his body, but then quickly averted. Quinn was beautiful. I knew his body as well as I knew my own.

"Why are you running?" This dude's eyes were burning with earnestness, and I wanted to trust him.

"Quinn's an Omega. He presented late."

Quinn gasped. "*Susannah!*"

I continued. Had to take a leap. "He's been promised to a really shitty person, and it would not be a good outcome for him. So we had to run. Quinn deserves to be happy, and not the fucktoy of some jacked-up Alpha douche three times his age."

The guy was silent for a long time, his eyes flicking between the two of us. "I know a little bit about being in that kind of situation." He sucked in a deep breath. "The name's Jericho. I think I can help."

1

SUSANNAH

Present

The sun shone through the window of the room I was currently nesting in. This wasn't my Packhouse. Wasn't my home. The Alphas outside these locked doors weren't my Alphas. But beside me was the greatest love of my life, so that was something.

Somehow, by some weird twist of fate, the Goddess —or Mother Nature, biology, whatever—had gone insane and spontaneously turned all unmated female Betas into Omegas in a mass procreation event, complete with simultaneous heats and a town-wide frenzy.

And guess who got caught up in that? Yep, this girl.

Quinn was wrapped around my body like he was

trying to soak me in, and I was hoping the pungent *fuck me* pheromones I was throwing off were enough to disguise the scent that was starting to seep through his skin. He hadn't taken Jericho's suppressant meds since this whole Omega bullshit started, and they were starting to wear off for the first time in a decade. We'd been religious about ensuring he'd taken them every day since we'd been discovered in California by a group of Legion soldiers.

That month had been the best of our lives. We'd been free, even though we'd lived basically like hermits in a flea-ridden hotel under an overpass. It hadn't mattered; we'd been fucking happy. So damn joyful.

But in the end, like all good things, it ended. We'd been dragged back to Maxton like errant children, but at least the drugs had time to take effect, meaning we were brought back as two naughty Beta teens and not a fucking runaway Omega. That would've had far more dire consequences than being quickly paired off. Quinn's parents had mated him to Wilkie as soon as he'd arrived back, and I'd begged to go with him, convincing Wilkie we'd be better as a Beta pair. There was no doubt in my mind that I'd rather suffer in Wilkie's Pack every day than be separated from Quinn.

And damn, had I suffered. We both had.

If only Jericho could see us now. We'd ended up in the same position again. I'd only visited the handsome witch once after we made it back, just before the mating ceremony with the Wilkie Pack. I'd begged for something that would prevent our bastard Alpha from matebonding Quinn and I.

Jericho had provided, and to this day, neither Quinn nor I were bonded to that old fuck. Not that he'd admit it, even under pain of death.

I wasn't sure what Jericho had done, but every time Wilkie got naked within a certain distance of us, he couldn't get hard. Stayed as soft as a cheap ice cream in the sun. Obviously, you couldn't matebond if you had erectile dysfunction. And that psychopath had punished me for it every single day of our Pack lives.

More than once, Errol—another Beta—had stepped in to stop Wilkie from beating me into unconsciousness. Errol wasn't a bad guy; he was just weak and useless. It was his bite that was on my neck. He was the only real anchor to the Wilkie Pack we had, though Wilkie liked to pretend it was his mark marring the soft curve of Quinn's neck and my own.

No, Errol wasn't so bad. But Wilkie's second Beta, Green, and even Joseph, the third down the Pack hierarchy, were all monsters. Monsters I'd have to return to any minute now. This was just a brief respite in the shitshow that was my life.

Who would've ever predicted that I'd be an Omega?

I had a brief flash of Quinn poised over me, both of us fulfilling a biological need and connecting deeper than I'd ever thought possible. Mated Omegas. My heart thumped in my chest as it filled with emotion that threatened to choke me.

Quinn stirred behind me, his fingers pressing into the soft flesh of my hip. My body ached, and I was starving. As if on cue, Quinn's stomach rumbled where it was pressed against my spine. We'd fucked for a whole three days as the heat hit me hard, and it had taken that long for Quinn's meds to wear off enough to enact his natural Omega instincts. But there wasn't a single Alpha in this room to impregnate my Omega, and I intended to keep it that way for as long as goddamn possible.

"The heat is over," he said with a yawn, though his morning wood seemed to contradict his words. He didn't have to say more, though. The heat had been a surprising, lust-filled haze. Now reality was coming, and that bitch was going to slap hard.

I'd been hoping that we could milk this for another day or so before we had to go back to the Pack. "Get up and take your meds, babe. Paradise is coming to an end, and I refuse to give Wilkie the satisfaction of two Omegas."

My voice was light, but Quinn's face still folded into a frown as he reached into the pocket of his jeans, pulling out a pill bottle. Without fail, Jericho sent a new packet every month. He wasn't in his house on the outskirts of town now, and I didn't know where he'd gone. But the pills kept arriving in our prearranged spot close to town, and every time, I mentally thanked him for keeping Quinn safe, even if he'd moved on with his life.

Quinn's sigh was filled with years worth of suffering and worry. "He's not going to let the matebond slide anymore. He'd probably tape popsicle sticks to his dick just to fuck you." It'd be funny if it wasn't true.

I shuddered, pure disgust making the hairs on my arms raise. "The average heat without a secondary Omega goes for a week, right?" I whispered. "I say we drag it out another few days. Merrick and Murphy will let us stay."

Quinn frowned at the mention of the two Alphas who were currently letting us make use of their nest. Well, it was a spare room with all their pillows, blankets—hell, were those their shirts?—tossed in. I swallowed hard as I turned my face to sniff the tee beneath my head. Looks like I'd buried my face in Murphy's shirt as Quinn made me come. My Omega had wanted to roll around on the scent of those two Alphas, men I'd known since I was a kid. Men I'd loved for so many years before I'd had to make a choice between them and Quinn.

And I'd always choose Quinn's safety over my happiness. Every damn time.

"Considering Merrick bit off Wilkie's ear, I'm almost positive they'll let us stay as long as we like."

I flipped over to face Quinn so fast I felt woozy. "*Excuse me?*"

We hadn't spoken much about what led up to me waking in this nest with Quinn by my side. He'd given me the rough version—I was now an Omega, as were a bunch of the other female Betas in town. We were at Merrick and Murphy's place, because they'd been tasked by the Alpha General to retrieve us from Wilkie's Packhouse after I'd fallen unconscious and the rest of the Pack had gone kind of nuts.

When I'd woken up, there was just the heat and a whole lot of fucking. So much fucking. With no Alphas in here, it had all fallen to Quinn, and he'd stepped up admirably. I was deliciously wrung out.

His laugh was amused, but there was an undertone of bitterness. "When I called Radic because you'd collapsed—your eyes rolled back in your head, and then you were dead to the world—he sent Merrick and Murphy. I was so fucking scared, Zanny. Wilkie was prowling around and trying to drag your body back to his room, saying you were a much better lay unconscious."

I vomited a little in my mouth, but I was unsurprised. We'd lived for years with that piece of shit. Nothing he could say would surprise me anymore.

"Anyway, Errol was arguing with him that something was obviously wrong, and I took the moment to drag you into my room and barricade the door.

Merrick and Murphy showed up, and Wilkie fronted up to them. There was a fight, but Wilkie's no match for both of them. Anyway, in the fight, Merrick bit off Wilkie's ear, and apparently Doc was too busy to sew it back on."

I laughed, because Wilkie was going to be pissed about only having one ear. He was a vain Alpha, considering how he was so fucking rotten on the inside.

I tried not to think about why Merrick and Murphy would do this for me, for us. I tried not to think about what they'd want in return, because if I'd learned anything, it was that nothing in life came for free and that everyone could be bought.

"What are we going to do, Quinn?" I whispered to him, snuggling my face into his chest. I might not have bitten Wilkie's ear off, but it would be Quinn and I who'd be punished.

"We could run again?"

We were mated to Errol, and the strain of that bond meant they'd always be able to find us. We needed to break the bonds, and that shit would *hurt.* Right now, we could throw up a wall between them, but that wouldn't stop him from being able to find us.

"We can't run. What about the new Alpha General? You think he'd help? Maybe put Wilkie down for good?"

Quinn shrugged, his muscles tense as he held me

closer. "How about we hide out here for the rest of the week and then we'll deal with it, okay?" He kissed my forehead. "I love you, Zanny. I won't let anything bad happen. Let's go back to sleep."

I pressed my face right over his heart, taking a deep breath. Already his Omega scent was fading into something more like a Beta. The newly minted Omega whined at the loss, and Quinn tensed beneath my hands.

"One day, baby, we're going to escape this place and that Pack. Then we'll be happy, just you and me. I'm sorry."

I nodded, my eyes welling with tears that I refused to let fall. This wasn't his fault. It wasn't my fault, either. This was the system's fault, and I'd dismantle it one way or another, if it was the last thing I'd ever do.

2

MURPHY

This last week had been a masterclass in torture training. My control over my Beast and my body had been tested, especially when the Omega pheromones in our house had been so thick, I felt like I could actually taste them on my tongue.

After the first full day inside, in that sex-smell soup, Merrick and I had decided to set up a temporary campsite in the backyard. One of us would have to stay indoors—we'd never leave Susannah and Quinn unprotected during the heat—but being trapped inside could, quite literally, send us insane.

Cocking my head to the side, I looked back toward the barracks that used to be our home for so many years. After the first female Omega had been found, Merrick and I had decided it was time to move out.

She'd presented a possibility that we'd never thought could possibly occur. But if another female Omega had popped up, and we'd tried to woo her while living in the damn Legion barracks? Yeah, that wasn't going to work for any of us.

So we'd bought this cabin on the outskirts of town. It was beaten up a little by time and neglect, but it had good bones, and we'd restored it painstakingly by hand. We'd included a nest, and man, was I glad we had.

I tried not to think too hard about the fact that the girl who both Merrick and I had loved since we were kids had become an Omega. Fate seriously liked to kick a man in the nutsack sometimes. Susannah had always been perfect for us, and we would've loved her every day of our lives as a Beta. But as an Omega, she was a dream come true.

And she was mated to the Manix I hated most in the world. She was Pack Wilkie. The burn of that hard truth was like acid in my veins.

The back door opened, and Merrick walked out, shaking his head. As always, when I saw my best friend, my soulmate, my lover, my heart thumped a few times in my chest. Didn't matter that it was the millionth time he'd walked toward me, I still ate him up with my eyes.

August Merrick wasn't what any fashion magazine might call beautiful. His lips were a little too pale and thin, his eyes a disconcerting shade of icy blue, the structure of his face a little too sharp. He had tight creases between his eyes, like he'd spent decades frowning, and they seemed out of place on the face of a nearly thirty-year-old. He made an intimidating Legion soldier, but I'd seen those features as he came apart beneath my hands, so when I looked at him, all I saw was beauty.

He shifted his hand down his body and rearranged his cock. "I swear, if they don't stop soon, my dick's going to explode."

We were on day six of Susannah's heat, and I knew it was waning. My dick didn't get instantly hard when I opened the back door anymore. No, it usually held out until I was five feet into the mudroom instead. The only way we knew that Susannah and Quinn were still in there were the sounds of Susannah's orgasms, and the fact that all the trays of food disappeared. I wasn't sure when they showered or went to the bathroom, but sometimes I'd pick up Susannah's scent in the small bathroom, and I'd rush to fuck my hand until I was exploding against the tiles with her scent swirling around me.

It was kind of creepy if I thought about it too hard. But it wouldn't be the first—or hundredth—time I'd found release to thoughts of Susannah and Quinn.

"Let them take all the time they need. I'm not in a hurry for them to have to face the world." Or go back to that piece of shit, Wilkie. Walking into that mausoleum he called a Packhouse, finding him banging against the door of Quinn's room, seeing Quinn's pale face and terrified eyes... It was too much. My Beast growled at even the thought of them returning to that place, and I was in agreement. But Susannah had always had free will, in abundance, and I wasn't going to be the one who caged her.

Merrick looked pensive, but nodded. "I heard that by the time they'd managed to fit Wilkie in to reattach his ear, the flesh was dead." He grinned ferally at me, and I couldn't help but laugh. The very image of Wilkie walking around with one ear would entertain me until the day I died.

Just then, the back door opened, and we both spun toward it, instantly on high alert. But it was Susannah stepping through the doorway ahead of Quinn. I had a brief flash of her small, pale body on the hospital bed unconscious after we'd picked her and Quinn up from their Packhouse, and I flexed my fingers to release the panic that still welled in my chest at the thought.

You'd never know it now. She looked better than I'd seen her in so long; her blonde hair was shining in the afternoon light, and the sweet curves of her hips were hugged in a pair of my sweats, though they were baggy everywhere else. She was still too thin, as was Quinn, but a week of the high-calorie food we'd been feeding them to keep their energy up had filled out the more gaunt edges. The fact that they could fuck like rabbits, doing that high-intensity cardio, and still put on weight over the last week made me wonder just how psychotic it was over there at Wilkie's Packhouse. Was he starving them? The thought made me clench my teeth, but I forcefully loosened my jaw into a smile.

"It's good to see you're both okay." It was a lame thing to say, but what else was there? *Hope you had a good heat? Wish I was there?*

It was Quinn who answered, "We can't thank you enough. I can't thank you..." His voice was rough, and I got it. It had been scary there for a while.

Quinn and Susannah had always been inseparable. They were two parts of the same whole, much the same way Merrick and I had been our entire lives. You couldn't say Merrick without adding my name to the end, and it was the same way with Susannah and Quinn. Though unlike me and Merrick, Susannah had always been the leader, even when she was young. My Beast had always been drawn to the fiery Beta, but I'd always liked Quinn too. Hell, there'd been a time when we'd all been teens when my Beast had tracked Quinn around the room like a hunter who had spotted his prey. But they'd run away soon after, then had to be dragged back by the Legion before jumping into bed with Wilkie.

That had been the end of all our dreams, and what my Beast wanted no longer mattered.

I dragged myself back to the present to hear Merrick's answer. "You're both welcome here anytime."

Forever, even.

Susannah met my gaze, and I held it. She'd known, all those years ago, how we felt about her. Hell, at sixteen, I'd all but gotten down on my knees and begged her to be part of my Pack—*our* Pack—but then she'd run away. Even worse than that was she'd joined Wilkie's pack.

I needed to let that shit go. It was water under the bridge now.

Susannah took a shuddering breath in. "We should go, get back to the house." Not home—*the house*. If that didn't say everything about what it was like in Wilkie's Packhouse, nothing did.

I could see her folding in on herself, like she was trying to be smaller. Anger flared in my chest, and I growled. Her eyes snapped back to mine, and her chin jutted out. There was that proud, stubborn woman I knew.

"Like Quinn said, thank you. If you ever turn into an Omega in a freak magical event, we'll be happy to return the favor." Her voice was cool, and I resisted the urge to smirk at her.

Merrick watched her closely, and she was purposefully avoiding his gaze. He was good at reading people, my mate—always had been. And Susannah knew it.

"I have one question," Merrick said before they could step away.

Quinn barked out a laugh. "I'm surprised it's just one."

Merrick quirked an eyebrow. "All the other Betas who turned Omega were unmated. All except you. Why is that?"

Susannah's eyes flashed angrily. "Lucky, I guess. Besides, it's none of your business, August Merrick. Yours either, Owen Murphy." With that, she gripped Quinn's hand, towing him out of the backyard and through the gate onto the street. It was a scene that had been the same since we were kids. Susannah plowing ahead, dragging a befuddled but doting Quinn behind her.

We watched them go, then I turned to Merrick. His face was pensive, staring in the direction of Wilkie's Packhouse. "Something's off there."

Yeah, no shit. But Susannah was right; it was none of our business, no matter how much we wanted it to be. We'd learned that Susannah didn't want our help early on, the first time we'd seen bruises on her arms from fingers that gripped them too hard. Bruises on her neck. We'd gotten into a brawl with the Wilkie Pack, and it had ended badly. Susannah had made it clear she was happy and that we needed to fuck right off.

So we had, for so damn long it hurt. However,

Merrick was right. Something was off, and we were going to get to the bottom of it.

Standing, I moved stiffly toward the house. It would need airing if I didn't want to be hard for another week from the residual pheromones. I tilted my head at Merrick. "We'll watch and listen. Be there if they need us. Until then, we should get back to work."

This brief reprieve had come to an end. Still, I couldn't shake the idea that this was the beginning of something big for us and the Manix. I'd never been a particularly devout believer in some higher being, but it was hard to dispute it when the Betas had literally transformed.

The Goddess obviously had a plan, and we were just along for the ride.

3

QUINN

My gut churned as I stepped between the Corinthian pillars of the Packhouse. It was more like standing on the steps of a prison than in the welcoming embrace of home. The mansion was ostentatious and pretentious, just like its owner. But also much like the Alpha of the Wilkie Pack, the regal facade hid the horrors of what happened inside.

I tilted my head to listen, but the house was quiet. Susannah went to push inside first, but I grabbed her elbow, pulling her back. "Let me go first, Zanny." She looked like she wanted to argue, but I didn't wait and flung open the door. It was still quiet as I walked in. Susannah huffed something under her breath behind me before she strode into the house.

Errol appeared from the kitchen. I liked Errol, in a

completely non-romantic way. The stress of living in this Pack made him look haggard, and I still didn't know if he was thirty-five or fifty-five. He was too nice to be saddled with this fucking Pack. But he'd been injured as a child, so he walked with a limp, and no one would take him except Wilkie. Not because our Alpha was altruistic, but because Errol was an amazing cook. Wilkie and Green treated him like a slave, but otherwise they left him well enough alone. Hard to get three-course dinners if you beat the shit out of the cook.

We only got to taste some of his food—whatever was leftover after Wilkie and the other Betas had eaten. Sometimes, there wasn't much at all. Wilkie wasn't above punishing us for his inability to get hard and mate us into the Pack properly.

"You're back," Errol whispered. He never spoke above a whisper. He looked left and right, obviously waiting for Wilkie or Green to appear. The only other Beta in our pack, Joseph, was probably at work. He brought in the majority of the money for the Pack, working as an accountant for the Legion. Joseph wasn't too bad either—his meanness not quite cruelty, more just following orders and turning a blind eye—but he worked long hours. Partly because Wilkie liked to live above his means, and partly because it meant he didn't have to be here in this house with Wilkie and Green.

Understandable.

Susannah gave Errol a tight smile. "We're back."

He didn't look happy about that, though. None of us were. I reached out and gripped his bicep softly. He flinched away, and my heart hurt for him. "Thank you for what you did."

He shrugged, his eyes flashing to Susannah and back to me. "It was nothing," he whispered, moving back toward the kitchen.

It wasn't nothing, and we both knew it. He'd stepped in to defy his Alpha. He would have been punished for disobeying Wilkie like that, but I let it go.

Susannah dropped her voice low. "Where are they?"

Errol shook his head. "I don't know. I haven't seen them in a few days. They've been home, because they eat the food I leave out, but they're gone again when I wake up." His tone was a mixture of trepidation and relief.

Weird, but I wasn't looking a gift horse in the mouth.

Susannah stepped closer to Errol and kissed the older man on the cheek. Then she turned and strode up the stairs. Our rooms were on the top floor, right at the back, as far from Wilkie's room as we could physically get. We technically had two rooms, but we always slept in the same bed. Safety in numbers. We shared a Jack-and-Jill bathroom, which also kept us a little safer.

Locking the bedroom door, I unloaded my pockets

of all the protein bars and chocolate I'd stashed as we were leaving. We'd hide them in the room somewhere so Wilkie couldn't confiscate them. I stripped out of my shirt and jeans. These would have to be burned. Actually, it should all be burned. Susannah was obviously on the same wavelength because she was throwing her clothes on top of mine and heading straight to the shower.

God, she was fucking beautiful. She was pale, freckles dusting along her skin like small kisses from the sun. Her Beast form was the same tawny gold as those freckles, which was something that always made me laugh. Her body was all sharp curves, though they'd softened slightly from the abundance of food at Merrick and Murphy's home.

I needed everything that had been infused with my Omega scent gone. I couldn't give Wilkie any hint that I was an Omega. I didn't know what to do about Susannah, but she had that curl to her shoulders that said she was going to do something self-sacrificing. Probably lay down and take that fuck, all in order to protect me.

I hated it. I turned so she couldn't see me as I screamed silently at the wall. Helpless. We were so fucking helpless.

Sucking in deep breaths, I gathered all our clothes, stuffing them into the bathroom trash can and pouring a whole bottle of cheap cologne over it. Manix didn't typically wear scents, but I'd burned out my olfactory senses using this just to give me an extra layer of protection. If even a whiff of my Omega pheromones snuck out, the shitty cologne would mask it.

My inner Omega whined at the thought of the perfect nest we'd just left, a place we'd felt safe for the first time in nearly a decade. But it wasn't ours. It could never be ours.

I wanted to climb into the shower behind Susannah, but she needed this moment. It was a lot, this sudden revelation that your life had been a lie and now you were something else. In any other pack, it would be a miracle, but in this one? It was a death sentence. A curse.

So I'd let her have her moment under water so hot that it was steaming up both rooms, and I'd pretend I didn't know it wasn't just water pouring down her cheeks, that I couldn't see her shoulders shaking with sobs.

Her pain burned my nose, and I was helpless to do anything.

There was a soft knock at the door, and I froze. I looked at the trash can of scented clothes, hoping it was enough to throw whoever was on the other side off the scent. Shutting the bathroom door, I walked over and undid the deadbolts that gave us the illusion of protection. Pulling open the solid door, I saw Errol on the other side. He was holding two plates of food and gave me a tight, unsure smile. He smelled like anxiety, but beneath that, he smelled of hope. And that was more pungent than anything else. Because there was no hope for our Pack.

"I thought you might be hungry. You and the, uh, Omega." He shifted from foot to foot, his eyes meeting mine briefly and then flicking away.

I swallowed hard and pasted a grin on my face. "If you start calling her Omega, Errol, she's going to get mad. She's still Susannah. The last thing any of us wants is to make a big deal out of this."

Errol finally met and held my gaze. "I don't think we'll have too much choice in the matter." With that, he turned and walked away.

I thanked his retreating back for the food, then spun back into my room. Susannah stood there, dressed in one of my hoodies and looking wide-eyed. I guess she'd heard Errol's words.

I walked over, handing her a plate and kissing her forehead. "One problem at a time, Zanny. First, eat. Then we'll figure everything else out."

She nodded, and I placed my own plate on my nightstand. I needed a long shower. Stripping off my underwear, I moved under the water and rested my head against the tiles. The muscles in my shoulders ached from being tense for so long. Nothing I did ever released them, but the burning hot water soothed them for a moment. Everything was better under a deluge of water. Maybe it could wash away all my fears and troubles, along with my Omega scent.

Susannah might think she was going to offer herself up as some kind of appeasement, but I wouldn't let that happen. She'd once sacrificed everything for me, and it was my turn to return the favor.

I needed to get hold of Jericho, because he was the only outsider we knew. Everyone else was a part of this suffocatingly small community. If we ran, we'd have no one to turn to, nowhere to go, except to a stranger we met one night so many years ago who may or may not still live close by.

I steeled my spine. If we couldn't run, I'd do what I had to do. Even if I had to cut off Wilkie's head in his sleep and suffer the consequences.

At least Susannah would be free then—from Wilkie and this Pack. And free from me.

4

MERRICK

The town still buzzed from the frenzy. There was a weird vibe in the air, and it set my Beast on edge. He'd been riled for a week, but today, it felt like there were invisible fingers running over my skin. It was making me fidgety. The added Omega pheromones around town were going to take a little to get used to, but hopefully, everyone would settle in the coming weeks. It was impossible to even contemplate how insane our lives had gotten since last week when all the Betas had turned.

I tried not to think about Susannah and Quinn being back home with Wilkie, because it made me want to shift and tear that bastard limb from limb.

Murphy walked behind me drinking his coffee, his eyes shadowed from lack of sleep. We'd fucked all night in the Omega's nest. I wasn't proud of it, but I'd been incapable of resisting. I wanted to roll in the sweet scent of her heat, even if we couldn't be a part of it. And it was heady.

Murphy looked exhausted and was downing caffeine like it was his only lifeline. He wasn't much of a morning person anyway. I scowled at every person who looked in our direction, and a bunch of people crossed the street to avoid us.

Actually, most people wouldn't even look at us. *Weird.*

"Does something feel off to you today?" I asked Murphy, and he scoffed, but I noticed the way his body went on alert, though his muscles remained relaxed. He was the consummate soldier.

He didn't say anything, but people avoided his gaze. "Might be a Susannah thing," he said softly, and that could be true. Some of the elderly members of Maxton were old school and would've taken issue with Susannah holing up in our Packhouse during the heat. It was almost unheard of to spend your heat with a Pack other than your own.

They could suck my dick. Let them say something.

A low growl bubbled out of my mouth, and Murphy gripped my forearm. "Let's head to work. They can go fuck themselves if they have a problem with how things went down."

I rolled my shoulders and nodded. Stepping back into the Legion building for the first time in a week, I couldn't help but marvel at how quiet it was. Where the hell was everyone?

Gunfire sounded, making me startle, but I had my gun out in the blink of an eye, as did Murphy, his coffee dropping to the floor. We found cover, looking for an assailant, but no one appeared.

Slowly, we moved deeper into the building, toward where the shots had sounded. I wanted to tell myself that perhaps it was an accident—some of the Legion soldiers were pretty abysmal with firearms—but I knew it wasn't true. The vibe in the town right now was off. Like everyone knew something big was happening, except us. This wasn't good.

We cleared out offices as we moved, hunting out personal assistants and the odd bureaucrat hiding beneath their desk. They weren't soldiers, despite coming from a warrior race. We sent them out the front doors and moved further into the building.

When we came up to the Alpha General's office, I smelled the unmistakable hot tang of blood. Signaling Murphy, I moved with Manix speed into the room, my gun raised. But there was no assailant. Moving further in, I saw Radic on the floor, a pool of blood spreading around him like crimson wings.

Fuck!

Murphy swept past me into the connected office that belonged to the Alpha General, but it was empty.

Holstering my gun on my hip, I raced to Radic. "Don't be dead. Don't be dead."

Radic was the best the Manix had. He had heart and smarts and had kept so much of this town from going under the leadership of the former Alpha General. He was the reason the less fortunate members of town survived and weren't chew toys for the Alphas. The half-bloods, the Betas, the orphans—they all owed their lives to Radic, even though he'd never accept the praise.

He couldn't die.

I felt his throat. He still had a pulse, though it was faint. "He's still alive, but barely. We have to get him to Doc." Murphy nodded. Pulling out his gun again, he waited as I shifted the bleeding Beta into my arms. "Hang in there, man. Bonnie needs you," I murmured softly. He was gray, and judging by the pool beneath him, most of his blood was soaking into the carpet of his office. "We need to move," I grunted at Murphy, and he hurried out of the room, his eyes scanning for threats.

We took the back streets, avoiding as many Manix as possible so we didn't incite panic or the shooter didn't return to find us and finish the job. Every unsuspecting Beta we came across, Murphy barked at them until they scurried away.

Finally, we were outside Doc's surgery, but there was a black SUV haphazardly parked near the door.

My stomach sank. It was one of the Alpha General's vehicles, and the scent of blood permeating from it had my skin buzzing.

This wasn't a random attack. This was something bigger. Something far more insidious.

Murphy banged on the door, but there was no answer. "Wait here," he growled, then moved in with his gun still raised. His hissed, "Hey, we're cool, we're cool," had me on high alert. I wanted to give him backup, but I couldn't.

"Merrick!" he called from inside the medical room. I stepped through the door and came face to face with Dominic, the Alpha General's second-in-command and Packmate. Dominic was pointing his own weapon at Murphy, who held his hands up in front of him. "We heard the gunshot and found him like this—I swear it, Dom," Murphy implored. It looked bad; I could recognize that. We were both doused in Radic's blood.

Murphy looked around Dom's body at a bleeding Bonnie. She was a new Omega, and another of the Alpha General's Packmates. His eyes went wide. "What the fuck is going on?"

Dominic let out a snarl that raised goosebumps on my skin. "A coup. A motherfucking coup. They have Pryce. I can't find Doc, and Courtland isn't answering his phone. Is anyone else medically trained?"

Every cell in my body froze. Was this what we'd come to? Trying to murder Omegas in cold blood? I shook my head, trying to clear the shock. Carefully, I placed Radic down on the examination table beside Bonnie, glad the thing was huge and made for shifted Manix. "Not really. Bonnie was Doc's backup, and even she can't do anything more technical than field medicine. Can Loren do any kind of magic to heal it?"

Dominic's face went blank. "Loren is dead. He took the bullet meant for me." His face might be blank, but the pain in his voice was a gut punch.

"I'm sorry, man." And I was. Loren had been a good guy, as much as a former witch in a drug cartel *could* be a good guy. At least he didn't try to kill women and children, unlike the so-called good people in this town.

Dominic whipped out his phone, and I instinctively knew who he was calling. We needed help, and there was only one species that was an actual legitimate threat to the Manix in this day and age. The vampires.

I put pressure on the wound on Radic's chest, and Murphy did the same for Bonnie as we listened to Dominic's conversation with Convocation Member Raine Baxter on the other end of the phone, who promised to send reinforcements. We just had to keep them alive for as long as we could.

Dominic turned to us after he hung up, his eyes more wolf than man now. "I have to find Courtland." There would be no talking him out of doing that.

"Merrick will stay and keep them stable until help arrives. I'll go with you and call in reinforcements,"

Murphy stated. It wasn't a request, but I nodded my agreement anyway. I was already moving around, pulling out the things I'd need to give them blood transfusions and stem the bleeding the best I could until someone could fix what was broken.

"No, no Legion Force. The kid from the Sanctum said it was a guy in a Legion Force uniform who shot Bonnie. I don't know who to trust."

I froze. It was the Legion who was doing this? The organization I'd devoted my life to? Murphy was agreeing, already on the phone as they walked out the door. I had to trust that Murphy and Dominic had it handled, even if I feared for the man who was my mate. He may be my partner, but he was also one hell of a soldier. My job was to keep two people—these two amazing Manix—alive until help arrived. I wouldn't let them go out like this.

Because the Alpha General might never forgive me if I let them die. I would never forgive myself either.

I packed gauze into Radic's wound, hooking him up for a blood transfusion. My field medicine skills were rough, but I hoped they'd be enough. For what felt like a lifetime, I ran between the two injured Manix, praying to the Goddess the whole time, even though I'd never been particularly devout.

When two vampires burst through the door of the doctor's office—one dressed in a Hawaiian shirt covered in cats with party hats, and the other one huge, tattooed, and scarred—I'd never been more relieved in my life.

"I heard there was a blood buffet?" the scarred one said in a gravelly British accent. I froze, my eyes twitching toward my gun.

The other vampire might've looked less scary, but his power made my Beast prickle beneath my skin. He elbowed the big one. "He's kidding. He's actually a very good surgeon, though he hasn't managed to find his decorum. I'm Nico. This is X. You'd better show us the patients, because the scent of death in here is getting stronger. I fear we don't have any time to lose."

"Bonnie has a collapsed lung, and Radic has lost far too much blood," I told them as dispassionately as I could so I didn't Beast out at vampires being so close to my injured friends.

With that, all mirth left the big, scarred one, and he became all business. "Get a line in that one." He pointed to me. "We're going to need a few more infusions and a hell of a lot more blood, so he's the walking, talking Red Cross for now." He rolled up his sleeves and got to work, while Nico expertly slid a needle into my vein, draining me of all the blood I could afford to lose.

As they worked, I sent a thanks to the Moon Goddess that these psychos existed.

5

SUSANNAH

I woke up to Quinn wrapped around my body, and my brother hovering over my bed next to an unknown vampire. My body went rigid, and I scooted up toward the headboard, my eyes flicking between Mikhail and the vampire.

"What the *fuck*, Micky?" I screeched. Quinn rocketed up in bed, his body curling toward mine protectively.

The vampire just looked bored. "Where is your Alpha?"

I shook my head, because what the fuck was going on right now?

My brother lifted his chin, casting a cool look at the vampire. "Sorry to intrude. This is Wilfred; he's a part of the Convocation Member Raine's personal guard. We're looking for Wilkie. Do you know where he is?"

Quinn peeled himself off me slowly. Mikhail was my second-oldest brother, and a Legion soldier through and through. But he'd loved and protected me when my father had succumbed to grief at the loss of our mother, and he'd more or less stayed in that role for years afterwards.

Quinn cleared his throat. "We haven't seen him in a week. Errol said he's been returning home late, but he hasn't seen him in a couple of days either. We've been holed up somewhere else since the frenzy." He didn't drop Merrick and Murphy in the shit with my protective older brother, who barely tolerated Wilkie, but would have definitely had something to say about me spending my heat with two unmated Alphas. "Why are you looking for him? And what is with the bloo—er, Wilfred?"

Micky's face went hard. "Get dressed and pack a bag. There's been a coup, and your Pack Beta, Green, just murdered Doc. The Alpha General is injured, as are his Beta and Omegas. I'm taking you back to Father's home until we get this shit sorted out. I am not leaving you here with this *Pack*. Do not argue with me, Susannah."

Micky's voice was hard, like he expected me to put up a fight. And I had, earlier in my relationship with Wilkie's Pack. Because Micky had wanted to murder Wilkie when he'd seen the obvious signs of violence on my skin, but Quinn's parents had beaten the shit out of him when he'd asked to come home, told him he couldn't leave his Pack and he wouldn't be welcome. Wilkie had made threats. So while my family would have welcomed me home, it would have meant leaving Quinn alone. So I'd fought against Micky's good intentions and stayed.

No longer. Things had changed, and I wasn't a stupid kid anymore. Quinn had options now that there was new leadership. We weren't trapped, so we'd take the out that was being handed to us.

"We'll come." I couldn't keep the relief from my voice. "Quinn comes too."

Micky shook his head, a fond curl tilting his lips. "As if I'd have it any other way."

Quinn was shaking his head, like he couldn't believe Micky's words. "Doc is dead? Bonnie's hurt?"

Pain constricted my chest. Doc was a stalwart in this town. The last of the old-world Manix who treated each of us with rough respect, not as servants. He'd healed all my wounds, even delivered me into the world. Maxton wouldn't be the same without him.

And Bonnie was going to be devastated. She was one of the few who saw past the bitch persona I showed the world to keep Quinn's lie protected. She saw too much, and her heart was too big. She didn't deserve this.

"How did Doc die?" I gasped past the lump of grief in my chest.

"Beheaded by your Packmate." Wilfred's top lip curled, like he thought we were all primitive beasts. As if he wasn't a blood-sucking predator himself.

Micky looked over at him, his eyes narrowed. "We'll wait for you in the living room. We need to question Errol."

Quinn stood. "Whatever Wilkie, Green, and Joseph were up to, Errol had nothing to do with it. He's..." He trailed off, like he wanted to say Errol was beaten down, but then Mikhail would know we were equally as stomped on. "He's innocent of anything. He keeps to himself, keeps his head down." Micky seemed to understand what Quinn was trying to say, because he just nodded and left.

I climbed out of the bed quickly, pulling on a pair of sweats, then throwing shit into the duffles in my closet. I looked over at Quinn. "Pack everything you can't live without. We're never coming back here."

Green was a murderer, but I had no doubt in my mind he'd done shit on Wilkie's orders. They'd pushed too far, and I didn't want to be connected to them when shit exploded.

Quinn just nodded before hurrying into his own room. It didn't take long before I could hear him dropping armfuls of things into his suitcase.

In a surprisingly short amount of time, I'd gathered everything I needed. I sat on the top of my suitcase to zip it up, then I wheeled my life out into the hall.

Quinn closed his door behind him, and I could see him heaving deep lungfuls of air. This was the precipice. We took control back at this point. Right now.

We walked to the living room where Errol was sitting on the couch, as far from Wilfred as he could get. Micky was looking between them, like he was ready to spring up and defend Errol if the vampire got a little peckish.

Errol looked down at the suitcases, then up at our faces. An expression that I couldn't define flashed across his face, or maybe it was several emotions all rolled into one. "You're leaving."

I wasn't prepared for the guilt that niggled at my heart. "Yes." I swallowed hard. "I'm sorry, Errol." Sorry for so many fucking things. Sorry that he was stuck in this hellhole, sorry he was mated to a psychopath, sorry that we were leaving him behind and never coming back.

Errol stood and made his way over to me. We were bonded, in a very basic way. We were bonded between Betas, but that was basically like when humans spat on their hands and shook on it in the movies. You had to be bonded through an Alpha for the bonds to really cement, but we'd all just ignored that fact. Still, we were bonded enough that when I tried, I could feel his fear and anxiety, but also his happiness.

He wrapped his arms around my shoulders and

hugged me tight. "Don't come back, Omega. Stay away, hide if you have to. There's nothing good for you here."

I swallowed the lump in my throat. Errol didn't deserve to be stuck here either. "You should take your own advice, old man," I whispered. Errol shook his head, tilting his chin slightly so I was forced to look at the ragged scar that was meant to be a matebond mark but was more an example of Wilkie's savagery. Wilkie hadn't accepted the bond back, oh no. Wilkie didn't want partners. He wanted Beta slaves. He'd chained Errol to him, but he had no such chains on himself.

"I have no choice but to be here. I thank the Goddess that it didn't stick with you two." Well, it wasn't the Goddess he had to thank—just a stupidly hot witch in the woods—but I didn't tell him that.

Mikhail was giving Errol what I considered his all-seeing expression. "I'll check in with you," he stated, like offering him his protection was no big deal, no matter how small the gesture seemed.

Errol's head whipped to the side, his brows high in surprise. But he didn't have time to ask questions, because Wilfred was hustling us outside and over to Mikhail's ATV. He loaded up our heavy bags like they weighed the same as a feather in the wind.

"We must continue on," he said to Micky, and my brother grunted in agreement, handing me the keys to the ATV.

"Straight home, Susannah. Things are... difficult

out there. The Alpha General is barely hanging on to life, there are factions that have turned friends against each other, and I'm unsure who to trust. Father had nothing to do with the push by Eldridge for leadership, and it's fairly safe to say that Raiden's Pack are trustworthy. Otherwise, unless they're your blood relatives, trust *no one.*" The unsaid statement was that we couldn't trust Quinn's family—like we ever would.

Quinn and I both promised that we wouldn't stop for anyone, especially not Wilkie or the rest of our Pack, and Micky and the vampire Wilfred disappeared into the trees. Little did my brother know that I would rather hit Wilkie with the ATV than stop for that fucker.

I was shell-shocked as Quinn hopped behind the wheel of the vehicle. "Holy shit," he breathed before starting the ATV and heading down the road a little faster than we probably should.

He wasn't wrong. This was a lot. A coup to overthrow a ruler wasn't how we operated. It was supposed to be a battle between two Alphas, a test of strength and cunning. We didn't hurt Omegas. Abduction and maiming, the lack of honor? It wasn't the Manix way.

Though I'd thought our society needed a shakeup, this hadn't been what I meant. But despite the uncertainty, despite the fact I felt sick about what had happened to Bonnie and Doc, I could see the light at the end of my own tunnel of torment. If there was going to be a silver lining to this tragedy, I was going to grab it with both hands. I didn't care if that made me a ruthless bitch.

I'd do worse things to protect the other half of my soul.

6

QUINN

I t rained the day we buried Doc. As it should. Everyone was solemn, and grief was a heavy blanket that lay over the entire town. The coup had changed things, though, and now everyone eyed each other with suspicion. Friends side-eyed each other, and no one would look at Bonnie, sobbing like her heart was being torn out of her chest as they lowered the only father she'd ever known into the earth.

No one said anything about how the remaining Legion Generals had found Wilkie not guilty of participating in the coup, despite Green's actions and subsequent death. There'd been an uproar, but the Alpha General was still injured, so he'd acquiesced to the decision given by the Legion Generals. I wasn't dumb enough to think he was going to take this betrayal lying down, despite his soothing words of forgiveness and democracy.

Dominic, his second, had no such need for political niceties. He glared at everyone like he was death and vengeance in one pissed-off package, and I didn't blame him.

It had taken weeks for the town to calm down, but it had reached an uneasy equilibrium. We were currently standing outside the Alpha General's Packhouse to celebrate his Pack bonding officially. Their Pack hadn't wasted any time, but I guess almost dying would do that to a Manix. Life was too short not to tell people how much they meant to you.

Susannah stood beside her father, and I bracketed her on the other side. We'd spent the last few weeks in Susannah's childhood home, and no one would go against a Legion General to insist we went back to our Pack. When my parents had come over and even suggested it, Joshua had threatened them so quietly they left in a hurry. Not before they gave me a look that said I was the biggest disappointment of their long lives, but who fucking cared? They'd been friends with the old Alpha General, and I had no doubt in my mind that they'd been on the wrong side of the coup. Judging by the feral look on Legion General Joshua's face, he knew it too.

Almost everyone was here, even those who I knew disliked the new regime. But everyone was far too gutless to purposefully miss this event, like they'd turn Courtland's evil eye in their direction. *Spineless bastards.*

I stuck like glue to Susannah's side as she moved over to say hello to her brothers. Wilkie and the rest of our old Pack wouldn't dare appear, but we were guilty by association, and it was enough that everyone turned to stare at us as we walked in. I swallowed hard, pressing close to Susannah's back. I could hear the whispers and curious tones, and feel their accusing glares.

Raiden wrapped his arms around his sister, and the peaceful feeling of another Omega washed over me. Well, another-another Omega. Actually, Naja came up behind him, so there were four Omegas in a four-foot radius.

For the first time in over two centuries, it didn't feel like we were dying out anymore. There was hope.

"Are you okay?" Raiden whispered into Susannah's hair, and the heavy weight of guilt lodged in my chest again. It was my fault she was estranged from her family.

Susannah shook her head solemnly, and Raiden's face softened. He loved Susannah, who had raised him like he was her own child, despite only being four years older than him. That was a lot of pressure for a small child to take on.

"We're here if you need us."

Susannah snorted. "Gatlin would love that."

If I was protective of Susannah, then Gatlin was rabid about Raiden. He would stand in front of a pack of raging Lycanthropes for his Omegas.

Naja made a rude noise. "You let me worry about the Alphas. Your brother is right; if you need anything, you come to us. If you need a place to lay low, or have questions about anything at all, you're always welcome. Both of you."

I looked at the half-breed Omega with a baby in her arms. She was an outsider, and I wondered what she saw that everyone else missed. Could she see our lie? It was impossible, but the way she was looking at me made my skin prickle.

Susannah gave her a hesitant smile. "Thanks."

The Alpha General stood a few steps up in his living room. "Friends, family. It's my pleasure to present the De Léon Pack."

There was a cheer, and I clapped along with everyone else, glad that the Alpha General looked healed in the few weeks since the coup. He stood strong, his Pack spread around him, his gaze shifting fondly between his Omegas and Betas. There were kids all around; some were Bonnie's orphans from the Sanctum, and some the Alpha General's charges, but it made the mood of the room much less stuffy.

The new Pack moved quickly into the crowd, accepting the surge of hand-shaking and ass-kissing.

One of Raiden's Betas, Ellar, appeared with a plate of food. He kissed both Naja and Raiden on the cheek, his eyes filled with love.

I sucked back oxygen, pasting a smile on my face. I liked Ellar, but the love in their Pack was a shining example of what Susannah and I had always wanted but never gotten. That unconditional adoration and care—it was like catnip for my inner Omega. I might be hiding as a Beta, but some of those Omega urges still consumed me from time to time.

As if she could sense my turmoil, Susannah wrapped her hand in mine, tugging me closer. She gave Raiden another quick hug. "I'm going to find Micky," she told her baby brother.

Raiden smiled around some kind of pastry thing. "Love you, Zanny."

I sensed more than saw her emotions spike. "Love you too, kid."

We moved away quickly, because she hated being vulnerable in front of Raiden, as if she always had to be that stoic mother figure. People moved out of our way almost instinctively—like we had traitor cooties—as we headed toward the food table. I grabbed a handful of cheese puff things and fed one to Susannah, then threw two down myself.

Before I could grab another handful, I looked over and swallowed hard at the sight of a vampire. Unfortunately, that meant I choked on the puff still in my mouth.

The vampire reached out and thumped my spine. "Easy there, mate. Gotta chew before you swallow. Deep throating is for masturbation, not mastication. That's what my maker always said."

I blinked at the vampire. I knew he was a vampire because his perfectly white fangs glinted in the overhead lights. "That makes zero sense," I croaked. He smiled wider, his fangs pressing tightly into his full lower lip.

Susannah was suddenly in front of me, like she could protect me from a fucking vampire any better than I could protect myself. I'd never say that to her, though; she was fierce.

The vampire raised his eyebrows as he stared down at my soulmate. "Sorry, Omega. Didn't mean to upset you. Just didn't want your, uh, Omega, to choke."

I froze, swallowing hard for a whole different reason. "I don't know what you're talking about," I hissed.

He frowned. "You're not an Omega pair? Your scents are really entwined, and she's an Omega, and you're an Omega, so I just assumed—*oof.*"

Susannah had reached out and punched the big vampire in the tit. She'd hit a fucking *vampire* in the chest to shut him up. Fuck, we were going to die.

"Be. Quiet!" she hissed, and the guy just looked really confused.

He opened his mouth to either yell at Susannah or eat her, but luckily he was interrupted by a familiar voice. "Is everything okay over here?" I dragged my eyes from the tall, blond, and stupidly attractive vampire to the Alphas who haunted my daydreams. Murphy was smiling pleasantly at me. "I see you've met the new town doctor, Tanner."

Merrick stood behind him, looking us over like he was trying to work out what the hell was going on. My gaze flicked between the Alphas and the vampire, my tongue frozen solid in my mouth.

"Just introducing myself to one of the new Omegas. Telling her about the Alpha General's genealogy project. I haven't met..." The vampire paused, looking pointedly at the fiery Omega in front of him.

"Susannah," she huffed. "This is my *Beta* partner, Quinn."

"Oh, Susannah and Quinn—Packmates of that bloody wanker, Wilkie. What a toolbag. No offense."

I snorted. "Uh, none taken."

"Though you don't smell like Pack. Actually, there's no scent of anyone on you, other than each other, and maybe the lightest hint of another Beta? Are you sure you matebonded properly?"

We all froze like prey. Me, Susannah, even Merrick and Murphy. Fuck me, this vampire had a big mouth. If looks could kill, Zanny would have him flayed on the ground by now.

"What I mean to say is that most Packs smell like a finished dish. They have an overall scent, but if you try hard, you can smell the individual ingredients too. You guys don't smell like anything other than each other."

I knew my eyes were too wide, and I could feel the hot gaze of the Alphas beside me, their eyes boring into my face. It was Susannah who broke the silence though, her voice pitched low. "That's because we never properly bonded to an Alpha. We aren't really Pack Wilkie."

I could have sworn the whole room went silent. Or maybe it was all just muffled by the sound of blood rushing in my ears as Susannah casually revealed one of our most closely guarded secrets.

"Tanner!" The sound of the Alpha General calling for the vampire in front of us broke the five of us from our spell.

The vampire gave us a toothy grin. "I feel like there's definitely some kind of personal convo that needs to go on right here. Susannah, come and see me down at the clinic so I can map out your DNA. You should bring Quinn too, if it'd make you feel more comfortable."

I had a feeling that it had very little to do with Susannah's comfort and everything to do with the fact he knew I was an Omega too. I nodded quickly. "Sure.

No worries." I didn't know why he was keeping our secret for us, but he needed to leave before he changed his mind. He disappeared faster than I could follow.

I met Susannah's eyes. She silently apologized, and I forgave her in a heartbeat. When I turned, I expected Merrick and Murphy to be livid. Instead, both of them were absolutely expressionless.

Looking around the crowded room, Merrick cleared his throat. "We should step outside."

Susannah looked like she wanted to tell him to fuck off, but instead she sighed. "Let's go."

7

MURPHY

My mind was churning Susannah's words over and over in my head. Unbonded Omega. She wasn't Pack Wilkie. She wasn't legally attached to that psychopath. Something in my chest fluttered like a dying butterfly.

Finally, Susannah must have deemed us far enough away from the building, almost on the edge of the woods, because she stopped, turning to face us. Her jaw was lifted in that stubborn angle I knew too well. You could almost superimpose the teenage girl she'd been over the image of the beaten-down woman she was now.

I raised a single brow at her. "Are you going to explain?" I growled, and she narrowed her eyes at me.

"Why do we owe you any explanation?"

My growl turned into an ominous rumble. *Why? Is she serious?*

"Why? You want to know why we want an explanation?" Merrick snapped back. "How about for the *years* of torture where we had to look at the bruises on your arms, your neck, your face, and do *nothing* about it? Quinn's black eyes, and that time his fingers were all broken? What about all the nights we spent in lock-up after fighting Wilkie and Green, because the horror of your injuries was *too much,* and the old Alpha General punished us for interfering in another Pack's business?"

He stepped closer until he was in her personal space. "How about the time you stood in front of us, with that same expression on your face, and told us you loved Wilkie and that we should mind our own business? You broke our hearts, and you *didn't even bond* the piece of shit!"

Quinn threaded an arm between Susannah and himself, pulling her back a few steps until she was safely by his side. I gritted my teeth. "We would fucking pluck out our own eyeballs before we touched her in anger, Quinn," I snapped, but he just tilted his head at me and gave me a blank expression.

"So you say."

I ground my molars, but sucked back my anger. "Help us understand how you went a full decade without bonding to Wilkie? He doesn't seem like the 'wait for you to be ready' type of guy."

Quinn and Susannah looked at each other quickly, and there it was. Shared secrets that they'd buried so deep, no one would dig them out without their help.

It was Quinn who answered. "Wilkie had erectile dysfunction."

My mouth dropped open, because I hadn't seen that one coming. It smelled like the truth, but I'd have to be an idiot to think that was all there was to it. Pretty sure Wilkie would've downed an entire bottle of little blue pills if it meant he got two more people to subjugate.

Susannah definitely saw my skepticism. "This really isn't any of your business. I never asked you for help, or to fight my battles"—her voice broke a little—"or to give me anything as fragile as your hearts. That's all in the past."

The silence around us was almost preternatural. "You've left Wilkie's Pack then? For good?" Merrick's voice was hopeful. Not for our chances—she'd made her feelings on the matter clear years ago. No, hopeful that both her and Quinn had escaped that prison.

Quinn's face softened, and he lifted a hand hesitantly, gently laying it against Merrick's tight shoulder. "We're never going back. We're done. We've talked to the new Alpha General, and I think if he finds Wilkie alone in a darkened alleyway, Wilkie will cease to breathe."

I shuddered with relief. "Good." Susannah was still an unmated Omega, but Wilkie was arguably the worst Manix had to offer.

Quicker than a heartbeat, I was in Susannah's space, her jaw clutched softly in my hand so she was forced to look up at me. She could have pulled away, but she didn't. She just looked up at me with those huge eyes that were a little too shiny.

"This is your second chance, Spitfire. This is your chance to be happy. You *don't* accept the suit of anyone who doesn't worship the very ground you walk on. Who doesn't accept you and Quinn for who you are. You deserve to be treated like perfection, not as some fucking backwards Alpha's chew toy. You deserve the world. Don't accept anything less."

Inside me, my Beast screamed, CHOOSE ME, CHOOSE US, but I didn't voice it. We'd had our chance, and we weren't what she wanted.

She nodded, her head moving almost imperceptibly in my hand.

"Good." Unable to help myself, I kissed the top of her head, inhaling her scent like a creep. Releasing her, I strode away before I did something desperate and pathetic, like drop to my knees and beg them to give us a chance.

I was halfway back to the Alpha General's house

before Merrick caught up with me. I couldn't hear what he'd said to them, but I had no doubt it was something to do with the mystery of how two Betas could end up unbonded to the most vicious Alpha in town for a whole decade. That wasn't an equation that could go unsolved, and quite frankly, the math wasn't mathing.

"There's something not right," he said, confirming my suspicions that he wasn't just going to let this go, no matter how much Susannah demanded it. They were a lot alike, Merrick and Susannah. Both were too stubborn for their own good. Both were too willing to give up everything for the people they loved.

We knew Quinn's parents, and I'd wanted to knock the old couple down off their bigoted high horse more than once. I had no doubt that if Quinn had been forced into a mating with Wilkie, Susannah would have gone too. It made way more sense than Susannah's claims she was swept off her feet.

Her dad, who was as absent as a man could be while still living under the same roof, might have accepted it. The old Alpha General might have signed off on it too. But I'd known Susannah and Quinn. And I knew when her happiness was faked.

The main reception room of Courtland's house was a cacophony of scent and sound that gave me an instant headache. The overly sweet scent of new Omegas, combined with the mix of shifters—hell, even that slightly sticky scent of children and old food—was intense. "Let's give our congratulations to the De Léon pack and get the hell out of here. We can talk about this at home."

Merrick nodded, and we beelined for Radic, who was looking way better. He was standing beside Dominic, who was rocking from foot to foot like he couldn't wait to kick everyone out. We waited until the group of people they were currently speaking to moved away, then quickly slotted in front of Radic and Dominic.

Radic raised an eyebrow at us. "Slinking away so soon?" You wouldn't know that a few short weeks ago, I'd held my hand to his chest and tried to keep his blood inside his body.

Dominic grumbled beneath his breath. "Lucky."

I laughed at them both. He was right; we were the lucky ones. Lucky that our leadership wasn't a pack of prehistoric assholes anymore, who did more damage to our people than any outside threat.

"These kinds of things aren't our scene, you know that. Give me a training yard and a sword, and I'll hang out with you guys for hours."

Dominic snorted. "Fucking swords. Archaic bastards."

We were pretty stuck in the past here. Most of the Legion had been trained with hand weapons, as if the world hadn't progressed, and guns would never be used by our enemies. Merrick and I had trained pretty intensively with firearms, though, even before the new regime came to Maxton.

"Hey, I'll meet you at the gun range anytime if you want to lay down a challenge," I teased Dominic, and he winked.

"Going to hold you to that." He looked over my shoulder, his face softening. Turning my head, I saw the De Léon male Omega, Pryce, with one of his cubs. "I'll see you guys later," he said distractedly, moving toward the Omega like he was floating on a cloud, but not before his fingers ran down the spine of Radic. A violent man with a violent past, but he was a marshmallow for his Pack.

Radic watched him go with an amused smile on his face, then refocused on us. Merrick cleared his throat. "We just wanted to offer our congrats again."

Radic dipped his chin in acknowledgment. "Thank you." The silence stretched tight between us, until finally, he sighed. "Just ask. I know you want to."

"Susannah and Quinn are unbonded. The Alpha General is going to protect them, right? From Wilkie?"

Radic's face hardened. "Yes. Let's say that the protection of those weaker is one of Courtland's personal crusades—especially protecting them from Alpha abuse. If Wilkie tries to take them back by force, he's going to find himself headless as well as heartless." Radic's voice was cold, and I knew he was remembering the bruises and black eyes, the way Quinn flinched away from Alphas. His voice dropped lower. "That Alpha is a dead Manix walking—he just doesn't know it yet. Dominic doesn't forgive and forget. Wilkie used Green to kill Doc, because we all know that dumb fuck didn't have the sense to operate under his own steam. In doing so, he hurt Bonnie on such a fundamental level she might never be the same. He's on borrowed time."

I nodded, because that was all I needed to hear. "If you need help, you know where to find us."

Radic squeezed my arm. "We all appreciate what you did when shit went down." He dropped his hand, and his gaze flattened. "I know you guys and Susannah and Quinn have some unfinished business from when we were teens, but hear me when I say this: I don't care how much we like you guys—you force that Omega, or Quinn, into anything they don't want? It won't matter how much we like you, Courtland will kick your ass. They've had it hard, so if you're pursuing them, it's on their fucking terms. Hear me?"

Radic might be a Beta, but he didn't fuck around. He had power in his position, and he'd wield it to protect those who needed it. I could respect that.

"You have our word," Merrick said solemnly.

Radic nodded and smiled at us. "That being said, I know you guys will finally treat them how they deserve, so I'm rooting for you."

Someone called out to him, so we said our good-byes and left. Walking home, we were mostly silent, lost in our own thoughts.

Finally, standing outside the Packhouse we'd bought hoping to convince an Omega to join our Pack —never dreaming it could be Susannah—I looked over at my long-time friend and lover, the man who held a piece of my heart in his calloused hands. "What do you want to do?"

He held my gaze. "We take the gift that's been given to us and take our second chance. Show them that we're the Alphas they were always meant to be with."

We wouldn't fuck it up this time.

8

TANNER

My first assignment as a responsible member of the undead world, and I was already making a dog's breakfast of it. I'd let it slip that someone's Omega was pregnant, in a very public place, and then almost outed a hidden Omega. But mostly, I'd failed to live up to the ghost of the previous town doctor, whom the town had very obviously adored.

From the previous doctor's notes—which were nearly illegible, but he'd kept plenty of them—the need for a doctor in Maxton was twofold. Firstly, to hold hands and lend a supportive ear, and secondly, to stitch the odd finger back on and deliver babies.

No one was lining up for either service from a vampire. I'd been relieved when Courtland had given me the genealogy mapping project. Honestly though, their problems reproducing with each other had probably been a divine intervention, because that family tree was gnarly.

I hoped the new Alpha encouraged them to fish outside the Maxton lagoon for potential mates, otherwise their little Manixlettes were going to have more heads than a Kings Cross brothel.

I looked at the new Omega in front of me, a woman in her mid-twenties with dirt under her fingernails and sporting a frown. Her notes said she was a mechanic and worked with her father. Her Beta mother had died during childbirth, so she'd been raised by just her paternal parent.

I continued writing down names as she rattled them off, and we were only up to second cousins. Half of Maxton must have been listed here.

Now was the time for me to put my professional doctor's hat on, because this part was about to get awkward. "As you've probably been made aware, the heat will hit once every six to eight months. It's important that you have a plan in place for that time, whether it be potential partners or a secure location to ride out the heat. I can give you painkillers and hormone stabilizers that'll ease the uncomfortable nature of the heat symptoms, but I can't lie to you— from all accounts I've found, it's miserable without, uh... *other things* to take your mind off it."

Mischa snorted. "Have you seen the list? I'm related

to every single one of the eligible Manix in this town. And the ones who aren't genetically related to me somehow aren't people I want to fuck, if you catch my drift."

I winced, because yeah, I definitely got her point. "No one said they had to be Manix. Or from Maxton."

She blinked at me. "What?"

I shrugged, flicking through the notes I had in front of me. "Nothing in my research says that another supernatural can't satisfy the heat urges, especially one with a knot. Or hell, even a human. Obviously, proper birth control would be necessary, because offspring between full-blooded Manix and full-blooded two-natured shifters can have some serious birth defects, but otherwise, let a thousand blossoms bloom," I finished, my voice kinda strangled. Why did I have to spend the day having the birds and the bees talk with Omegas?

"The old Alpha General prohibited it," she whispered, like it was still treason.

I snorted. "No offense, but the old Alpha General sounded like a tosser. Honestly, talk about a hypocrite."

I'd done the Huxley-Grey Pack first in my genealogy quest, considering Naja Huxley-Grey was kind of the reason for this whole thing. I'd learned that one of her Alphas was the half-blood son of the old Alpha General and a human. *What a tool.*

"My father would have a heart attack if I spent a week shacked up with a shifter."

"Not going to lie, Miss Hayles, the Manix are going to have to learn to think outside the box. Otherwise, it won't matter if you have dozens of new Omegas—your bloodlines will start looking like that of European royalty, if you know what I mean."

"They'll all have knobbly knees and weak chins?"

I grinned. "Exactly." Fear flashed through her eyes, and I cursed the fangs. *Dammit.* "Anyway, let me know if you have any questions or develop any concerning symptoms."

Mischa nodded and stumbled out of the office, like this was all just too much. I couldn't even imagine what it would be like to move through your life thinking you were one thing, and then magically being turned into something else.

Oh, wait.

I sighed, resting my head on the smooth wooden desk. The work was interesting, and given the Manix had been considered extinct until a little while ago, it was quite an honor to get this post.

The entry door tinkled, and I lifted my head up from its defeated position. It would take me a little while to get my shit together, and the town needed time to get used to me. Or hell, maybe they wouldn't, and they'd train someone else up to be the town doctor. It was easy to forget I was immortal. I would always look like a twenty-three-year-old bush doctor who spent too much time swimming the Sydney beaches. I'd always have the bite mark on my thigh where the Great White took a nibble while I was swimming, though my turning had healed the wound without any lasting damage. I'd been lucky that my maker, Steve, had stumbled across me, washed up on the rocks off Domain Beach, and changed me.

Steve was absolutely fucking insane. The guy had spent too much time in the sun, and it'd baked something in his head. We might've been able to withstand the sun here in the States, but in Australia? There was no fucking ozone layer, so we burned like a crisp in the mid-afternoon glare. It was definitely not a place for vampires, who dwelled better in the darkness.

I'd moved here not long after I was able to control myself around humans, but Steve had stayed. He liked to go swimming in the ocean at night, punching sharks in the nose, or fighting them over bleeding prey. He explored the depths of the coral reef, free dived until the pressure forced him to emerge, and lived in a cave off the coastal cliffs.

For a time there between the 1860s and the 1920s, he'd lived exclusively off shark blood. He'd insisted it was better for us, since the red blood cells weren't created by dirty bone marrow, but by specialist organs near their gonads and their esophagus.

Anyway, there'd been a downturn in shark attacks

over those decades, because even sharks didn't want sharp teeth near their gonads.

After that, surfing had come to Australia, and the Aussies took it up with force, me included. But it meant there were way too many people in the water, and no one was going to miss some guy who looked like he was trying to suck off a shark.

The scents in the waiting room finally permeated my senses. My fangs dropped and ached, which was an entirely inappropriate response. Manix tended to smell good, like a barbeque in the distance. But the two Manix in the waiting room? They smelled like perfectly cooked porterhouse steak after you'd been on a diet of bamboo for a month.

It couldn't be an Omega thing, because Mischa hadn't smelled like that. Maybe it was a mated, unbonded pair thing?

I bit back a groan, pasting a professional smile on my face as Quinn and Susannah Wilkie walked into my examination room. No, not Wilkie, apparently. I wondered if unmated Omega pairs took each other's names? Did they decide on one until they had an Alpha, or did they keep their own family names? A question for another time, that was for sure.

"Susannah, Quinn. Thank you for stopping by. Come on in. Or you can do your appointments separately, if that would make you more comfortable?" My eyes drifted to Quinn, the Omega masquerading as a

Beta. He was handsome, but after a century of keeping the gene pool small and the male-to-female ratio being so skewed, the current generation of Manix were all oddly attractive. When your options were limited, sometimes something as mundane as the physical attractiveness of your partner mattered most.

Quinn had light brown hair that had a slight curl to it, so it was a little chaotic. He had that warm skin tone most of the Manix had, and eyes that bordered on aquamarine. His chin had a slight cleft, and his nose was slightly crooked, as if it had been broken and never set correctly. He was handsome; it was undeniable.

As the muted light from the skylight hit Susannah's cheekbones, and the freckles spread across them, I recognised that they both had a quiet kind of beauty. Not as flashy and cover model beautiful as some of the Omegas I'd interviewed since my arrival, but a quiet sort of intensity, like they were trying to hide their uniqueness under the radar. Which, if I was right, was exactly what they were doing.

"Let's get the truth out in the open, and I'm sure we'll get along like a house on fire." I turned to Quinn. "You're an Omega." A furtive nod. "But everyone thinks you're a Beta?" Another nod. This was going to be slow going, then. "Even the Alpha General thinks you're a Beta? Your parents?" Courtland De Léon had senses almost as good as a vampire. If whatever Quinn was doing to keep his designation under wraps could fool him, it was probably something I should know about.

It was Susannah who answered. "Nobody knows. Except Quinn and me."

"And now you," Quinn added.

I nodded solemnly. I wanted them to know that I understood the gravity of their trust. "Everything you tell me is confidential, from everyone. Even the Alpha General."

Quinn hoisted himself up onto the examination table. "It almost doesn't matter anymore. I'm tired of hiding."

Susannah's head whipped toward him, her brow folded into a frown. "It's too soon. What if the Manix forgive and forget Wilkie's betrayal, and they make you go back? You know if your parents found out, they'd have you mated off to the next available Pack."

"I'm not a kid anymore, Zanny. I can stand up to them." Susannah snorted derisively, making Quinn bristle, but I could smell her fear beneath the bravado.

I lifted a hand to stop the argument. "There's no need to rush into anything. Take your time to decide. But I think you should start from the very beginning."

The tale they told me filled me with rage. Their former Pack Alpha was a dead man walking.

9

MERRICK

This was creepy. Logically, I knew that. Well, the man knew that. The Beast? He thought this was the best idea we'd had since last night. In fact, every night for the last nine nights I'd sat in the front yard of a Legion General's house.

I'd snuck out of my bed beside Murphy, leaving out the same note I'd placed on the dining table every night. But Murphy was a notoriously heavy sleeper—not a good thing for a soldier, but great when his life-long partner was doing his best impression of a stalker. I didn't trust Wilkie not to steal them back. If he tried, I wanted to be here to put him down permanently.

Hidden in the trees behind the house, I knew which room used to be Susannah's, and given the soft light that glowed behind her curtains, it was still her room. We'd been nine the first time I'd snuck into her bedroom. It had been an innocent thing back then; we'd whispered ghost stories and eaten candy I'd managed to hide away from my brothers.

Those nights had just been us. Both Quinn and Murphy's parents were strict, so they stood no chance of joining us, and at the time, I hadn't minded. I'd always been exceptionally good at hiding my scent, which was the only reason I hadn't been pounded by her brothers as I got older. I'd enjoyed it being a small moment for just Susannah and I in those darkened hours, when we'd whisper our greatest hopes, and I'd hold her in my arms as we talked about our greatest fears.

When we'd hit fifteen, and it was clear I was an Alpha and she was a Beta, things changed. The innocence of those nights disappeared, to be replaced by hormones and my first kiss. Well, my first kiss with a girl. Murphy had been my first everything else.

"I should be surprised you're out here, but I'm really not."

The soft, lilting voice behind me made my chest leap with happiness, like it did every single time I heard it. Closing my eyes, I breathed in her scent, taking in the feel of the air around us. Then I straightened my face, because she wasn't ready for that expression.

"I should be surprised that you managed to sneak up on a trained Legion soldier again, but I'm really not." I turned, and there she was. My childhood crush, the dream who'd turned into a nightmare. "You shouldn't be out here; it's late."

She raised a single eyebrow. "I could say the same to you."

I inclined my head. "Then we'd both be right."

Instead of moving back toward the house, she sat down beside me. "It's weird being home. I kind of expected you to climb through my window again."

"I didn't think it would be quite as welcomed as it once was," I murmured, giving her a crooked smile.

She sighed and tilted her head back to look at the stars. "No, probably not. Things got so complicated."

I grunted my agreement and just sat beside her, soaking in her presence, like I was a plant who'd been deprived of water for so fucking long that I was basically just a husk. I pretended to concentrate on the stars like she was, so she wouldn't think I was looming.

Shrugging off my jacket, I laid it on the grass behind us, then lay down. I didn't tell her to join me, didn't put any pressure on her at all. This moment felt fragile, and I was determined to hang onto it as long as possible.

I held my breath as she lay down beside me, her body pressed to my side softly. "Are you ever going to tell me what went wrong?"

She stiffened but slowly relaxed, though she was

still silent. "I guess I can probably tell you now, but you have to promise you won't tell a soul."

With those words, I was transported back to being a twelve-year-old kid again, staring at the glow-in-the-dark stars on her bedroom ceiling. "I swear it. Except for Murphy."

She snorted a laugh. "Nothing's changed, then."

I turned my face to look at hers. "No. I love him more now than I could've even imagined back when we were kids."

She met my eyes. "You'd do anything for him, right? Anything to keep him safe?"

My brow creased. "Of course."

"What if you thought he was an Alpha but really, he was something else, and you knew if his parents found out, his life would be miserable?"

"Susannah..."

"What if you *tried* to save him, and instead it backfired horribly, and then the only thing you could do to keep him safe was to become the shield between him and a monster? Even if it meant giving up your own happiness. Even if it meant lying to everyone. Would you do it?"

I swallowed hard, feeling the slight tremble of her body beside mine. I wanted to grab her, drag her into my arms and tell her that I'd be the shield between her and the monsters now. The shield for both of them.

Instead, I reached out and twined my fingers

through hers. "You know I would. What's this all about, Zanny?" I used her childhood nickname for the first time in a decade. It had felt wrong calling her something so intimate when she'd belonged to another Pack.

She blew a large breath out her nose, and I could feel her tensing. "Quinn is an Omega."

Of all the things I thought she was going to say, that wasn't it. "No, he's not. He doesn't smell like an Omega."

She turned to me, and if looks could castrate, my balls would be sashimi on the floor right now. "Are you Alpha-splaining Omegas to me, an actual Omega, right now?"

Ah shit. Backtrack, backtrack. "Of course not. I just... I've stood next to him. Had entire conversations with him. I've breathed him in. He *smells* like a Beta." I squeezed her hand. "Is that why you guys ran away? I knew there had to be a reason—other than teenage rebellion, like the grapevine said." I cleared my throat. "I always thought that it was perhaps because of what we said. What we asked."

Yeah, we'd told her that we wanted her to be Pack —Quinn too—because even back then, they were a package deal. Murphy had told her he loved her, an emotion we both felt, but I still didn't have the balls to say it out loud. Less than two days later, she was gone, and when she came back, she'd walked right into Wilkie's arms. Or so I thought.

She closed her eyes against the night, and I wanted to drop it. She seemed even more vulnerable out here in the darkness, like the moon had stripped away all her armor and left her bare to the elements.

"That wasn't it at all. It had nothing to do with you and Murphy." She let out a mirthless laugh. "Okay, maybe a little to do with you, but not in the way you think." She rolled onto her side, and I was forced to stare into those pretty eyes that had haunted my dreams. "This is really Quinn's story to tell, but he doesn't like talking about it, so I'm pretty sure he won't care. It happened the night after you and Murphy walked us home from Roch's party. You'd given me your hoodie to keep me warm, and I was pretty sure you and Murphy were the most perfect Alphas in all of Maxton. Way better than the rest of those drooling bastards, who only cared about me because Raiden was my brother and they wanted to use me to get a little closer to an Omega."

Raiden was nice, but we'd never had the spark we had with his older sister, that was for sure. You only had to see him with the Huxley-Grey Pack to know there were no other men or Manix for him. The addition of Naja had only cemented that. I made a soft sound of assent so she'd continue.

"Anyway, that night, I was still in your hoodie when Quinn came over to tell me that his parents had promised him to Wilkie as a Beta when he turned eighteen. He was stressed, terrified even. Quinn is beautiful, obviously, and I knew enough about Wilkie even back then to know he liked to break pretty things. I was holding him, promising him everything would be okay, that Murphy had said he loved me and I'd insisted on Quinn also being part of the Pack when it happened. He buried his face in the hoodie I was wearing—*your* hoodie—and he let out an Omega whine. And his scent, it filled the air, thick like melted chocolate. I might never have seen an Omega in the early stages of the yearning, but I knew that sound instinctually. Later, we figured it was because he smelled your scent in the fibers of the hoodie."

I shifted a little closer, pressing the side of my body against hers to share my warmth, and maybe also because I just wanted to touch her. "It's coded into our DNA. Alphas for sure, but Betas too. It's our instinct to take care of Omegas when they make that sound."

Susannah chuckled softly. "You aren't kidding. I almost tore his pants off and sucked his dick just so he wouldn't be in pain, but I knew that would have to wait. I doused him in one of my mother's perfumes, packed two bags, and we ran away that night. I was still in your hoodie. Because if Wilkie would break him as a Beta? He would *destroy* him as an Omega, and there would be no way Quinn's parents would let us bond with you."

All this fucking time, I thought she'd rejected us. That she'd run away because we'd pressed her too fast, or hadn't shown her that Quinn mattered to us too. She should have run to us; instead, she ran out into a world that was filled with evil and danger.

"We would have helped you." It was a naive thing to say, and I thought I was past that. But the boy who'd given his heart to this girl was still inside me.

She laid her head on the crook of my arm, snuggling close. It was like the last ten years melted away in that moment, and reality was pushed further into the darkness. "I know you would have. But you were kids too. You weren't Legion soldiers yet. You weren't asskicking Merrick and Murphy, the dynamic duo. We were all just kids with big dreams and no good sense."

"So you ran."

"Yeah. To California. Best month of my life holed up in San Francisco, in a dingy pay-by-the-hour hotel with roaches, dipping our toes in the ocean, eating cheap food from back-alley dives. We had no plan, but I would have done anything to save him." She smiled, but it melted away slowly, painfully. "And then we were dragged back. You know the rest."

Quinn's parents had made him bond with Wilkie immediately, Susannah had confessed her undying love for the older Alpha, and Murphy and I nursed broken hearts for years after. All because Quinn's parents were scheming assholes and biology had decided to kick Quinn while he was down.

So many mistakes and misunderstandings. So much time lost.

"I still don't understand how Quinn smells like a Beta."

Susannah looked away from me, staring up at the stars once more. "We had help. An unlikely friend. But I can't tell you more than that."

I gritted my back teeth, breathing deeply to push down the hurt that she was still keeping secrets. Susannah didn't owe me a damn thing. Not her secrets, not a new chance, nothing. It was my job to prove to her that we were worthy of both her and Quinn's love. That we were the Alphas who would protect her from the people that would try and tear her down.

I didn't say anything for a long time, just wrapping my arms around her and breathing her in. Finally, as the sun started to turn the horizon purple, and my eyes were heavy with sleep, I asked *the* question. "What will you do now? Now that you've left Wilkie behind for good and no one's going to make either of you go back." I squeezed her tighter, so she knew that I would personally harm anyone who tried to force her or Quinn to do a single thing.

"Tanner suggested that Quinn should go off his Omega suppressants. He said it wasn't healthy to deny biology for so long. Plus, they prevent him from shifting." A soft smile curled her lips, and I felt jealousy that the vampire could elicit that response from the woman who was in my very soul. "He said he would personally ensure that there'd be no blowback from Wilkie or the Alpha General. I got the feeling that he'd inform the Alpha General, but his conversation with Wilkie would be a little more permanent."

A low rumble vibrated my chest. "He might have to take a number and get in line if he wants a pound of flesh from that fucker."

She grinned at me, an expression that was like a thousand volts to the heart. "I get ticket number one." She blew out a breath. "I don't know if we're ready for the questions that come with both of us suddenly being Omegas. Or the feeding frenzy that'll come from being an Omega pair. I just got out of a Pack I didn't want, one filled with users. I don't want that again."

I squeezed her tight, knowing I was going to be a part of that frenzy. Fuck, I felt like the worst person. "You take your time, Zanny. Or don't—you don't *need* a Pack, if that isn't what you want. You can just have Quinn and be happy. Don't let anyone tell you differently, because I'll set them straight in a way they won't soon forget."

She laughed softly. I could feel her inhaling my scent as her eyes drifted closed. "I've missed you guys so much. Missed your friendship."

I shouldn't have done it, but it was impossible to resist. I kissed the top of her head softly. "You'll never have to miss us again, Zanny. I promise you that on my scales and claws."

But she was asleep, and I was once again that boy holding the girl he loved until the sun lit the sky, then I'd wander back home, counting down the hours until I could be with her again.

10

SUSANNAH

The night with Merrick almost seemed like a dream I'd conjured from the past. I'd woken up on the grass in my backyard alone, the early morning sun pressing against my eyelids. The only sign he'd even been there was his jacket that he'd wrapped around me.

I'd crawled into bed beside Quinn and confessed that I'd told Merrick everything. And I meant *everything*. I couldn't work out what it was about that Alpha, but he made me want to bare my soul to him. It had been that way for as long as I could remember.

Quinn hadn't been particularly impressed, but he'd gotten over it quickly. The weight of keeping the secret had always been a lodestone around his neck. The sooner we could shake free of it, the better for us. But not yet. We were heading to get coffee in town, and the eyes of the townsfolk on me were already heavy. I wasn't sure I could deal with being in public if the full extent of our subterfuge came out. Soon, maybe.

However, beneath the weighty judgment of public opinion was a feeling of freedom that I'd been denied for so damn long. With my hand wrapped in Quinn's, the sun beginning to dip behind the mountains giving us a reprieve from the heat, and the heavy weight of having to return to Wilkie's Packhouse gone? Well, it was like a high I hadn't known was possible.

We hadn't attended the burial of the Pack's Beta, Green, and given that he'd killed Doc and was just a shitty person in general, I doubted many others had either.

Walking into the coffee shop, no one spoke to us. We were shunned by extension, but whatever; I didn't want to talk to most of these judgmental fuckers anyway. My nonchalance didn't stop the sounds of gossip swirling around the room after us, though.

"Did you hear about the Wiley-Fletcher-Reid Pack's feral little Omega? Apparently, Corvin and Beckett had her hidden away in a private love nest in the middle of the woods like a heathen, just out there, scraping away in the dirt. I heard she hissed at Radic the first time she met him. If I were Darius and Cooper, I'd have left their asses in the dust."

I didn't turn around to see who was gossiping. Honestly, it was probably the same poison that had passed dozens of sets of lips. It was shit, but at least they weren't talking about me and Quinn.

We hadn't told anyone that we'd left Wilkie's Pack. We'd been holed up in my dad's house, but very few people knew that either. Everyone thought that Wilkie had stashed me there while he figured things out after the "betrayal" of his Beta, Green. Apparently, Wilkie had been telling everyone how happy he was that the Goddess had granted him an Omega, like he'd been found particularly worthy when none of the other mated Beta females had been turned. That had swayed more than a few people to Wilkie's side, because they didn't know he'd never actually bonded either of us. Who would stay in a Pack unbonded for nearly a decade?

No one, that's who.

"Wilkie told me he wanted to have his new Omega pregnant and the next generation running around his Packhouse by the end of the year. A new, pure generation—unlike the rest of the cubs that have been born in the last few years. Someone has to keep the Manix purity alive."

My good mood disappearing through my fingers like water, I moved up to the counter and ordered my coffee. I wanted to be out of here *now*. Taylor, the kid behind the counter, took our orders and gave the stink eye to the gossiping old bastards.

Eventually, the old guard would die off, and then

kids like Taylor—who lived up at the Sanctum—would finally be able to breathe without being judged as a half-blood.

Quinn looked around the room. "We'll take the coffees to go."

Taylor nodded, and I could tell that to him, we were guilty by association. I couldn't blame him. I wanted to scream that I'd rather cut out my uterus than have a child with the sociopathic fuck, but instead I just clenched my jaw so tight my teeth threatened to crack.

Finally, coffees in hand, we got out of that cesspool. Maybe I wasn't ready to come outside yet, wasn't ready to face the world and its judgment. The sooner we could distance ourselves from Wilkie and his shitty ideologies, the better.

I swallowed down my anger. "We should go talk to the Alpha General and Radic. See if we can't get out of here for a little while."

"Drop the bombshell and run?" Quinn asked, raising an eyebrow.

I smiled at him. "Exactly."

We were walking past the alleyway behind the bakery, when Quinn was yanked hard to the side. His coffee went flying, splattering hot liquid over my bare legs and feet, burning me. It felt like I was moving in quicksand as I looked down the alley beside me.

Wilkie, in Beast form, had Quinn by the throat,

pressing him against the wall as he drove his fist into Quinn's gut.

"*NO!*" I screamed. I rushed Wilkie, but the guy was fucking huge and he wasn't budging. I freed my Beast, giving myself claws and fangs, and tried again, but he hardly moved an inch. I screeched helplessly as Quinn's face turned purple. I hammered Wilkie uselessly with my claws, but they just bounced off. Reaching up, I tried to dig them into his eyeballs, but he grabbed me and flung me further down the alley.

"You stole my Omega from me, you worthless little fuck. And because of you, I lost my fucking ear. You think I was just going to let that pass?" Another hard blow against Quinn's stomach made him retch and moan. I was up, grabbing at Wilkie's hand, trying to pry it from Quinn's throat as his face went a sickly blue shade and his eyes began to roll back.

"Stop it! You're *killing* him!" I screeched at Wilkie. "*Help!*"

But no one came. I knew the people inside the bakery must have heard, but no one came to help. I kicked at his knee, at his balls, I scratched and clawed and bit, but nothing worked.

The next thing I knew, Wilkie was yanked away, and Quinn slid lifelessly to the ground.

"No, no, no... Quinn?" I whispered, shifting back, feeling for his pulse. "Baby. Wake up."

"He still has a pulse. He's just unconscious."

I whipped around, my teeth bared. Tanner stood behind us, his foot on Wilkie's throat. The Alpha's arms were at odd angles, and he was breathing hard, either in anger or pain. Or maybe both. Beneath the effortless strength of Tanner, he struggled uselessly.

"You're a dead man!" Wilkie howled. "Fucking bloodsucker. Your time in Maxton is done."

Tanner actually laughed in his face. "Ya think so?" He pulled out a phone, swiping the screen and lifting it to his ear. "Hey, mate, it's Tanner. I just found your favorite Alpha beating the shit out of his former Beta. Yeah. Nah, don't worry about it. Wasn't hard to overpower him. Like putting down a kitten."

Wilkie thrashed even harder at that. Clearly, he didn't like it when someone used their brute strength against him. *Boohoo!*

"Quinn's unconscious, so I'd like to get him back to the surgery as quickly as I can. Yeah, with pleasure. I'll just put the Alpha in the garbage bin where he belongs, and you guys can come and get him. Alley by the bakery. Okay. No worries, I'll keep you updated." Tanner hung up and stuck his phone in the back pocket of his jeans. He looked down at Wilkie, and there was a flash of the predator on his face. "Lights out, mate."

He kicked Wilkie in the temple so hard, the Alpha slid across the alley and into the side of a dumpster.

Lifting the lid, Tanner threw Wilkie in like a bag of trash.

"What a waste of good oxygen," he muttered, before shutting the lid and locking it. Then he was in front of me, carefully picking up Quinn. "Let's go and get him checked out, hey?" His voice was gentle, and I realized I was shaking. I nodded, following behind him, and I knew he was moderating his steps so I could keep up.

I avoided the eyes of the other people in Maxton, none of whom had come to help when I'd needed it. No, it was a vampire, an outsider, who had come to our aid. These fuckers and their backwards views hadn't really changed, despite the change in leadership. They still believed a Pack should deal with its own issues. No, not everyone, but so, so many.

Plus, not many people wanted to get on the bad side of Wilkie, that vindictive asshole. Very few Manix would ever challenge him and get away with it. I was just unfortunate that none of those people had been within hearing distance today.

We stepped into the doctor's office, and thankfully, the waiting room was empty. Tanner laid Quinn down on the table and got to work. As soon as his body touched the cool metal, Quinn's eyes opened, and he groaned. Then he whimpered.

I was beside him in an instant. "Shh, it's okay. You're at the doctor's. You're okay."

"Hurts," he moaned, and I felt physically sick. This was my fault. No, it was fucking *Wilkie's* fault.

"I'm going to kill him, Quinn. I'm going to put him in the ground, then I'll shit on his grave. I promise. Somehow, it will happen."

Tanner cleared his throat. "I'm just going to take some X-rays of his ribs. I'm also a little worried that given the amount of bruising, he might have fractures in the cartilage around his larynx and trachea." He looked down at Quinn. "Sorry, Q. This might hurt a little." He prodded around Quinn's throat, his face filled with professional concern. "Let me know if you feel any crackling or popping sensations, okay?"

In the end, Quinn had two broken ribs, but thankfully only soft tissue damage to his throat. Given the rate we healed, Tanner thought he'd be as good as new in three to four days. Well, on the outside.

The terror Wilkie had inflicted on us for so long would take an age to heal, if it ever did at all. Because how could you heal from your wounds if the monster was hiding in the shadows, ready to cut you open all over again?

11

QUINN

Susannah hadn't left my side in days, playing nursemaid. My injuries were slowly healing, but I wasn't sure she'd ever forget the terror of watching me go down anytime soon. She'd told me everything that happened, her voice breaking toward the end, and that hurt me more than anything.

Susannah was strong; she didn't cry, even when she needed to. She didn't break, even if sometimes she bent beyond what she should. As she hovered, I wished I was an Alpha. Bigger and stronger so I could protect her against men like Wilkie, instead of just being another liability.

When she'd told me about Tanner coming to our rescue, I knew I owed a debt to the vampire. None of our own kind had come, but a near-stranger—a "vicious predator" if you listened to some of the gossip —had rushed to help.

I had my follow-up appointment today, and I didn't know if I should bake him a cake or give him a year's worth of blowjobs for saving me. Saving us. Shaking my head, I gently nudged Susannah awake. I'd leave her asleep if I didn't think she'd panic when she woke up and saw me gone. This was our life now. He'd filled our moments with terror.

"Babe, wake up. We're going to be late."

She nuzzled closer to me, and I breathed in the scent that was so quintessentially her. Kinda sweet and spicy, like gingerbread or Christmas. "It's too early," she grumbled.

I kissed her soft cheek. "It's almost ten. We have to be there in fifteen minutes."

Her eyes snapped open. Her dad was a literal General, and he'd drilled into his kids that if you weren't fifteen minutes early, you were late. "Why did you wait so long? Get up, get up!" she insisted, nudging me gently out of bed.

We had the world's quickest shower, where I only groped her slippery boob once—okay, twice—and then we were dressed and downstairs with five minutes to get across town.

My feet stilled at the front door. Merrick and Murphy stood there in their Legion uniforms, lazing on the front porch, talking to Susannah's father. When we appeared, they straightened.

Murphy nodded a greeting. "Quinn, Susannah. The Alpha General thought it would be best if you had an escort for a little while, until things calm down."

I frowned. "Isn't Wilkie in the cells beneath the Legion building? How much more calming should he need?" That was where Tanner had said they were going to take him when I'd asked what happened to him.

Every Alpha on that porch frowned, and the stink of anger burned my nose. "No. Someone let him out," Susannah's father, Joshua, growled.

I felt sick. I gripped Susannah closer to me, like a security blanket. I could still feel his fingers around my throat, choking me, like he enjoyed watching the life leave my eyes.

There was a rumbling noise from Merrick, which was somewhere between a purr and a growl. Like he was swallowing down his anger and trying to soothe me all at once. "You're safe here, and we'll make sure you're safe out there as well, until I can track that fucker down and rip his other ear off."

That made Susannah laugh, but it was a wild, hysterical sound. I had to push my own panic down, for her. Steeling my spine, I wrapped my arm across her shoulders. "Thanks. We better get going or we'll be late."

And just like that, we had a military escort to town. My bruises had faded to a disgusting yellow color that made me look like I had jaundice and not like I'd had the shit beaten out of me. I kept it all covered in a long-sleeved crew-neck shirt, refusing to be fodder for the gossipmongers.

We climbed into Merrick's ATV, and I wrapped my arm around Susannah's waist, holding her tightly to me as we drove down the dirt tracks that made up most of the roads in Maxton. Paving anything but the road in and out would raise too many questions.

I watched the trees, and with every slight movement I wondered if it was Wilkie. I hated this. Every bump made my ribs ache. Jumping at shadows. The acrid smell of Susannah's fear.

Finally, we were outside the clinic. "We'll be fine from here. Tanner will keep us safe."

I watched the play of emotions that raced over Merrick's face at Susannah's words. Murphy merely raised his eyebrows. "Tanner, is it? Sounds comfortable."

Now it was my turn to frown. "When he saves you from being strangled to death, you're allowed to be on a first-name basis."

Merrick dipped his chin. "Of course."

They let us go, holding open the door as we walked into the surgery. Tanner appeared almost instantly, his face devoid of its usual professional mask, instead twisted in concern.

"Come in, come in." He ushered us into the examination room, his hand lightly on my spine as I walked past. I tried not to tense, not because it felt wrong, but because it felt kind of right. Ignoring the weird response, I hoisted myself up onto the examination table, wincing as my ribs twisted the wrong way. Well, that's what I got for trying to subtly flirt.

Both Susannah and Tanner were looking at me with concerned eyes. "Sorry, I forgot they were broken for a second." Susannah gave me her *bitch, please* look, and I flushed.

Tanner grinned, those fangs peeking out. "I guess that's a good sign if you forget they're broken, even just for a bit. Though you should probably rest them a little more over the next couple of days."

I nodded. "Susannah and I decided that while I was resting, it might be a good time to go off my Omega masking meds too."

"Oh?" he asked, examining my throat with cool, gentle fingers.

"They stop me from shifting. I would be fully healed if I could shift, and I don't want to be helpless ever again."

I could almost hear his teeth grinding, and I slid my gaze to his. He straightened, looking down at me.

He was well over six feet, and I wondered if they just bred them tall in Australia.

"I'm sorry that some fucking coward has forced you into a decision you weren't ready to make. I'm kind of regretting not taking him to jail myself and possum-stomping him on every gutter between that alley and the Legion building," he muttered, more to himself than to me. "Take your shirt off, and I'll restrap your ribs." I did as he asked, flushing under the intensity of his gaze. He tilted his head to the side. "I can tell you've gone off your meds. Your scent profile has changed slightly. You should be careful of a possible hormonal pushback. After being denied so long, you might go into the yearning if you just quit cold turkey. You should ease them off slowly, if you can."

Susannah was sitting in the corner, uncharacteristically silent. She was watching Tanner with an expression I'd rarely seen in the last ten years, unless she was looking at me.

Desire. *Interesting.*

I mean, not unwarranted either. Doc Tanner was handsome as hell. The quintessential Australian surfer: hair bleached by the sun, a tan that not even death could steal, tall and broad in the shoulders, and lean in the hips. I bet if he was naked, he'd have a six-pack.

Well, there was only one way to find out. "Do you have a six-pack?"

"Quinn!" Susannah gasped, like I'd just asked to see his dick and not his stomach.

I shrugged. "Don't pretend like you weren't wondering." I gave her back the same imperious look she was using on me.

"*Definitely* some hormonal kickback," Tanner said with a laugh. "Not going to lie, mate, I'm pretty cut under this white coat. That 1800s lifestyle of hard labor and no food—not to mention being turned into the undead—will do that to you." He artfully stuck medical tape on me, like he was wrapping a football to put under the Christmas tree.

"I think I might need proof. You should show us," I purred, and Susannah buried her face in her hands, her cheeks pink. "I'll show you mine if you show me yours." It was like my tongue had been possessed by the Demon of Horniness.

Tanner pulled my shirt back over my head, still laughing. "Tempting offer, but I've never been with a bloke." He smirked, and it made his eyes dance with mirth. "Too many human hangups, but you know what they say—never say never. What's the point of living forever if you don't try everything once, right?"

"Bloke?"

"Men, Quinn," Susannah growled. "He doesn't do men."

I raised an eyebrow. "That's not what I heard. But oh well, what about pretty Omega women with too much loyalty and a little bit of a martyr complex?" I teased, and Susannah was immediately up, dragging me off the examination table and over to the door, like she would shove me out of it if I opened my mouth again.

"Oh my Goddess, Quinn. *Shut up*," she hissed. She looked at a spot in the middle of Tanner's chest. "He's good to go, right?"

"Sure, Omega. Make him rest, though." Susannah nodded and pulled me through the doorway. We got to the outer door of the waiting room when Tanner called, "Quinn?"

"Yeah?"

"That's definitely my type."

Susannah made a high-pitched whining noise and slammed the door. Stuffing me in the back of Merrick's ATV, she hissed, "You are so embarrassing. Fucking horny Omegas."

But I knew my girl. I knew under some of that embarrassment, she was wondering what it would be like to go to bed with the vampire. She'd denied herself so much to protect me over the years—a proper Pack, love, someone to depend on—and now that we were free, I intended to give her everything she wanted. Even if it was a tall vampire doctor with a funny accent.

I looked at the two Alphas in the front of the ATV, and Murphy's gaze met mine in the mirror. "Everything went okay?" The way his eyes ran over me, like he was checking me for damage, told me it was more than professional interest. I held his gaze, letting the armor I kept around my heart, hard and cold, crack a little at his obvious concern. He could have been our Alpha. We could have been so damn happy; I knew that in my soul.

Merrick and Murphy were the best kind of Manix. Strong but kind. Giving. They'd have loved Susannah and I like we were the suns that they rotated around. I'd fucked that up for her. For me.

But not anymore. They mightn't want us anymore, but I was trying to give Susannah everything she'd ever desired, and I was going to start with these two Alphas.

My inner Omega whined. Maybe not just for Susannah.

"Do you guys remember that watering hole, up past the Olsen house? The kids got banned from going there about five years ago when one jumped off the rocks and broke both legs?"

Murphy nodded. "Of course."

"Can we go up there? I don't want to go home and sit inside, hiding from the world."

Merrick and Murphy shared a look. "It'll be busy on a hot day like today, but we have somewhere better," Merrick said with a grin. "You're going to want to hold on—the trip is a little bumpy."

Susannah was giving me a confused look, and I shrugged, leaning over to kiss her cheek. "Better hold on, babe."

She shook her head. "Damn Omega hormones."

12

MURPHY

We'd found this swimming spot once when we were doing a perimeter check for the Legion. It was the most perfect swimming hole you could ever ask for. Large boulders hid it from the world, and you had to squeeze through a tiny gap to get down to it. But once you got there, it was spread out before you like a hidden world. It was on a tight bend in the river, so the water pooled into a small rocky outcropping. A tree grew up from a gap between the stones, like it had pushed its way to the surface just to provide the perfect amount of shade to cool some of the stone for swimmers to escape the blazing summer heat.

Merrick and I had sex under that tree more times than I could count on two hands.

Quinn spun in a circle. "This is amazing," he

murmured softly, and my Beast preened at his words. We'd put that note of wonder in his voice. We'd done that.

"The water drops to quite a deep pool, so you can swim properly," I told them, taking my shirt off and setting it on the ground so they could sit on it. "It comes from the mountain, so most of the time the water is pretty cold, but I like it."

The scent of desire swirled around us, and I bit back the grin that wanted to consume my features. Unbuckling my belt, I pulled it out with a one-handed snap and laid it beside my shirt, my pants quickly following until I was in nothing but my boxer shorts and a smile. Quinn was looking at me as if he wanted to lick me like a lollipop, and I was so close to obliging him.

Susannah swallowed hard, dragging her eyes from my naked chest to my face. "You should know that Quinn is going off his Omega masking meds, so he's a bit more..."

"Volatile?" Merrick supplied.

Quinn snorted. "Horny. All those denied urges are just racing back to the surface, so I apologize if I stare at you like you're a piece of prime rib."

I gave him a cocky smirk. "Anything you need, Omega. You just have to ask."

Quinn blinked in surprise at the honorific. We often called people by their designations as a sign of respect, or sometimes in the bedroom. I would never call Merrick "Alpha" while he was fucking me, but if Susannah was beneath me, whispering "Alpha" to me as I fucked her?

Mmph.

Crap, my cock was getting hard. I needed to get in the water ASAP to cool down a little before everyone got an eyeful.

Merrick rolled his eyes at me. "Apologies, Quinn. We won't refer to you as Omega if you don't like it."

Quinn shook his head. "No, it's not that. It's just... weird, is all. I wasn't really an Omega for long before I started taking the pills and pretending to be a Beta. It's just weird to hear it directed at me."

Susannah snorted. "You aren't kidding."

I laughed, wading into the water until it was deep enough to dive in. The frigid water made me surface with a gasp, but my body relished the cool that it hadn't felt in so long with this damn heatwave.

I groaned. "This is so nice." And it had a positive effect on the hard-on I was beginning to sport.

Susannah was never one to be outdone. She stripped off her shirt and wiggled out of those tiny cutoffs that had made me hard for at least sixty percent of the day. We'd been to the swimming hole with Susannah a lot when we were teens, but this wasn't my teenage fantasy in front of me. Susannah the woman was everything I'd dreamed of and more. Soft curves that weren't nearly as sharp as they'd been when she'd lived with Wilkie's Pack, which added credence to my guess that he'd been starving them both. She had full boobs in a white lace bra, and I wanted to bury my face between them and never emerge. Soft thighs that were way too biteable. Fuck, I was getting hard again, even with the cold water.

She tiptoed in, hissing a little at the cold but continuing to wade out until the edge dropped away and she was forced to swim. "Holy fuck, that's cold," she grumbled at me, and god, it was adorable. "You're a fucking liar, Owen Murphy."

It was weird hearing her say our given names. No one used them. Merrick and I didn't even use them with each other. We'd always gone by our surnames, and the only people who used our given names were our parents, and Susannah.

"You'll get used to it. Don't be so soft," I teased. It was so easy falling back into that naturally playful friendship we once had. Susannah had always been a stubborn, prideful Beta. She'd always hated to think she was weaker in any way than her Alpha brothers, or me and Merrick for that matter. That hadn't changed with her new Omega designation.

She splashed water at my face, and I ducked away with a laugh. "Just because you're part lizard," she grumbled, floating on top of the water to allow the sun to warm her skin.

I clenched my hands to stop myself from reaching for her. I wanted nothing more than to pull her close, to wrap her body around mine, to kiss her until she begged me to lay her on the warm rocks and make love to her like I'd dreamed of for so many years.

Instead, I looked over at the rocks. "Are you coming in?"

Merrick shook his head, which I knew he'd do. He would stand guard. I looked at Quinn, and he shrugged. As he pulled off his clothes, the waft of Omega pheromones hit me hard.

"Holy shit," Merrick grunted, reaching down to adjust his dick in his pants.

I gritted my teeth as my dick hardened even more. I wasn't getting out of this water anytime soon. "Are you close to the yearning? My Beast is going crazy."

Susannah sat up until she was treading water again. I reached out an arm to her lazily, and she took it, using my body to keep her afloat. It was just a single hand, and not wrapped around me the way I'd like, but I'd take it.

"Tanner said that now he was off the meds, his hormones might act up and throw him into a yearning."

There was so much there to unpack. "You're going to reveal yourself as an Omega?" I asked softly, knowing how big of a deal this was going to be for them.

Quinn swallowed hard, then dragged his shirt over his head. I growled low at the tape on his ribs that couldn't hide the bruises on his flesh, putrid shades of green and yellow. I'd seen the ones on his throat, and they'd made my Beast rage. But to see the full damage Wilkie had caused made me so fucking angry. I wanted to give all that pain back to him, tenfold.

Who was I kidding? My Beast wanted to rip out his goddamn *heart.*

Quinn's sadness burned the back of my throat. "I don't want to be helpless ever again."

Merrick gripped his shoulder, pulling him into a hug. I stared, because Merrick wasn't a hugger, not really. But he held Quinn's tense body until he relaxed into his arms. I had no doubt that he was thrumming for the Omega, a soothing, silent purr that Alphas did for their Omegas.

"I'll end him before I ever let him touch either of you again," Merrick growled, his voice dropping to a low timbre that told me his Beast was closer to the surface than he would have liked.

Susannah's hand on my arm tightened, and I turned to face her. Fear, sadness, and anger all played across her face, and I pulled her closer, needing to hold her at the very real evidence of Wilkie's brutality. I knew in my soul it wasn't the first time for Quinn, and probably not for Susannah.

She let me hold her, and something happened in

the stillness of this little cove. No one said anything until Quinn pushed gently away from Merrick, clearing his throat. "Okay, that's enough of that," he said in a rough voice. "The water is calling to me." He took a run-up and jumped into the deep water right by us, splashing cold water up over our heads.

Susannah sputtered, rubbing water out of her eyes. "Quinn, you shit!" she screeched, diving at the other Omega, and they wrestled around in the water until we were all laughing.

I looked over at Merrick, wondering if he felt the same thing I did at this moment. How very right this felt, our tiny Pack, laughing and playing. I wanted this every single day for the rest of my life.

Merrick was watching them with a soft smile, but his eyes moved to mine, like he could feel my gaze on him.

Can we keep them? I mouthed in his direction.

He grinned back at me, before mouthing back, *Absolutely.*

13

MERRICK

Escorting a freshly bonded Omega into a human town was not high on my list of favorite duties, especially when I'd made progress with my own Omegas a few days ago at the swimming hole. I didn't want to piss them off by smelling like another Omega. Everyone always said that Omegas were notoriously territorial.

But the new Wiley-Fletcher-Reid Omega was a cute little thing. She had sass, and as her name, Kitten, would imply, she had some claws too. Not my type, but she fit with her Pack perfectly.

The stench of humans here was strong, and it was always a little like stale beer and death. Give me a room of humans, and at least one of them was dying, even if they didn't know it yet.

Murphy had the Omega on his arm like she

belonged to us, keeping her positioned between us so we could protect her efficiently. The scent of the Wiley-Fletcher-Reid Pack was so thick on her, it was burning my nostrils. They'd marked her up good before sending her out into the world with two unmated Alphas.

I looked at the bartender, an older man with a three-day-old beard and a dispassionate attitude. "I'm looking for Sam," I grunted, threading a little of the Alpha into my words to grease the wheels, as they say.

The guy narrowed his eyes. "Whatcha need Sam for?"

"He was the last person to see an old friend of ours, and we were wondering if he had any information on their whereabouts."

Seemingly appeased by my answer, he slid a bottle of beer down the bar to a man at the end. I looked at the guy as he caught the beer, then did a double take. There was something off about him, like the shadows had gathered around him, even though the bar was well-lit.

He met my eyes, and I held his. Neither of us wanted to look away first, and that was how I knew he was definitely a supe. Didn't know what flavor, but not shifter, judging by his scent.

I took stock of him: the long, black trench, the dark eyes and hair, the tattoos that ran up his neck to his chin. The taste of his power. There were other supernaturals that came through Maxton, but very few settled close by. The Manix reputation of being extinct had relied on that fact. But with our reappearance, it stood to reason that a few more would come out of the woodwork just to take a look.

Someone knocked on the bar in front of me, and the man grinned, raising his beer. I dragged my eyes back to the bartender, though I made note to mention the guy to the Alpha General.

The bartender was frowning at me. "Sam sold the bar to a company down in the city and retired last year. He lives around back. Take that door back there, and it'll drop you into the side alley. He's the one across the street—the house of sticks that looks like it's about to fall down around his ears, but he's too cheap to hire a damn contractor to fix it." It was clear that the old bartender grumbled with love.

"Thank you," I replied and turned back to Kitten, just in time to see a young-ish human with a patchy beard come up to the Omega.

"Kate?"

The Omega winced. "Oh, hey, Garth."

It didn't take a rocket scientist to realize that she'd known this guy intimately. I was kind of glad none of her Alphas had come with her. Otherwise, I had no doubt that Corvin, at the very least, would've had this guy laid out.

Kitten did some backtracking, politely fobbing him

off, and I stepped between them as the guy went in for a hug. *Yeah, no.*

"Come on, *Kate*," I said, emphasizing the fake name. "Sam retired and lives around back, according to the barman. Let's go." I started herding her toward the hallway the bartender had mentioned, ignoring the guy's stammering questions and Kitten's soft replies.

Soon enough, we were out of the building and across the street, banging on the door to the ramshackle cabin. There was some grumbling, and more than a little swearing as someone thumped toward the door. The old guy who answered looked like he'd been kicked around by humanity and had come out tougher on the other side.

"What do you wan—*Leandra?*" The quick progression from surprise to sadness in his eyes told me this wasn't going to be a happy ending.

Fuck.

THE TRIP HOME was filled with the scent of melancholy from the back seat. I couldn't wind down the window, though, because one, it was hotter than hell outside, and two, a wind had whipped up while we were in town and it was flinging dust everywhere. The Omega was silent, and Murphy and I didn't interrupt her thoughts.

That had been rough on the poor thing, and

honestly, kind of hard to hear. The old Alpha General was definitely her father, and I'd swear it on my bond with Murphy that he'd killed her mother. He'd been a sociopathic old fuck. Lived too long with too much power. He'd always been hungry for it, and had enjoyed flexing it over those who couldn't challenge him back. I was glad he was dead. I'd hated him when I worked for the Legion and he was still in power.

Murphy kept an eye on the girl as we drove back up the mountain away from town. I would be relieved to drop her off with her Pack so they could soothe her hurt. She mightn't be mine, and I might have no interest in her, but her sadness still riled my Beast.

"Can you stop the car?" she called softly from the back. I looked into the rearview mirror to see her staring out the window in horror. "Seriously, stop the car!" she yelled, and I slammed on the brakes.

"What is it?" Murphy yelled back, but she was up and out of the car, running toward the woods. "Kitten, where the fuck are you going?"

Another scent replaced her sadness. Fear. "Wildfire!"

We raced after her, Murphy getting in front. "Are you sure?"

I caught up, and she stopped dead, looking at us wide-eyed. "I'm sure. Smell the air? You can taste the smoke. Feel it. Hear it. The animals are disturbed— they're running to find shelter already. That hot wind?

It's going to pick up this evening, or maybe even sooner, and with it the fire will rage."

I lifted my nose again, filtering out the scent of the Omega beside me. As soon as the acrid smell burned my nostrils, I knew she was right. "I believe you. But what are you going to do running toward it? We have no water, nothing we can use to put it out."

Real terror made her face scrunch, and she shook her head. "The kids are out here with the goats. It's their third day as goatherds. They should be in the western quadrant."

Fuck. I'd forgotten that the new Alpha General had sent some of the teens to herd goats through the underbrush so they could eat back the overgrown foliage. Too little, too fucking late. We'd needed Kitten and her forest expertise two years ago to prevent this very moment.

Murphy swore violently. "Let's go. Merrick, call the Alpha General." They both took off, and I pulled out my phone, calling Courtland's private phone.

"Merrick?" he said by way of greeting.

"We have a big fucking problem. There's a wildfire on the north-western border of the Packlands. Kitten spotted it. We're just going to get the kids out goat-herding, and then we'll check it out. You might want to be on alert and start implementing the emergency protocol."

Courtland didn't panic. He just covered the phone

and started rattling off orders to Radic, then came back on the line. "Get the kids and the Omega, then get back to Maxton. I'll get the Legion out there with some of the fire-fighting vehicles and see if we can put it down before it gets too wild."

"Yes, sir. Kitten says that if we can't get it under control by this afternoon when the winds pick up, the fire will rage."

Courtland swore. "Let me know what you find."

"Yes, sir." I hung up and ran in the direction that Kitten and Murphy had gone. She was a half-blood and couldn't shift, but she still ran like the wind. I could hear them calling for Rosa and Eris, two teens from town. There was a shout in the distance, and we switched directions.

My heart sank at what we found. An unconscious, bleeding Rosa and a frantic young Alpha, Eris.

"Be calm. What happened?" I pushed all my Alpha power at the boy. We needed answers, and we needed them quickly.

He told me hurriedly that they'd had lunch, and all their stuff had been on fire when they returned. They'd gone to get the goats and herd them into town to get help, but at some point Rosa had tripped and hit her head. Now she was unconscious.

Kitten was checking the girl, and soon looked up at me with worried eyes. "She needs to see Tanner right now."

Shit. "Do you have an ATV out here?"

Eris shook his head. "We herd the goats out here on foot, then herd them back to their pen in the evening."

Fucking hell, this was all going to shit. "Fuck." I fished my keys out of my pocket. "Give her to me and shift. Now, Eris!" Taking the unconscious girl from his arms, I forced him to shift, then gave him my car keys and the girl back. "Go quickly, but don't jolt her around." I hoped to hell she didn't have neck injuries or she was already in trouble. "My car is on the road south-east of here. Take her straight there, and then drive to the new doctor, Tanner. *Do not stop*—do you understand me?" Again, an Alpha command. The kid was an Alpha too, but he was young. He wouldn't be able to shake off the compulsion to follow orders.

Eris ran off, gliding like he was a damn gazelle across the forest floor, barely jostling the girl. There wasn't anything else I could do for them.

Kitten scaled the tree to get a better look, but I could smell the smoke and hear the crackle of flames from here, and I knew. I just fucking *knew*.

We were already out of time.

Kitten dropped down beside my feet, agile like the animal she was named after, and Murphy gave a choked laugh. "I see where you get the nickname now."

She looked over at me, the solemn look on her face confirming everything. "There's nothing we can do. Call Courtland and tell him to get ahold of the human authorities. There aren't even any fire trails out that side. They're going to need to do aerial drops." Then she started running again.

"Stop, Omega!" I shouted, using my Alpha command once more. "You're going toward the flames."

She gritted her teeth at me as she slowed, and I knew I'd fucked up. I was glad she wasn't my Omega because I was pretty sure I'd have been castrated before the night was out.

"I'm aware of that, *Alpha*." She said the word with so much derision, it could have been a curse. "But the goat herd is just there, and if we can push them south, they'll have a better chance of surviving."

Murphy let out the kind of whistle that made me want to punch him in the face. "Go, Omega." She didn't need to be told twice. "I'd sleep with one eye open until she forgives you, Rick."

Soon enough, a herd of goats were thundering toward us, the Omega shouting, "Hyuh!" behind them. "Keep driving them back toward town," she shouted at me, like she was the Alpha. Then she turned and ran in the opposite direction. Not toward the flames this time, but not toward town either.

"Where the fuck are you *going?!*" I shouted after her.

"Home!" she yelled back, not slowing.

Murphy looked at me, wide-eyed. "Fuck. I'll go with her. I'll drag her back to town bodily, if I have to."

I looked at those fucking goats, then back at him. Gripping his shirt, I kissed him hard. "Safety first, okay? I don't care how much she hates it, you get both of you back to town alive. Got it? I'll get our Omegas and get the hell out of Maxton." I shoved my phone at him, so he could contact help if he needed it.

He gave me another hard peck on the lips. "I got it. Go play the sexiest goatherd on the prairie."

I flipped him the bird, but watched him until he disappeared into the trees. This was a goddamn nightmare.

14

TANNER

The little Alpha who burst into my medical office was almost hysterical. I'd heard the car as soon as it pulled up, as well as someone saying very loudly that they'd need the spinal board. Probably to give this frantic baby Alpha something to do.

"You gotta come because she's unconscious and she keeps drifting in and out and she was bleeding so much..." It all ran together in a single breath, not making much sense until you took the time to unpack it. I got the general gist, but I was worried the little Alpha was about to pass out from the anxiety of it all.

"What's your name?"

"Eris."

I opened the door and ran out to the parking spot in front of the clinic. Darius, the Wiley-Fletcher-Reid

Omega, was standing beside an open car door. I could smell the blood from here. I turned my attention back to Eris. "Slow down, mate. Now, start from the beginning." I looked at the girl. Her eyes were closed, and her color was quite gray. "Where did she hit her head?"

I put a collar around her neck to support her spine, then checked her over for signs of more injuries they may have missed. So far, I could only see the head wound, so that was good. We moved her gently onto the spinal board, but I was hopeful that nothing else was wrong. Striding quickly, I had Cooper, an Alpha from the Wiley-Fletcher-Reid Pack, move her onto my examination table while I grabbed my portable X-ray machine. The thing was a godsend, really. Who knew I'd have to use it so often in a colony of supernaturals who should have superior healing?

I had to get the young Manix Alpha to wait in the other room because he was underfoot and refused to leave the young shifter's side. It was hard to work with someone growling softly in your ear.

Cooper left, but not before telling me about the incoming wildfire. *Fuck.* This was bad. I needed to get this kid patched up and offloaded to her parents so I could pack up the clinic for the worst-case scenario. Reading the X-ray, I sighed with relief. Nothing broken or doing what it shouldn't do. She definitely had a doozy of a concussion, though.

She woke up while I was dressing the head wound.

Her eyes met mine, then dropped to my fangs, and I saw panic flash in her eyes.

"Woah there, tiger. Get it? Because you're a tiger." I cleared my throat. "My name is Tanner—we met at your Packhouse, if you remember? You hit your head chasing goats, and now you have a concussion, but you'll be right as rain." She still seemed on edge, like a cornered wild animal. I raised my hands and moved away, being as non-confrontational as possible. "I'll get Bonnie in here as soon as I can. If you could shift, it would help your healing."

It was like she didn't need any more encouragement, turning into an almost fully grown tiger right there in the clinic examination room. She was massive —bigger than a normal tiger, that was for sure.

She turned to me and snarled, and I raised my hands again. "Not gonna lie, kiddo, I've already been eaten by one apex predator and I'm not looking to do it again. Bite wounds are a bitch."

The door suddenly swung open, and Bonnie was there, panting softly. "Rosa, are you okay?" She looked pale as well, and I wondered if she'd sprinted down the mountain from their Packhouse. The tiger in front of me let out a pitiful chuffing whine as she curled around Bonnie's legs.

Bonnie stroked her fur soothingly. "It's okay, beautiful girl." Bonnie's eyes shot to mine. "She's okay, right?"

I nodded. "She had a pretty serious concussion, but hopefully the shift would have cleared up any lingering effects. Keep an eye on her anyway, and if she seems drowsier than usual, or has a headache or any shifts in behavior, bring her back."

Bonnie frowned. "If there's a back to come to," she said softly.

"It'll be okay. I was just about to start packing up the necessities."

She sucked in a jagged breath, her scent stressed. "Do you need help?" When I shook my head, she sighed. "Anything you don't think you'll need urgently can be stored in the cells beneath the Legion building. It won't be perfectly safe, but better than here if things go... pear-shaped."

If the town burned to the ground. That was what she meant by pear-shaped.

"Mate, I'm Australian. If we know one thing, it's that some things have to burn to grow. Like eucalyptus trees in a forest. Fire tears through and bursts open all the seedpods. Where there was one old tree, there's now hundreds of new seedlings just waiting for the right conditions to grow."

Bonnie raised an eyebrow at me. "Is that an allegory?"

"An allegory? No, ma'am. I'm Irish Catholic."

She threw back her head and laughed. "I know you're messing with me right now." She squeezed my arm. "We have to go, but be safe. This town needs you."

I nodded my head solemnly, all my mirth gone. "I'll be here for as long as I'm wanted."

Bonnie disappeared, the tiger on her heels. I could hear her calling for the little Manix Alpha, who'd taken up post in my waiting room. "Let's go, Eris. I'll drop you back to your parents."

A breath rushed out between my teeth as I stepped out onto the footpath in front of the little building. Tilting my head to the side, I used my vampiric senses for more than just finding a good spot in someone's carotid artery. I let all the stimuli rush in, until it was almost painful, then filtered out what I didn't need. Panicked voices. Cars and shouting. But beneath all that was the unmistakable whoosh and crackle of a raging fire. And the smoke threatened to choke me. The wind was shifting, and too soon there'd be nothing left of this town.

I'd never been more thankful for my vampiric speed as I sorted and packed everything into three categories. Firstly, the stuff that needed to be packed into a van so it could be evacuated—things like dressings, medicine and ointments, topical steroids, and the Doppler machine. The second pile was for things that were too big to come with us, but were expensive pieces of equipment. Not irreplaceable, but better if they were preserved. The third category stayed in the office and we'd all hope for the best.

I hefted an armful of the stuff that needed to go somewhere safer and ran over to the Legion building, not even asking for directions to the cells below. They'd been hewn directly into the stone and were definitely the safest bet for rogue Manix. Very few things in the world could stop a frenzied Manix in their shifted form.

Seemed like I wasn't the only person storing important things in this rocky tomb. Files and equipment—as well as half the armory—had made it down here.

An efficient-looking older Manix man was directing people around. "Ah, Doc Tanner. I thought you might be over sooner or later. I've left a corner for the clinic's equipment in cell four." He smiled sadly at me. "I've never been more thankful for your help than at this moment. If we had to divert workers to help clear out the clinic, so many other resources would be lost."

I gave him an imaginary tip of my hat. "Glad to help. I've probably got six boxes and the X-ray machine to come. Everything else will have to be in your Moon Goddess's hands."

He nodded. "We appreciate it." Just then, a Legion soldier with a box in each arm descended the stairs, and the man went back to directing traffic.

I rushed back up into the belly of the Legion building, stopping when I saw a familiar but harried face. "Radic!" He turned, giving me a tight expression. "Just wanted you to know that Rosa is fine."

"Yes, thank the Goddess. And you too, of course. Bonnie called; they're evacuating the Sanctum now. We didn't want to take any chances with the kids. Courtland is ordering all the elderly, children, and half-bloods to evacuate as they'll be the most susceptible to smoke inhalation, but I think more will want to stay."

I shook my head. "Nah, mate. Everyone wants to stay and defend until they're staring at an eighty-foot-high wall of fire roaring toward them. They want to stay, fine, but they better be prepared to run. And if they get circled..."

I didn't need to finish because there were very few supernaturals impervious to fire, and I'd never personally met any of them. The Ifrit, a type of Djinn, some fire elementals. My maker Steve had once told me about a fire elemental who lived on a tiny volcanic island in the middle of the ocean. That was it.

Radic nodded sadly. "I know." He pulled a card from his pocket. "If things get that bad, this is the location we're evacuating to. You should know, it's a colony of witches. I know how vampires feel about witches."

"Nah, I don't have any of those ancient prejudices. Comes from being turned by a recluse who talks to sharks." I slapped his shoulder. "I'll stay while I can, and then I'll set up shop in town for any injuries."

"Thanks, Tanner." He turned to stride back into his office, but something niggled at me.

"Radic?" He looked back. "Susannah and Quinn—do you know if they're evacuating? I wanted to check in on his injuries."

Yeah, sure. That's what it was. Professional curiosity. *Not.*

Radic frowned, like he was going through his mental filing cabinet for the information I needed. "Courtland has assigned Merrick and Murphy to be their guards while that fuckhead Wilkie is still wandering around. I'm pretty sure they'll find them and evacuate them."

"Thanks, Rad."

They'd be safe. They weren't mine to worry over, but I couldn't help it. There was something about them both that stirred my protective instincts. Well, Susannah stirred something else, but even Quinn made me want to hold him close and protect him from harm.

I couldn't shake the feeling that something was coming for them, and I didn't think it was the wildfire raging outside.

15

SUSANNAH

My phone had been going insane. My dad had called first, telling me about the wildfire, and that he wanted me on the first bus out of harm's way as soon as possible. That was A-okay with me.

Part of me hoped this town burned to the ground. I had no fondness for this patch of land at all. It was just the shackle that kept us all locked in the past.

After my father called, I'd assumed that the news about the fire only got worse, because every single one of my brothers had called to ensure I was going to be all right. I'd been taking care of myself for longer than they knew, but now that I was an Omega, I was apparently helpless.

Raiden was on the phone to me now. "Do you need us to come and get you? You can evacuate with us."

Raiden had cubs and toddlers, as well as a life to pack up. He didn't need to be taking care of me as well.

"We'll be fine, little brother. Quinn and I are getting on the first bus out, like I promised everyone else who called before you." I softened my voice. "You take care of your Pack. I know it won't be easy leaving again." They'd only just rebuilt Raiden's Packhouse after it had been torched by a psychopath.

"Everything is easier the second time around, and honestly, I'm almost glad we hadn't made too many memories in this place yet. I'm not sure I could have coped otherwise."

My heart ached for my little brother, but he had a wonderful Pack, and they'd get through whatever happened. "It'll be okay. No matter what happens, remember your home doesn't rest on stone foundations, but in those tiny arms that call you Papa."

Raiden made a choked noise. "Zanny?"

"Yeah?"

"I'm not sure I ever told you this, and I'm not sure I ever appreciated it until I had the cubs, but thank you for being the best mother figure a little Omega kid could want. I—" He cleared his throat. "I know it wasn't easy for you, and it's not something you should ever have had to do, but the man I am today? The father I am today? It's because of you."

Tears rushed to my eyes, emotion balling in my chest. I'd spent every one of my early teen years resenting having to be someone's mother, since I was just a kid myself. But I'd loved Raiden. I'd never resented him personally; we'd both been victims of the cruel whims of fate.

"You were the best kid, Rai. Even when you were a little shit, I loved you. You were my baby, even if I was only four years older than you." I sniffed, now *this close* to a full-on crying session. "Okay, go and pack. We can have this heart-to-heart when we reach... what's the place called?" I looked down at the slip I'd written the address on. "Moonburst. You're going straight there, right?"

I could almost hear Raiden rolling his eyes. "Of course we are."

"Love you, Rai."

"Love you too, Zanny. Be safe."

I hung up the phone, swiping my arm across my eyes to wipe away the tears that threatened to fall. Quinn came up behind me and wrapped his arms around my waist. "Everything okay with your brother?"

I nodded, leaning back into him. "Yeah, they're packing up and evacuating now. I feel sorry for them, though, to have to do it all over again."

He kissed the top of my head, his Omega presence soothing my sadness and my frazzled nerves. "They're a resilient Pack. If anyone can rebuild twice, it's the Huxley-Grey Pack."

With a sigh, I zipped up the last of my suitcases. It was sad how we only had three bags between the two of us. We'd lived light since the day we'd run away, and we'd kept very little stuff with us at Wilkie's Packhouse. But this place, my childhood home, had more memories for all of us—some good and some bad. Raiden had taken his first steps here. My mother had died in the bedroom down the hall. Quinn had taken my virginity here, and we'd discovered he was an Omega in the same room.

My dad had come by and packed his own go-bag. I'd watched him touch all my mother's jewelry and little things he'd kept all these years. He'd loved her so much. Eventually, I told him to pack whatever he wanted, and Quinn and I would take it with us. I would help him preserve the memory of a woman I'd barely known, but whose death had forever altered the course of my life.

We dragged our things down the road toward the center of town, where the Alpha General had arranged buses to ship out everyone who wanted to go, and those he deemed "at risk." Basically, everyone he could Alpha-order without causing a fight.

More people joined us as we queued, the air filled with the scents of fear and sadness. This might be the last time they ever walked out their doors again. It might be the last time they'd see friends or loved ones who stayed to fight the fires, though my father had declared that a fool's task. No one spoke as we reached the center of town.

A man I recognized as one of the supply managers was there, directing people to where they could put their luggage. "Everything has to fit under the bus. If it's too big, it will have to stay behind in the Legion building," he said firmly, but with a lot of compassion. He knew what people were feeling; I had no doubt he was feeling it too.

Quinn helped me push our suitcases beneath the bus, then we moved out of the way for the family behind us. Walking over to the supply manager, we waited until he was done reassuring a group before he turned to us.

He bowed his head. "Omega. It's good to see you here and safe."

"I'm hoping a lot more people will see reason," I said, giving him a sad smile.

He lifted a single shoulder. "Only the Goddess can know what will happen. We just have to plan the best we can. The bus should leave in about twenty minutes. Another will come straight after. Don't be late, because we aren't doing a roll call—if you aren't here, we won't know."

We'd be left behind to fend for ourselves. "Fair. We'll be here."

"Young Murphy is looking for you too," the older man said, his eyes twinkling, despite the fact he must've thought we were still mated to Wilkie. We hadn't made that little tidbit known throughout town just yet.

"Thank you. Be safe."

We stepped out of the way as the small square filled up with more and more people. I was relieved that they weren't being stubborn and insisting on staying. Soon enough, the crowd swelled, and I was a little worried we wouldn't get on the same bus as our bags. Everything smelled like smoke and fear, and it was giving me a headache.

I dragged in oxygen, and froze. A scent that chilled me to my bones clouded around me, making me want to throw up.

Something hard and sharp pressed into my spine. "If either of you shift or yell out, I'm going to sever this bitch's spinal cord, and she'll have to drag her useless cunt around for the rest of her short life." Wilkie's voice swept over my skin like acid. "I don't need you to be able to walk to sire my cubs, bitch. Now, *move.* We're going to go home."

I didn't turn around, but I could see the fear in Quinn's eyes. He was nodding with his hands raised as he turned and walked down the small path between the buildings. Wilkie had his fist wrapped in my hair tightly so I couldn't run without ripping off half my scalp, but it might still be worth it. I just didn't believe that we could outrun him. He was an Alpha—

primed to be physically superior to Omegas and Betas.

My body trembled, making the knife press harder against my skin. Wilkie led us down the shadowy back alleys of the buildings, past the dumpsters, avoiding all the incoming people. It was a small mercy that the smoke and the trash were still covering Quinn's burgeoning Omega scent. Maybe I could shift to the left a little, try and move the knife to a less deadly position, then Quinn could run and get help.

As if he could sense my thoughts, he looked over his shoulder and widened his eyes almost imperceptibly. Years of love and friendship meant I knew that expression was a *don't even think about it* look.

As we walked toward a dead end in a nearly empty part of the Legion training grounds and saw Joseph and Errol, I knew this was only going to be bad. Errol looked pale, standing as far away from Joseph as he could without being in the middle of a fire zone. Joseph sneered at us, his eyes twitching around the trees, like he expected the Alpha General to fall from the sky.

"Look, Betas. I've brought home our wayward Omega and her bitchboy Beta," Wilkie crowed. "Bring me the cuffs."

Joseph walked over, swinging two sets of cuffs from his forefinger. He was a handsome man, which fucking sucked because on the inside he was almost as ugly as

Wilkie. He didn't want power—not like his Alpha. No, Joseph wanted money and prestige. He wanted to hide away in the background, hoarding dollars and ripping off his fellow Manix just so he could be the richest man in Maxton.

It was a pity that Wilkie liked to spend money as fast as Joseph made it. He resented his Alpha, though not enough to cut ties with him and all his connections.

"Are the cars ready?" Wilkie snapped at Errol, who wouldn't meet anyone's eyes. "I asked you a question, Beta." Wilkie Alpha-growled when he didn't reply fast enough.

"Yes, Alpha. Everything is packed." Errol looked up just enough to give me a guilty look, but I held no beef with the weak-willed Beta. He didn't have the strength to resist an Alpha command.

Yanking my arms behind my back, Wilkie snapped a set of the handcuffs on me. "Tight enough that if you decide to shift, they'll cut off your goddamn cheating hands."

He snapped another set on Quinn. He paused, leaning a little too close for comfort, his hand coming up to grip Quinn's face. The ugly tattoo on his hand had always amused me: a crest with his own name in the middle. Like he was going to forget his own name? How douchebaggy could you get?

His hand clenched around Quinn's face, looking

like a brand on his skin. He inhaled Quinn's scent deeply, his eyes going wide with shock. "You're a fucking *Omega?*"

I flinched as I waited for the blows to come, but they didn't. When I opened my eyes, I would have almost preferred a fist to the face than to see the gloating look.

"You're an Omega pair?" Wilkie crowed. "The Goddess has fucking blessed us, Joseph. A fucking *Omega pair.*"

I looked at the despair in Quinn's eyes, a sensation that matched the sinking feeling in my own gut. We were fucked now.

16

QUINN

"On your knees, Omega," Wilkie growled at me. "I'm not taking any chances that you'll slip through my claws again. Oh no. I'm going to bond you right now until you're tied to me forever, and your only dreams will be how good you can suck my cock and bear my young."

The Alpha compulsion had me dropping to my knees with a grunt, and I whined in frustration. It was almost worth losing my hands to get out of this. I couldn't be tied to this man, couldn't *stand* the thought of his teeth on my body. Or any part of him in Susannah.

I'd die first.

I looked over at a shaken Susannah, her eyes wide and her skin pale. I tried to reassure her with my gaze, tried to reassure her that we'd be okay. I didn't know how yet, but we would. This wasn't the end.

"Never," I growled at Wilkie, spitting at his feet. He laughed, then kicked me in the face, my body lurching up and backwards as darkness threatened to close in on me.

No. I couldn't leave Susannah alone.

I struggled back to my feet. "You limp-dicked fucker. You're too weak, too cowardly to be called an Alpha," I growled, though my words were slurred and my jaw hurt. Fuck, had he fractured something?

"Weak?" Wilkie snarled, prowling forward. "*DON'T FUCKING MOVE.*" The amount of Alpha bark he'd put into his command had my whole body stilling. Me and my big mouth.

"Wilkie," Errol started, his voice almost a whine. "We should go before the fire gets here."

Wilkie turned toward the older Beta with a snapped curse. "Shut the fuck up and get the cars then."

While Wilkie was distracted with Errol, I mouthed to Susannah, *Run.* She shook her head, and if my jaw didn't ache so bad, I would've gritted my teeth.

But then it was too late; Wilkie was concentrating on me again. "*Suck my cock,*" he purred with Alpha persuasion. He freed his dick, and I felt myself lean forward without any conscious will.

No. No. My jaw opened, and I yelped in pain. Definitely broken.

Then Susannah screamed. It was a blood-curdling, ear-shattering sound that threatened to burst my eardrums. Wilkie whirled around with his cock in his hand and a snarl on his face. "Shut her the hell up before everything goes sideways," he hissed at Joseph, who stepped close and slapped Susannah, before stuffing what might have been a handkerchief from his pocket into her mouth. Who fucking carried handkerchiefs these days?

Hands handcuffed behind her back, Susannah's voice was muffled as Wilkie turned back toward me, kicking me in the chest until I fell face-first into the dirt. "Well, I guess there's no time for foreplay. I'm going to bite you now, and I'm going to make sure it fucking hurts," he growled at me, his expression inhumanly gleeful at the prospect of making me hurt.

He dropped down and placed a knee on my back as he started to tear at my clothes. I turned my head back toward Susannah. *Run,* I mouthed silently to her again. I didn't want her to see this. I didn't want her to have to succumb to this either. *Please.*

Again, she shook her head. And then Wilkie's weight was gone. There was a roar as a fully shifted Manix tackled him into the dirt beside my face.

I scented Murphy immediately. Joseph shifted and launched himself into the fray, but he didn't have a hope against a fully shifted Murphy. But a solo Murphy against Joseph and Wilkie together? He'd be in trouble. Wilkie was powerful, which was why he'd gotten away with his shit for so long.

Struggling to my feet with no hands was not easy, but I was up and in front of Susannah quickly. She was hissing with anger that we couldn't shift and help. I hip checked her. "You need to go and get help."

"No! I won't leave you."

"Fucking *go!*" I shouted, and with one last anguished look, she sprinted back toward town. I breathed easier as soon as she was out of sight. Throwing myself into the brawl, I knocked Joseph off Murphy's back where he was trying to claw at his jugular. Fucker couldn't even fight clean. I fell hard on my arms and felt something pop, but I didn't have time to think about the pain. Back on my feet, I grimaced but ran at them again.

Wilkie swiped at me with his shifted claws, and I felt them peel open my skin. I just needed to keep him distracted enough that Susannah could be long gone. And so Murphy had a chance. Panting through the pain, I did my best impression of a wrecking ball until I was bleeding too much and my limbs felt impossibly heavy.

"Murphy," I croaked out, the words feeling too big to pass my throat. They were pummeling him now. Wilkie was bleeding heavily, but between the two of them, they'd managed to get Murphy on the ground. "Get up," I grunted. "Fucking get up!" It was easy to say as I lay on the ground, bleeding out.

A flash in my peripheral vision told me that help had arrived. It might be too late, but at least Susannah was safe. That was all that mattered, really. Hot liquid splashed across my face, streaks of red washed through the darkness. A voice pleaded for mercy in the background as I drifted in and out of blissful unconsciousness.

I was definitely dying this time. Susannah was going to be pissed.

A face appeared before me, a stranger smeared with blood and gore. Not what I thought the Goddess's Handmaidens would look like, but I mean, it fit.

"Are you okay?" the Handmaiden asked.

Was it a Handmaiden if it was a guy? Handbachelor?

"Okay, so head injury and blood loss at the very minimum." I hissed as he moved my head from side to side. "What hurts?"

I wanted to laugh because *everything* hurt. It would even hurt to tell him everything hurt. The Handbachelor looked over my head. His face turned scarier as blood dripped down his cheeks.

"Wilkie kicked him in the face, so his jaw? There's —I mean, I *think* there's a gash on his side and maybe broken ribs?" The male voice was wobbly and filled with fear. Well, I guess that made sense.

The Handbachelor cursed softly. "Bloody hell. What have you gotten yourself into now?" A low growl sounded across the clearing, and the Handbachelor raised a brow at me. "He sounds pissed."

With that, a shifted Manix form slammed into the Goddess's chosen one. I sighed. I didn't think I was dead anymore, no matter how much that would make the pain stop.

"Calm down, mate. I found them like this." A slight pause. "Well, not *him*. I did that. But Quinn and Murphy were like that when I arrived."

I realized that the Handbachelor was really a blood-soaked Tanner. *Shit.*

Susannah was suddenly leaning over me, kissing my face. "You're alive. Thank the fucking Goddess, you're alive."

I groaned, rolling onto my side to spit out the blood that was welling in my cheeks. Maybe I'd bitten my tongue? My whole face hurt, so it was hard to define what part hurt the most. "Kinda." She helped me sit up, and I looked over at Murphy, who looked just as banged up as me.

But it was the rest of the clearing that made me want to vomit.

Wilkie lay unseeing on the ground between Murphy and I, his chest now gaping open and his heart gone. The appendage in question was lying on the dirt ten feet away. His throat had been savaged, and his lifeblood pooled around him, the smell dulled by the scent of smoke. His hands, which had hurt us so often, had been ripped off.

A shifted Merrick and Tanner were still staring off with each other, uncaring about the fact that Joseph, with his throat torn out but his chest still unopened, was dead at their feet.

"I heard the scream, so I came to investigate," Tanner said defensively. "I might've gone a little overboard, though." He stared down at the dead bodies, looking remorseful. "Fuck, this is going to get me into trouble."

Merrick transformed back, and he helped a now naked but much healed Murphy to his feet. Tanner walked over, ignoring the growls of the other Manix in the clearing. Grabbing my cuffs, he tore them off, like they were made of plastic. "If you shift now... Have you come off the drugs enough to transform?"

If it hadn't hurt so much to shrug, I would have. Since I'd stopped taking the tablets, I hadn't tried to shift. If I was honest, I was a little scared. Scared that after keeping my Omega repressed for so long, my Beast wouldn't rise. I'd be forever locked into my human form.

Susannah's hand squeezed mine. "It's okay. If it doesn't happen, it probably just means we have to wait a little longer. Your Beast is in there. I can feel him."

I nodded and closed my eyes, trying to remember the shift and how it felt. Magic rippled over my skin as my body stretched and contorted, aching as my bones meshed and elongated. It was like being in a cramped space for so long, all your limbs forgot how to work.

Finally, I opened my eyes, and Susannah was beaming down at me. "Hello, handsome," she purred, and my Beast thrummed low. I lifted my hand, but I'd only shifted into my half-form. Soft, multicolored fur covered my body, as well as small but sharp claws. My ears twitched on my head, so I knew that my face had shifted too. I'd been aiming for a full shift, but this would do for now.

I stood up tenderly, Tanner's hand under my elbow, and I turned at the sound of Murphy growling. "Take your hands off him," he grunted.

Tanner laughed, but moved away. "Easy, Alpha." I guess it was hard to be scared of a man who was threatening you while his dick hung in the breeze.

I looked past him at where Merrick was standing over Errol. Whatever he was saying was making the man's shoulders shake. It wasn't Errol's fault. He'd been just as much a victim of Wilkie and his Pack as we were —he just didn't have a Susannah to lean on in the hard times.

I moved toward them, but Susannah grabbed my arm. "Wait."

Merrick pulled the Beta into his arms and held him tight. I watched as Errol shook and cried. Then Merrick pulled away, patting the man on his shoulder and pushing him in the opposite direction. "Go. Don't come back. Start again somewhere else."

I knew what he was doing. People hated Wilkie, but if the story ever came out, they wouldn't understand why Errol had stood by and let his Packmates be killed. They'd judge him, and he'd be a pariah.

Errol looked over his shoulder at us one last time. "I'm sorry I failed you two. I'll live with that forever."

I shook my head, happy it didn't slosh my brains around again. "We failed each other. Be happy, Errol. When shit dies down, we'll come and visit you. I promise."

He shook his head. "Don't worry about it, kid. I'll be fine."

Then he was gone, and I knew deep down I'd never see him again.

17

TANNER

As touching as it was, we had bigger problems at the moment. First, there was a wildfire raging toward us at an alarming rate. Second, there were two dead bodies that needed to be dealt with. Third, I'd broken the Dark River covenant, and worse, the vow I'd made under the purview of the Vampire Council. When I'd taken my post among the Manix, I'd promised I'd do everything in my power to ensure the health and wellness of the Manix community. I was pretty sure it didn't include exsanguination or open-heart surgery with rather permanent results. All of this would have to be dealt with while the majority of our party was naked and I was doused in blood.

Well, I could solve problem number two quickly and easily. Picking up Wilkie's heart, as well as his hands—ignoring Susannah gagging a little—I stuffed it all back in his gaping chest cavity. Then I reached down and hefted the other huge Manix under my other arm. "Excuse me for a second. I'm just going to…"

"Clean up after your meal?" Susannah suggested.

"Take out the trash?" Murphy added, and I smiled. I liked this guy.

I cleared my throat. "Something like that."

I raced off toward the fire. Soon enough, Mother Nature would take care of these wastes of oxygen. A niggling part of my humanity tried to raise its head at the fact I'd rather cavalierly taken two lives. After hearing what they'd done to the Omegas, and then seeing them almost kill a man I knew to be honorable, it had set off the predator inside me that I liked to pretend didn't exist. But he did. Part of the man I'd been—the one who'd vowed to do no harm—had died the day a shark had taken a munch out of me. In his place was a predator with the morals of a human. It made for an awkward balancing act.

I was so close to the flames now that I could feel the shift in temperature. The heat was blowing toward me like a hairdryer, and I dumped the bodies onto the dry grass.

Two choices. I could dig a hole so deep that they wouldn't be found, and just hope the fire destroyed any evidence. Or I could leave them to burn, and when someone eventually stumbled across them, they'd assume they'd accidentally been caught in the flames. Tough choice.

In the end, like an ostrich, I went with burying my problems in the sand. Grabbing a rock, I started digging a hole, because I didn't want to tear up my fingers on the rough earth. I dug for as long as I could before the fire felt too close. Six feet down, I dug, then threw the bodies into the ditch and roughly covered it back over. Blood and dirt was now coating my body, and I hotfooted it back before I was either discovered or barbecued for my sins.

When I arrived back in the clearing, everyone was now dressed. Fair enough; no one wanted their tackle hanging out during a wildfire. Wrong kind of sausage sizzle.

One of the Alphas—Merrick, I think—threw me some clothes. I knew the Manix had small stashes of clothes all over town for inconvenient shifting, but I hadn't thought I'd ever need to make use of it. "We're gonna have to burn yours."

With a shrug, I started to strip out of my duds. Everything was dirty and smelled like smoke, ash, and the blood of that filthy fucker. As I threw the last of my clothes onto the ground, I looked up to see everyone staring at me.

"What? I thought you shifters were good with public nudity?" I looked down, in case I'd missed something, like a knife in the kidney. "Is it the shark bite scar? She's ugly, and she itches when it's humid, but no real damage that a little vamp turning couldn't fix." The large, jagged scar stood out prominently on my thigh.

Crickets. Well, not literal crickets—those were all fleeing for their tiny little hippy-hoppy lives. *Proverbial* crickets.

Finally, Susannah threw back her head and laughed. "They aren't looking at your shark bite, Tanner. They're looking a tad up and to the right. Put some clothes on so we can all get going."

Oh. They were looking at my dick. I thought there was some kind of supernatural etiquette that said you didn't look at a man's junk while he was changing, but hey, if it made them look that awed, then I was here for it. I winked at Susannah, then pulled on the clothes they'd found for me.

Quinn looked between us. "What do we do now?"

Ah, the age-old question. What did you do after you'd just witnessed the murder of your abusive Pack Alpha during a catastrophic fire event?

"You guys should head to that town the Alpha General secured. Safe and out of the way of harm. I have to go and confess my sins to Convocation Member Baxter, and probably the Vampire Council and Titus. Then I'll probably be punished for a bit, but it'll be right. I should be back in a year or so, depending on the punishment."

"What?" Quinn whispered.

Ah, fuck. Me and my big mouth.

Merrick frowned. "You were protecting the lives of two Omegas—that has to count for something."

I shrugged. "You never know with the vampires. Some of them have been around so long that they've reduced everything to black and white. But Raine's all right. I'm pretty sure she'll forgive me." *I think.* But I didn't want to freak these guys out any further.

Susannah folded her arms across her chest. "No."

Now it was my turn to blink and gape. "Excuse me?"

She raised an eyebrow. "You aren't getting punished for saving Quinn. I won't allow it. We're coming with you and we'll corroborate your story. I'll tell them all about how Wilkie treated us." Her voice cracked a little at the end, and I wanted to drag her into my arms. Yeah, that wasn't good either.

"No offense, Omega, but there's no way I'm taking anyone who smells as good as you anywhere near a room full of hungry vampires."

She stepped into my space, her blue eyes staring me down. "I don't believe I was asking permission, vampire."

Was it bad to want to kiss her right now? Was that breaking some kind of doctor-patient professional boundary? I mean, technically, she wasn't *really* my patient... right?

"I agree with Susannah," Merrick said firmly. "You protected our own. You put your own safety on the line. You cleaned up our mess. We're coming with you."

I sighed. Well, if it was unanimous... "We better go. It's a long drive. Let's hope no one catches on fire while we're gone, hey?"

They all looked at me, shocked again, and I decided to leave the comedy for the professionals—at least for the night.

TURNS OUT, the second car that Wilkie had stolen for his abduction attempt was a Legion car. So we decided to save it from imminent destruction and drove it out of Maxton, with the fire on our heels. Even with the flames in eyeshot now, there were still a few Manix out preparing their Packhouses. They were leaving it too late to get away safely. I knew that.

I was almost relieved to see the Alpha General climbing into the back of an SUV with Radic as we rolled through town, leaving his sinking ship. I knew the man well enough to know that he wasn't the type to stay and fruitlessly argue with people too stubborn to change their minds. He had a Pack, cubs, and a family to live for.

We followed the highway, first east and then north, until we came to the turn-off toward Moonburst. I looked over at Susannah and Quinn, both of whom looked exhausted. "You should go to the town where all your family will be. They'll be worried if you don't turn up."

Susannah stubbornly shook her head. *I shouldn't find that so bloody attractive, right?*

"I've already messaged my father and told him we were out and fine, but we were going to lie low for a while." Then she grinned, and I realized I was in trouble. "Sorry, shark boy. You're stuck with us for a little while yet."

I sighed, but deep down, I wasn't mad about it. I'd spent decades being alone. Leaving Australia as soon as I could on a red-eye flight, then slowly realizing that not all vampires were like Steve. Most were brutal and vicious, deranged from years of being an apex predator. It was only in the last decade that I'd stumbled across Dark River, and Raine, and they'd shown me a new kind of life. One where I could hold on to the small amount of humanity I still had left. But for all their camaraderie, I was still alone.

There was something about Susannah and Quinn that made me feel like I was a part of something. Like my soul was reaching out for a friend.

Or maybe I was losing it.

We drove to the Canadian border, but unfortunately, no one had any documentation except me. Right before the border, long after the sun had set, I let them out on the side of the road. They'd run across the border, and I'd drive the car over, then collect them at the north fork of the Belly River.

Watching four half-shifted Manix melt into the darkness was like watching a magician while you were drunk. Your logical mind knew that it was a trick of the light, or your brain, or something, but some other part of you—maybe your inner child, if your inner child drank cheap beer—thought it was magical.

If I wanted what was best for them, I'd just keep driving. Take the left, instead of the right straight out of the Customs gates. But I didn't, because I was selfish. I just drove to the Big Belly campground and waited.

18

MERRICK

When Quinn shifted, his Omega scent perfumed the clearing. I bit back a groan as my cock went hard. *Fuck.* How had I missed it for so long? He smelled so fucking delicious. Susannah shifted too, and I took a moment to admire her Beast. She was slighter than a male Manix, and tiny in comparison to an Alpha. But she was still strong and fierce, and my own Beast wanted her bad.

We were only half-shifted, because the soft, dappled fur and shorter claws were best for stealth through the forest and going across the border.

You know what was not stealthy in this form? My raging fucking hard-on.

Luckily, it was an unwritten rule of etiquette not to stare at people's dicks when they were shifted. I mean, sure, we'd all broken it with the vampire earlier, but we'd all been raised better than that.

I could hear Murphy's soft laughter behind me, and I shot him the finger over my shoulder. Okay, maybe we weren't all *that* well raised. He was lucky he was upwind; otherwise, he'd be eating his words right about now.

"Let's go," I grunted, turning so I could shift my cock around.

We set a steady pace, a slow jog that should've been easy, even for children and the elderly. I was aware that despite the fact he wasn't broken anymore, Quinn had just taken some serious injuries. I wanted him to shift back so I could carry him, maybe prevent some exacerbation of his wounds, but a furry giant carrying a human through the woods? It was unlikely we would be spotted, but if we were, the Bigfoot conspiracy theorists would have a coronary.

So instead, we just moved slower than I'd like. We headed north-west until we came to the almost dry bed of the Belly River. Come the spring melt, this would be another flowing river, but right now, it was as good a marker as any to run beside. We'd stay deep in the shadows of the trees, but soon enough, we'd come out the other side.

If we ran across some hikers in the meantime? Well, we could always shift back and pretend we were kinky naturists having an orgy in the forest. I mean, it wouldn't be the first time in history.

I tried to think how long it had been since I'd run in my shifted form through the woods in a Pack like this. Not since we were teens, that was for sure. Murphy was bringing up the back, still slightly injured and probably enjoying the leisurely pace with the two Omegas between us.

Two fucking Omegas. They'd always been inseparable, Quinn and Susannah, two halves of a whole, and it was even more so now. It made so much sense that I felt stupid for not seeing it before. Though how could I have predicted that the Goddess would suddenly turn the Beta I'd loved into an Omega?

Not even my skills of prediction were that good. But I felt like I should have known about Quinn. What kind of Alpha, even when we were teens, didn't recognize the beginnings of an Omega presentation? He was late—that I knew, but still. The way he used to flush in the locker rooms after Phys Ed. The way he was always touching Susannah, like she was a security blanket. The way he eyed me sometimes, like he was hungry. I'd just thought he was a Beta responding to an Alpha. It had never occurred to me that he was in the hormonal throes of transitioning to an Omega.

My own response to him was even more telling. I'd always loved Susannah, but I was also super protective of Quinn. I'd told myself it was because I liked him, and because Susannah loved him more than she loved anyone. More than she loved her own family. More than she'd ever possibly loved Murphy and me. She'd stand between Quinn and a bullet without blinking.

I'd always thought of him as Pack, but if I looked back, I was a little too growly with other Alphas around him. A little too protective. A little too hurt when he'd chosen Wilkie too.

"You're thinking real hard up there, Alpha," Quinn gritted out, and I stopped, turning to check on him. He looked pale, and a light sheen of sweat spread across his face, making him glisten in the moonlight.

I gave him a tight smile. "A lot to think about, *Omega,*" I replied. "Are you doing okay?" I pulled out my satellite phone, checking the GPS. "We aren't far away now—maybe another two hours of jogging, or four if you want to walk the rest of the way. We're just over the Canadian border now."

Quinn shook his head. "I'm fine. The quicker we get there, the quicker…"

"The quicker what?" I asked softly.

He shook his head. "I don't know. I don't know what to do now." He swallowed hard. "And I think the yearning is catching up to me now that I'm not on my meds, you know?"

My dick went instantly rock hard. *Fuck. The yearning.* It was like the heat for male Omegas, and usually, it would push the female Omegas into heat as well. It was like a fuckfest of epic proportions, with only one goal: to be bred.

"Goddess," Murphy breathed.

"Just Quinn," Susannah said quietly. She looked flushed too, probably responding to the *fuck me* pheromones coming from Quinn. She'd feel the effects first, but we'd all fall into the frenzy behind her. I was so damn glad we weren't in Moonburst, Montana. The joint combination of an unmated Omega pair in heat/yearning would've had every unmated Alpha in the vicinity banging on the door.

Murphy cleared his throat. "How long?"

Quinn shrugged. "I don't know. I've, uh, never technically gone into yearning."

I swore beneath my breath, but reached out and gently held his forearm. "If you need anything"—*a nest, treats, cock, my cubs*—"all you need to do is ask. Murphy and I are here for the both of you."

The Omegas between us both blushed, and I didn't have to wonder too hard about what they were thinking, especially when their scents bloomed together. Separately, they smelled delicious, but their scents together? It was fucking heaven.

Quinn's pretty aquamarine eyes were wide and shiny. "Thanks, Merrick." He looked over his shoulder at Murphy. "You too, Murphy. We owe you everything. You saved us." Susannah's face was solemn, but she nodded her agreement.

The memory of Susannah tearing into town, her face pale and her eyes wide with fear, was going to haunt me forever. Even thinking about the healing scrapes on her wrists where those cuffs had been on too tight made me angry. I wanted to dig up Wilkie and kill him myself. She'd run straight to me like I was her savior, and I'd never been more scared in my life. I could feel Murphy's rage and pain through our bond, but I hadn't been able to find him until Susannah had found me.

We all owed Tanner a life debt.

I squeezed Quinn's arm once more, then turned. We needed to get out of these woods and back to Tanner, then onto wherever we were going. I had my suspicions about where we were headed, though. Dark River. Home of the vamps who'd all sworn to do no harm.

My Beast rumbled low in my chest at the idea of walking our Omegas—*the* Omegas; they weren't ours yet, I chastized myself—into a town filled with vegan vampires. If I thought they smelled amazing, what would vampires think? Would we test their self-control?

Inexplicably, I trusted Tanner to protect them too. He wouldn't have saved them from Wilkie only to turn around and let them be eaten by his own kind.

By the time we made it to the campground where we were to meet him, the sun was lighting the sky and

Quinn was starting to throw off pheromones like they were fireworks on the Fourth of July. My dick had throbbed for the last mile and a half.

I could smell the faint scent that I associated with the vampire. It was more a blankness of smell, but with a hint of Murphy, whose clothes he was wearing. Shifting back, we pulled our clothes from the backpack Murphy was carrying and changed into normal clothing. Unfortunately for me, the hard-on just traveled from one form to the next, so I tucked my cock into the waistband of my boxers.

I fell back, wrapping an arm around Quinn. The Omega fell into my body, burying his face against my chest and huffing in lungfuls of my scent. I did my best to surround him, which would give him the most comfort, but he was only a little shorter than me so it wasn't as easy as it looked. Being close to an Alpha would ease the symptoms he was obviously suffering from.

Tanner was sitting on the hood of the car, and his head whipped toward us when we appeared from between the trees. "You made good tim— Why does he *smell* like that?" His words were choked, and even in the darkness, I could see his pupils dilate.

"He's going into the yearning."

Tanner raised a single eyebrow. "Fuck me swinging. I knew he must smell good to the Manix, but I didn't realize he'd smell good to other supernaturals too. Not enough outside data." He made a humming noise, but his eyes never left Quinn, except to flick to Susannah. He cleared his throat. "The research says that from the onset of pre-yearning symptoms, it's usually twenty-four to forty-eight hours before the full force of the yearning hits. I'm sure the last thing you want is for it to take full effect out here in the middle of the woods."

Murphy snorted. "We're Manix. We are literally *made* to have sex in the woods. But they'll need a proper nest."

Tanner nodded, sliding off the hood. "Get in. Slight change of plans. We're heading to Fox Falls."

Where the fuck was Fox Falls? Trust didn't come easily to the Manix, especially not when I had two Omegas to care for. But I slid into the passenger seat, allowing Murphy to comfort the Omegas in the back, and put my faith in a vampire I hardly knew.

The smell coming from the rear seats made me groan. Susannah's heat was rising up to meet Quinn's needs, and that was a scent I knew well. It still permeated our Packhouse from the brief time they'd stayed in the nest there. I wanted to roll in the scent of all three of them together.

"You probably want to break a few road rules and get us there fast."

Tanner didn't say anything, but when he peeled out of the campground, rocks and dirt sprayed out behind us.

19

MURPHY

My dick would forever have the imprint of my zipper along its length from being jammed against it tightly for so long. I was sure I was going to bust right through any moment now. Quinn was pressed between Susannah and I, but I was fairly certain that Zanny was about to follow him down the pheromone yellow brick road and on to fucking Wonderland.

And I would die a happy Alpha in the back seat of this SUV. Cause of death: blood loss from testicles exploding like overripe water balloons.

I thrummed hard, making Quinn's body languid against mine. So much of my history was caught up in these two. Merrick had been obsessed with Susannah, but I saw them more as a package than he ever did. They wouldn't be the same people without each other. It would be like loving the left hand but not the right.

Quinn made a soft whine, and I closed my eyes slowly, breathing in and out through my nose. This was torture. Actually, while he was still not in the throes of a heat-yearning combo, we should probably talk.

"Quinn?"

"Yes, Alpha?" he breathed. I cursed softly at the way that sounded falling from his lips. Dead. I was dead.

"Would you like Merrick and I to help you through the yearning?" I said the words softly, but the whole car seemed to hold its breath as we waited for his answer.

Quinn purred softly. "Yes." He sucked in a deep lungful of air, and I watched his Adam's apple bob. "If it's okay with Susannah."

I looked across his body at the other Omega. *Fuck. Two Omegas in one car.* Two years ago, this would have been a myth, an impossible dream. An Omega pair was the stuff of fairy tales and history books.

She looked between me and Merrick, and nodded. "It's okay with me. It doesn't mean anything more serious, though. No biting," she added, and I didn't miss her eyes sliding toward Tanner in the driver's seat. Neither did Quinn.

I noted the bunched muscles of the vampire's shoulders, and the way he was white-knuckling the steering wheel. "And if Tanner wants to help, you let him," Quinn murmured. His voice was strong and sure, like he didn't want us to try and talk him out of it later by blaming the yearning fog. He met Tanner's eyes in the rearview mirror, his lids hooded and his expression pure sex. "Just in case you want to try it out, just once."

Merrick's eyes met mine. I didn't know how the Beast would cope with a predator near vulnerable Omegas during their heat. The yearning was a wild time where the logical part of our brains got pushed back, until only the animal inside us was left. Breed, feed, and repeat. The addition of a vampire might be a problem.

"Quinn..."

"Non-negotiable, Murphy. Otherwise, Susannah and I will just hole up and ride it out the best we can."

I growled low in my chest, making Susannah whine. *Dammit.* "Fine. We'll try. If the Doc even wants to help."

"It goes against my profession to allow anyone to suffer," the vampire said, a small smile on his face as he looked back at the Omegas. "I never thought the cure would be my dick, but I did say I'd try anything once— right, Q?" He slid his eyes quickly to Merrick. "But if I think that my presence is causing undue stress, or becomes a danger to Quinn or Susannah, I'll get myself out of there. On my honor."

I let out a harsh breath. "I did say anything, I guess." I dipped my lips closer to Quinn's ear. "And Tanner is pretty damn hot."

"He also has above average hearing," Tanner teased from the front. I flushed a little, but smirked back at him. He wasn't really my type, but I wasn't going to lie —I wouldn't mind watching. He was beautifully made for a bloodsucker.

It was just under ten hours from the Canadian-US border to Fox Falls, according to Tanner, and I wasn't sure if we were going to make it. Quinn was beginning to become irritable, tossing and turning in his seat, like his skin was too tight. Susannah was breathing heavily, her cheeks flushed and her eyes glassy. I liked to think I was pretty good in bed, but not even I could satisfy two Omegas in the back of a moving SUV.

It was about ten in the morning, and we'd been driving for about four hours—the last hour with only the pained noise from Quinn's chest echoing around the otherwise silent car—when I called it. "We have to stop. Quinn and Susannah need food and fresh air at the very least, and they need to nest. They're hurting."

The solemnity in the car was at odds with the pure, unadulterated lust that hung in the air. Finally, Tanner nodded. "Okay. The harshness of the midday sun is giving me a headache anyway. There's a small town up ahead. We'll grab some supplies."

Merrick nodded, pulling out his phone. "I'll look for somewhere to stay." His voice was deep, a sure sign he was about to lose it himself.

The last twenty miles to town were the longest I'd

ever endured. Quinn's whines had turned to whimpers, and none of my soothing words were making a difference now. Merrick joined me in a thrumming purr, and while that calmed them for a moment, I knew it was a band-aid fix.

Pulling up to what was essentially a glorified gas station, Tanner ducked in. Merrick climbed out of the front seat and came round to the back, picking up Susannah bodily, then climbing back in with her on his lap. He ignored the looks from the nosy locals, slamming the heavily tinted doors. Susannah straddled him immediately, burying her nose in his neck and inhaled deeply.

Quinn whined, and I grinned, which probably made me an asshole, but it was cute. He could hate me later. "Come here, Omega. Let me make you feel better," I murmured. I unclipped him and dragged his face toward mine.

Then I kissed him hard. I'd never kissed a person who wasn't Merrick before, not even Susannah, and I marveled at the difference between them. Quinn wasn't soft, no, his jaw was sharp beneath my palm. His lips beat down on mine, gasping for something desperately. I was more than happy to provide, sliding my tongue into his mouth and tasting him. His moan echoed against my lips, and I pressed him harder against my body. The spike in his scent told me he liked what I was doing, so I slid my hand beneath his shirt, tracing my fingers over his searingly hot skin.

"My poor Omega," I whispered against his lips. "Soon I'll get you out of these clothes and into a nest. And then I'm going to fuck you, fill you full of my cubs, knot you deep until the only thing you can feel—the only thing you can *think* of—is the feel of my cock inside you."

The noise that emerged from Quinn was loud and pornographic. The busybodies outside were definitely getting some bang for their gossip buck. Quinn gripped my hand, dragging it down to where his cock was straining against his sweats. I could feel his slick, smell it like it was thick in the air.

"Then you're going to suck Merrick's cock while Zanny rides his face. Would you like that, Omega? Do you want a belly full of Rick's cum?"

Merrick groaned, and Susannah ground down faster. The SUV was definitely rocking now. "For Goddess's sake, Murphy, you're killing me here. Easy, baby," he crooned softly at Zanny. "Easy, I've got you. Tanner needs to hurry the fuck up."

As if we'd summoned him, the blond vampire stuck his head in the driver's door, a grin on his face. "It smells like a whorehouse on a two-for-one night out here," he groaned. "The natives think you're all perverts."

He climbed in, throwing half a dozen bags in the

passenger seat, now empty since Merrick had vacated it. Merrick muttered an address as Zanny leaned over and kissed Quinn from her seat in Merrick's lap. Watching their tongues tangle made my dick throb, like it had its own pulse point. Their combined scent was doing something to me, and it was torture.

Hell, who was I kidding? Their very *existence* did something to me.

Quicker than probably legal, or even humanly possible, we were pulling up to a secluded cabin. Sliding out of the SUV, I prowled around the perimeter, always keeping one eye on the car, scenting for anything suspicious. Anything that shouldn't be there.

My Beast gave a relieved chuff when all he could scent was the stale smell of whatever human had been out here to clean the cabin, and the smells of the woods. We were alone.

I grinned. This was going to be fun.

20

SUSANNAH

Two heats in two months felt a little excessive, but my body didn't care. My Omega was thrilled, because on top of her Omega, she had two handsome, devoted, strong Alphas to see her through it.

I felt like Omega Susannah was a separate entity, because she was desperate to be bitten and filled with cubs, while logical, rational Susannah was absolutely horrified at the very concept. But rational Susannah wasn't at the wheel right now. Horny, insatiable, fuck-me-sideways-then-inside-out Susannah was in charge.

I continued to kiss Quinn like I could climb inside him, like I would die if I didn't get to taste him. My body flushed hot and then cold, my head throbbed, and I *needed*. That was the last rational thought I had.

"Please," I whined, and suddenly arms were there.

I looked up into the golden, handsome face of Tanner. "Hello, little Omega," he whispered close to my lips. "May I kiss you?"

"*Yes!*" There wasn't anything I wanted more in that moment than to feel his lips on mine, except maybe his cock inside me. I whimpered and wrapped my legs around his waist, letting him walk me toward the small, rustic cabin. I tilted my head to the side and saw that Merrick had Quinn pressed tightly against the front door, one hand twined tightly in his hair, the other blindly pressing numbers on the combination lock that would open the door. I couldn't hear what he was saying, but when he kissed him ferociously, I whined again.

Then Tanner's lips were on mine, and all thoughts of Quinn and Merrick briefly escaped my brain. They were cool and dry, and unbelievably soft. When my tongue darted in and got his fangs, I moaned.

He moaned too. "Sweetheart, if you do that, we're going to have a way bigger problem. You're too fucking tempting," he grunted, then pushed my tongue back with his until we were almost dueling. He growled low in his chest, and the vibration sent waves of euphoria through my veins. He walked me to the small kitchen counter as Murphy hurried in behind us, his hands filled with grocery bags.

My eyes drifted straight to the huge tent in Murphy's pants. I wanted that, right fucking now. He pulled out one of the protein bars, unwrapped it and passed it to Merrick. I watched as the Alpha broke off pieces of the bar and hand-fed them to Quinn piece by piece, kissing his lips after each morsel.

I moaned at the sight until Murphy appeared with another unwrapped protein bar in his hand. "You guys haven't eaten, and I don't know when the heat will allow us up for air again. Eat, Omega," he purred, and I did as I was told, like a supplicant little Omega. A part of my brain would store that away to rehash with embarrassment later when I was back to being logical Susannah, but until then, the feel of Murphy's fingers touching my lip as he fed me was sending me into a primal frenzy.

He looked at Tanner, who still stood between my thighs, his cock pressing against the hard seam of my jean shorts. "No food for you in there?" It was a question, but also a statement.

Tanner shook his head. "I should be fine. They don't sell blood bags at the Stop'N'Go."

Murphy gave him a hard look. "If you need a snack, you take a bite out of me or Merrick, not the Omegas."

Tanner winked. "At least not until after the heat, right?" He leaned down until his lips brushed the sensitive skin behind my ear. "Don't worry, little Omega. Your big bad Alpha will like my bite. One day, so will you. My bite on that pretty neck will throw you into an orgasm so strong you'll scream my name."

The food turned to ash on my tongue, but I swallowed hard, knowing that Murphy wouldn't give me what I needed until I'd eaten something. I looked at Murphy imploringly as he fed me another piece. "Please, I need..."

"What do you need, Omega?" Murphy growled low.

"Quinn. A nest."

He pulled me off the counter, and I mewled at the loss of Tanner's heat. "Go make yourself a nest, Omegas." He stripped off his shirt and his pants, until he was standing there in only boxer shorts. He handed the clothes to me, giving me something that smelled like him to build my nest around.

Without prompting, the other guys did it too—even Tanner, who must have thought it was weird as hell. Except Tanner didn't have underwear on. He just got completely naked, and I was once again transfixed with the size of his dick. Manix were in proportion, plus the knot, so it was hard to dicknotize a female Manix. But there was something about Tanner naked, with his lean, muscular body, those washboard abs that were indeed cut, a V that fed down into an impressive-sized cock that just made you wonder what it would feel like inside you... Well, it was kinda magical.

"Stop staring at my dick, Omegas. Go build your nest so you can get to know it up close and personal," he teased.

I wanted nothing more than *my* Alphas in *my* nest with *my* Omega. I grabbed Quinn and launched myself down a short hall to the first bedroom I could find. We stopped outside the door as Quinn's skin burned against mine, and I had to kiss him. Had to, had to, *had to* do something. Needed.

Quinn grabbed me up into his arms, all the guys' clothes still tightly against my chest as he kissed me. It was messy and rough, and I needed more. Wiggling out of his arms, I dragged him into the bedroom that smelled like musty, stale humans. This wouldn't do at all.

I looked at Quinn, and we were on the same wavelength. We closed the blinds, darkened the room, and together, we worked to drag the mattress off the bed frame and onto the floor, rearranging pillows and blankets. More and more kept appearing, and I realized the guys were pilfering the rest of the bedding from the other rooms.

Someone slipped in and lit the fire, though I already felt too hot. But it did add to the room that made my Omega chuff with happiness, so I didn't protest.

Finally, having roughly pulled together something that was primal and basic, but good enough to appease the Beast, I dragged Quinn down onto our makeshift nest with me. "I love you," I breathed, suddenly realizing we'd incorporated our own clothes into the nest in the frenzy of activity, and now we were both naked. "I need you, Quinn. Need you inside me."

He crawled over me, kissing me as his hands roamed down my sides and then back upwards, over my breasts, kissing, and sucking any part of my skin he could find. We were already bonded, Quinn and I, which was probably why his yearning was affecting my heat so badly. He licked his mating mark on the underside of my breast, and I came. Slick flooded from my body, and someone groaned.

Looking over Quinn's shoulder, I saw my Alphas standing in the doorway. I beckoned them into our nest, but my attention was quickly drawn back to Quinn and the things he was doing to my body.

"Baby, I can't wait. Please," he whined, the head of his dick nudging at my entrance. God, I wanted nothing more. Not air. Not sustenance. Not even the Alphas whose scents were filling the room.

I thrust my hips up, my ankles locking around his butt as I dragged him into me. Hard. Fast. His hips slammed against mine, and we both moaned with relief. One of us was chanting, "Yes, yes, yes, yes," but I couldn't pull my thoughts together enough to work out which one of us it was.

Everything about being with Quinn like this felt right. Our sex life had always been amazing, but this? This was transcendent. We writhed against each other, and I sucked on my mating mark on his shoulder.

Sucked so hard, I made the old bite mark purple, and made Quinn pound into me until I couldn't breathe. I came on a scream, and he roared along with me.

And then I felt it—a sensation that was both foreign, yet completely right. A pulling feeling inside, and I knew he was extracting my eggs, which logically sounded weird as hell, but it was everything. My Omega keened with happiness, and the noises I was making weren't even remotely human.

Quinn sank his teeth into the curve of my shoulder, and fireworks danced behind my eyelids. I came, and came, and came until my body felt like I was the Wicked Witch, only someone had dropped a Pleasure Palace on me instead of a house.

Finally, after what felt like hours, Quinn dropped down on top of me with his full weight, his lungs heaving in oxygen. He was still hard, but the sucking/stroking sensation inside me had stopped.

He kissed up my neck to my ear. "Love you," he said, his voice rough.

Squeezing him tightly, I murmured it back, but I sounded drunk. Dick-drunk. When he slipped out of me, I whined, but I didn't have to whine for long. Strong arms were around my body, pulling me off my nest and onto someone's lap.

"Don't worry, baby. I've got you."

I looked up into Tanner's beautiful face, pulling him down to kiss me again. The coolness of his body was bliss on my overheated skin, and I wanted to rub myself all over him. So I did. I lost myself in the kiss, but when Quinn groaned, I dragged myself away with a whimper. I wanted to watch.

"Hold up," Tanner whispered, picking me up like I weighed no more than a feather and turning me on his lap, so my back was to his chest. "Now we can both enjoy the view."

And what a view it was.

21

TANNER

I t was like watching the best porn I'd ever seen in my life. I'd grabbed every packet of Magnum XL condoms I could find in the servo—I mean, gas station—when I'd gotten the basic supplies, but I wasn't sure that it was going to be enough. The two Alphas were moving Quinn between them, one at his front, kissing and stroking, and the other behind him, whispering reassuring things in the Omega's ear while rolling a condom down his cock. They were kneeling on the other side of the nest, and if I reached my hand out, I could stroke the sweat off their bodies.

With the amount of sex pheromones floating around this room, I didn't know how much of my hard-on was from watching the guys, the pretty little Omega on my lap, or how much was the reaction of the vampire inside me to the delicious scents they were giving off.

In the end, it didn't matter. I pulled Susannah tightly back against my chest, her slick dripping over my cock, begging me to enter her. She shifted around, and I reached between us to hold my cock as she notched herself against me and slid down slowly.

Holy hell. Jesus H. Christ.

She felt like perfection. I groaned as I held her hips, controlling the slide of her pussy up and down my cock, because honestly, I was one good slam home away from losing it and coming, like I was still an eighteen-year-old kid.

Wrapping my arm low around her hips, I held her tightly, keeping her still. Together, we watched as Merrick entered Quinn. The sound he made had Susannah clenching around my cock, making us both moan in symphony.

Shallowly, I moved inside her, letting the build up burn slow. Her pulse beat against my lips, and my fangs were aching as badly as my balls. Dragging my lips away from temptation, I buried my nose in the back of her neck and rolled my hips, hitting those spots I knew from medical school would drive her wild. She might be an Omega, but the happy spots were still the same as any other woman, mostly.

Sliding my other hand down to her clit, I stroked it gently, knowing it would be sensitive after what she and Quinn had just done. God, the sight of them together was going to be forever etched in my brain for as long as I lived. For eternity.

Quinn was panting now, and Merrick bent him in half so he could take Murphy's cock in his mouth. "That's it, my Omega. Take our cocks. I'm going to fill you up, make you ours. You're such a good Omega. Look at you, so ready for Merrick's knot," Murphy crooned. His hands fisted in Quinn's hair as he pulsed shallowly inside his mouth.

Susannah whimpered in my arms, and I wanted to whimper along with her. My arm still around her waist, I bent her forward, changing the direction of my strokes and fucking her harder. I needed her to come, and then come again before I could get off. I wasn't competitive by nature, but I'd be damned if I was going to embarrass myself in a room full of fucking primal Manix.

"Tanner..." she breathed. Her body pulsed around me until my eyes crossed, until an orgasm rocked her body. I had to think of something else before I blew my load.

Paul Hogan as Crocodile Dundee.

Men who wore footy shorts with no undies, so their balls fell out the side.

The word mayonnaise.

The Queen Mother.

Once I felt more in control, I pulled her back to me

again, turning her face so I could take more sipping kisses from her lips. She tasted like heaven.

"Bite me, Tanner," she breathed, and my whole body shuddered. God, I wanted to. I really, *really* wanted to. But she wasn't really giving me permission. She was so fucking high on pheromones, she was probably as high as a spider in an updraft.

Merrick's grunt of release was timed to perfection with Quinn's. It dragged my eyes back from Susannah's neck to the three Manix in front of me. Merrick was knotted inside Quinn, their bodies curled around each other on the soft blankets of the nest, but Murphy's eyes were on us.

Or more particularly, on me. Like he knew what I was thinking. He knew my weakness.

He appeared in front of Susannah, kissing her hard until all she could do was whimper against his lips. Pulling away, he looked over her shoulder at me. "Bite me, not her."

I gritted my teeth. "I'm in control."

The look he gave me held more clear-headed compassion than I would have thought possible, considering he'd just had his dick deep in the throat of another man. "You're suffering. Bite me, and let's both bring her the pleasure she deserves."

I was weak, and he was offering. At this point, it was just one more in a long list of sins I'd committed. Grabbing his wrist, I pulled it to my fangs and pierced his skin. His blood rushed into my mouth, and bugger me, it was everything.

I slammed hard into Susannah, and she moaned and squealed against me, riding my cock as I rode the wave of magic-fuelled bliss that was Manix blood. Fun fact: a vampire bite was pleasurable if we wanted it to be, and god, did I want it to be. I fed all my ecstasy back to Murphy, until he was kissing Susannah and coming all over her breasts and stomach.

As she clenched around me, I finally let go, filling her, holding her tight to me until her pussy stopped fluttering. I lifted her off me, then pulled her back against my chest, rolling us until we all laid together like cutlery in a drawer.

I was stuffed. How did Manix do that every twenty minutes for days on end? It was fucking lunacy.

Merrick laughed from where he was nuzzling against Quinn's shoulder. *Whoops.* I'd said that out loud.

"That's just the beginning," Murphy purred. "Welcome to the frenzy."

THREE DAYS. I'd never had an orgy before, let alone one that lasted three whole days. Apparently, due to the nature of Quinn's repressed yearning, it went on and on rather than being sated quickly by coupling with Susannah. But you know what? I didn't even care. It could have gone on for another five days and I would've been happier than a pig in mud. Probably a dehydrated husk, but a happy husk.

Finally, we ran out of food and stupidly large condoms, and had to emerge from our heat haze. You'd think that after seeing each other stretched and contorted in ways that were definitely not human, we'd be as close as five people could be. That wasn't how it went at all. There was the awkwardness of unspoken questions, like we'd been on a three-day bender with strangers.

We all showered and changed back into filthy clothes, none of us having had time to pack extra before leaving Maxton. It was okay, because once we got to Dark River, we could stop at my place and change.

When I'd stumbled into Dark River a decade ago, Raine Baxter was already the Convocation Member for Weird Supes. I mean, she had a proper title, but that was what it boiled down to, right? They had run me through the normal tests, made sure I wasn't a whack job—though that didn't seem to be a deciding factor, if you considered Raine's mates.

I'd gotten a job as research and surgery assistant in town, and obviously, as a loan-out by Raine, although technically I belonged under the purview of the Vampire Nation. The Vampire Nation didn't give a shit who I ate, though, as long as I didn't get caught by humans.

No, the people I had to answer to were my new people, and I was pretty sure I was about to be excommunicated for breaking just about every cardinal rule they had. *Don't murder people* was pretty up there.

"Let's go," Merrick said softly, and we did the combined awkward walk of shame. Yeah, they were going to have to have a talk, because even dead, I was still affected by the sheer chemistry the four of them had.

We climbed back into the misappropriated SUV, and Murphy slid into the passenger seat beside me. I tried not to laugh at the look of longing he threw at the back seat. They really, *really* needed to have that talk.

I pulled out onto the bumpy dirt road and made my way back to the highway. There were only four or so hours until we made it to Dark River. We should arrive about seven p.m., which was basically early morning for a vampire town. Hopefully, we could sneak in without raising too many questions.

I snorted at the idea. There were no secrets in Dark River.

The silence seemed to get heavier the further away from the little heat oasis cabin we got. Eventually, it was too much for me. I couldn't deal with the tension that came with unsaid things. "Okay, out with it. This is literally killing me for the second time."

Murphy startled, whipping his head toward me. "What?"

I sighed. "The amount of unresolved feelings is giving me hives. Merrick and Murphy, it is very obvious to everyone in this car with a heartbeat—me included—that you desperately want Quinn and Susannah. Am I wrong?"

Susannah glared at me from the back. "Tanner, it's not that easy."

"But why?"

"Because we've just come out of a relationship where we were someone's property. I'm not in a hurry to be someone's property again."

Merrick stared at her. "You think we want you as *property*?" he said incredulously. "We don't want to own anyone, least of all you and Quinn."

Quinn, who seemed less stubborn than Susannah, tilted his head. "Then what do you want? From our experience, and the experience of other Omegas, that's essentially what we become. Breeders. Possessions. Status symbols."

Murphy snorted. "You think Raiden is a status symbol? You think he considers himself a possession?"

Yeah, I'd met Raiden and Naja, the Omegas for the Huxley-Grey Pack. There was definitely a pecking order in that Pack, and it started with those Omegas. Their Pack adored them. They would lay down their lives just to make their Omegas happy.

But I'd seen other Omegas in Maxton's Packs, who were treated exactly how Quinn was describing, especially in the older Packs. It was even worse for the Betas. The Manix had definitely been designationist—probably not a word—in the past, and I didn't think the new wave of changes had been around long enough to create any real systematic change.

However, Quinn was wrong about these two Alphas. Anyone with eyes could see that, but I kept my thoughts to myself. They needed to work through this at their own pace, now that I'd nudged them in the right direction.

Who said my psych rotation wouldn't come in handy?

Susannah snorted. "We both know the Huxley-Grey Pack is the exception rather than the rule for just about everything."

Merrick gripped her hand. "And so are we. We've wanted you since we were kids—both of you." He looked between them, his face almost painfully sincere. "We wanted you even when you rejected us for someone who treated you like crap. Every Omega, every Beta, every other Packmate we've tried to take hasn't been right, because it's always been you."

Something got in my eye, and I blinked it away rapidly. Yeah. That's what was happening. There was no crying in baseball.

I snorted internally. I had let Quinn suck my cock like he was a Dyson, so I was pretty sure toxic masculinity had gone right out the window this week. But still, I swallowed down the emotion.

Murphy seemed to be panicking at Merrick's declaration. "We'll take it at your pace, Omegas. Let us show you that we aren't like the old Manix Packs. Let us show you how we think you should be treated. It doesn't matter to us if you're Omega, Beta or Alpha. It's you we want. It's always been you."

Quinn and Susannah looked at each other, having a silent conversation. As the heavy silence dragged on, I thought I'd have to intervene again. Finally, Susannah nodded. "We'll try, but no commitments. Not yet."

Merrick grinned and leaned forward, kissing her hard on the lips, then dragging Quinn across her lap and kissing him too. I swerved a little before focusing back on the road.

The Steve Miller Band was on to something. I really was "the Gangster of Love."

22

QUINN

Apart from our brief hiatus in California, neither Susannah nor I had ever been out of Maxton, or the tiny town beside it. We'd gotten our education at the school there, and Wilkie had never let us get any higher qualifications, so we'd never even done college online.

But we could have traveled the world and never found any place quite like Dark River. As we drove through, the place was lit up like it was summer solstice, with barely visible shadows that I knew were vampires darting around.

A diner with a striped awning out the front was glowing like a beacon, but Tanner drove straight past. The town square was lit up with fairy lights, and people stood in small groups, chatting and laughing. It was like a macabre Rockwell painting.

Tanner pulled into the space in front of a tiny cabin, no bigger than a two-room apartment. It didn't look particularly like anything, almost a blank canvas.

"Home sweet home. It's not very big, but we can shower, and you guys can borrow some of my clothes before we head over to talk to Raine," he said, climbing out of the driver's seat and stretching. I knew he probably could have run this distance in nearly half the time, but he'd stuck it out with us.

The big blond vamp made me feel soft, but I'd noticed when he was giving us our Pack therapy session earlier that he hadn't added himself into the equation. Maybe he wasn't interested in anything more with us, and I wasn't about to admit out loud how much that hurt. Tanner didn't owe us anything. He'd been more than good to us; he'd saved me and gotten me through the yearning. His responsibility to us ended there.

Hopefully, we could give him something back in the form of a reprieve for murdering Wilkie and Joseph, but then that was it, right?

I sat in the tiny open-plan living-kitchen area, jammed onto the couch beside Susannah while we waited for Murphy to emerge from the bedroom. I was wearing Tanner's sweats and a tee, and they fit pretty well. But they swamped Susannah, and they were basically like tights on Merrick. Honestly, it looked like he'd stashed a salami down his pants, given the camel tail he was rocking. Manix were just built bigger.

When Murphy came out, I snorted out a laugh before I could suck it back down. "Laugh it up, chuckles. I'll take it out on your ass later," he warned, pointing at me, and I winked back. Promises, promises.

Tanner swallowed hard, and his eyes danced with laughter. "We should go. You're probably hungry, and nothing is better dinner entertainment than watching me get my ass handed to me by a five-foot-three vampire who looks like she's eighteen."

He was joking, but I could see the very real worry around his eyes. I grabbed his fingers and squeezed them. "We've got your back, Tanner. I'll throw a full Manix Omega hissy fit if they don't see it our way." I raised an eyebrow at him. "I've never done it before, but I've seen it plenty of times. There's a lot of tears and snot. It's kind of disconcerting from a nearly seven-foot monster."

Tanner laughed, wrapping an arm around my shoulders and pulling me in tightly to his body. "Thanks, mate. I appreciate it." He kissed the side of my head, and I told my heart that it was just a friendly gesture, not romantic. If I'd learned one thing about the golden retriever vampire, it was that Aussies were huggers.

We took the SUV, despite the fact the place we

were going was less than a ten-minute walk away. There were no other cars on the road, mostly just people zipping all over the place at the speed of light. A car would almost be a slower mode of transport.

We stopped in front of a well-lit building. The sign hanging above the plate glass windows said The Immortal Cupcake, and the stained-glass windows glowed invitingly. Sucking in a deep breath, Tanner climbed out, holding the door open for Susannah and I.

Zanny brushed her fingers across his stomach, and he looked down at her with something close to adoration on his face. They'd definitely gotten closer during the heat, and anyone with eyes could see the attraction building there. I'd seen it all along, the way she'd watched him hungrily. They just had to get out of their own way.

He looked over at us all. "We can say our piece, and then you have to let the next events run their course. You can't interfere, yeah?"

I narrowed my eyes at him. "What's the worst-case scenario?"

He just shook his head, walking toward the entrance of the cafe. There were at least a dozen people inside. I followed in behind him with Zanny's hand in mine, and the Alphas brought up the rear.

The whole place quieted as we entered, and I could

almost hear their collective inhale. Every atom in my body stiffened in preparation for fight or flight, but then a girl behind the counter snorted. "Keep your fangs in your pants, or I'll eject every single one of you from here and give you an eight-week ban."

There was a collective mutter as everyone went back to pretending to eat. The girl wasn't the Convocation Member, and as I inhaled, I realized she was alive. A shifter of some kind, maybe?

"It's good to see you, Tanner," she said happily. "Who are your friends?"

"Everly, this is Quinn, Susannah, Merrick, and Murphy. They're Manix."

The girl's brown eyes bounced between all of us with interest—the academic kind of interest, not the sexual kind. "Bold of you to bring a bunch of Manix into a town of bloodsuckers, Outback Jack. Like whipping out the caviar at an all-you-can-eat buffet."

"Desperate times, Everly. Is Raine around? And why are you here and not the guys?"

Everly's smile was wide. If I had to describe it, I'd say it was a shit-eating grin. "Well, a lot has happened while you took your tiny hiatus to Whoville, Crocodile Dundee. Raine went on a gap year and came back with two new mates. She's probably somewhere having dirty, immortal monkey sex."

Tanner screwed up his nose. "There's a lot to

unpack right there, and I'm not sure I have the brain-power for it today. How was seven mates not enough? Nine just seems excessive."

Everly laughed. "Yep, she's definitely going to need some kind of vaginal facelift in a decade. Vag-lift?"

A voice cleared behind me. "I promise my vagina is as tight as it was the day I was turned. Could crack walnuts in that baby. Ka-pow."

I spun on my heel to see a tiny woman with blood-red hair. There was no doubt in my mind this was the Convocation Member. I hadn't met her, despite her trips to Maxton. We'd been… otherwise engaged.

The vampiress looked at Merrick and Murphy. "Good to see you two again. I just got off the phone with your Alpha General." Her face folded into empathy. "I'm sorry about your home."

Merrick cleared his throat. "It's all gone, then?"

She nodded. "Some of the Legion building stands, but most of the town was demolished by the force of the flames. It took out a lot of properties further down the mountain too, though the human authorities managed to save the main part of the little town you guys frequent for supplies."

Merrick's face was neutral, like she'd told him that they were out of his favorite flavor of ice cream rather than that our ancestral homes were gone. I mightn't feel much for the place, but that didn't mean everyone else felt the same way.

Susannah reached out and twined her fingers through his, pushing some of her soothing Omega essence toward him. He let out a shuddering sigh, nodding at the vampire in front of us. "Thank you. We've been out of touch for a couple of days."

Raine looked between Merrick and Tanner. "Indeed. You better tell me what you're doing here, instead of where you're supposed to be." She looked around at all the people pretending they weren't listening. "And perhaps we should do that in my office."

She disappeared, and we all filed out of the cafe at a normal pace. Tanner looked over his shoulder. "Good to see ya, Everly."

"You too, Shark Bait."

He chuckled, and I couldn't imagine the brass balls on a shifter to so openly make fun of a vampire, even one as good-natured as Tanner.

We walked at a human speed along the footpath, and I tried to ignore the fact that people were staring at us like we were a sideshow. Tanner did his best to play tour guide. "Dark River was set up by the vampire Nico and a few others, as a place for vampires who were tired of the endless blood and death of normal vampire society. To live here, you have to pledge not to feed from or turn humans. The penalties for doing so are... harsh. They are ruled by a Town Council, and every year, they get at least one or two new town members. Everyone is given a job in or out of town, depending on whether they're at an age where they can control them-selves properly around heartbeats. It's kind of like a Hallmark Christmas movie, if you couple it with a late-night horror movie, and a little snuff film."

"What the hell kind of movies are you watching?" Murphy grumbled, and I laughed.

"It's a pretty good place to live. People who think like you, who have the same morals and ethics as you. Kinda idyllic, really."

"Sounds like a cult," Murphy muttered.

Tanner chuckled. "Maybe a little." He stopped out the front of a non-descript door. "Nico is in," he said with a huff. "Guess it's better to get it over with in one go."

He pulled the door open, and we were met with an honest-to-god, nineties-style wooden bead curtain. Behind it was a short vampire with swirling blue tattoos and a presence so heavy it made my Omega whine. Merrick tensed beside me, an Alpha reacting to the Omega's distress—or maybe it just sensed a bigger predator in the room.

"With a reaction like that, you'd think that you weren't happy to see me, Tanner?"

I watched Tanner's face. He gave a one-sided smile, but it was resigned. "I was hoping we could put off the inevitable for a little longer." He walked over and gave the vamp a man hug, all back-slapping and grumbling questions on how he'd been.

Finally, Nico pulled away. "She's in her office answering another call. Come on in." The ancient vampire looked over us all. "Merrick, it's good to see you again." His gaze bounced to the rest of us. "I'm Nico. Who wants ice cream?"

23

MERRICK

My Beast was disconcerted by the energy in the room. He didn't care that our Omegas were happily eating ice cream, or that the two vampires in front of me looked about the right age to attend the local community college's Orientation Week.

He knew what they were, and therefore he couldn't relax. I couldn't relax. It didn't help that their faces were stony as Tanner gave his recount of what had happened in the last week or so. Though I did see something inherently terrifying pass through the Convocation Member's eyes as Tanner listed off Wilkie's systematic abuse of my Omegas, and I hadn't been able to hold back the growl. Quinn had grabbed my thigh, squeezing it gently, a reassurance I so desperately needed. That was behind them now. They would never be treated like that again, not while I still breathed.

However, when we got to the part where Tanner not only killed Wilkie and Joseph, but tore them to pieces, I winced. The way he recounted facts dispassionately made it sound way worse than it was. I mean, it was bad, but he'd done it for the right reasons.

Susannah interrupted. "Without him, Quinn would have been assaulted in the worst way, and I would have been too. We would have been bred against our will, captives to an Alpha who thought he owned our bodies and that free will meant nothing. Yes, Tanner took two lives, but he saved two lives—maybe even more—in the process."

No one mentioned Errol, and I was okay with that. The look of relief, of guilt, of hope that he'd had on his face as he looked down at his dead Alpha had been heartbreaking. That poor Beta had deserved better, and if anyone could survive in the human world, or greater supernatural society, it was Errol. I hoped he found something, or someone, who made him happy and he never returned to Maxton.

Well, there wasn't a Maxton to return to. I should feel something, knowing that my home had burned. That the place where I'd been born, grown up, fallen in love, had my heart broken, and fallen in love again was no more, but I didn't. Murphy was my home. And if I had my way, the Omegas beside me would become the heart of it.

Raine was nodding at Susannah's impassioned plea. "I understand, and as the Convocation Member, I give him a total reprieve for the deaths of those two Manix. I'm not above an eye for an eye." Relief swamped Susannah's face, but when I looked at Tanner, he was still expressionless. When Raine continued, I understood why. "But it's not just *my* rules he broke. I don't think I need to bring this to the Vampire Nation—it sounds like you cleaned up your mess—but the Dark River Town Council will have to meet."

Nico nodded, looking a little sad. "You were acting within the purview of your duties as a representative of the Convocation Member in the very general sense, so I'll ensure execution is off the table—"

"*What?*" Quinn gasped, his eyes whipping to Tanner. "You came back here to confess, knowing they might decide to kill you?" He punched our vampire in the arm, hard. "*You fucking dick.*"

I ignored the fact that I'd mentally referred to him as our vampire. In this room, he was ours. Not like, in a Pack sense. In, like, a familiar sense.

Yeah, let's go with that.

Tanner grabbed Quinn's hand and squeezed it gently. "I didn't think they would. I was at least ninety percent certain. They might be strict about their rules, but they do have some fairness."

Murphy was shaking his head. "This is bullshit. I literally saw the vampire Lucius tear a Manix's head off."

"Different set of rules. They're a part of Raine's guard," Nico replied, holding a hand up as we growled our protests. "Calm down. I promise I won't let that happen. The best-case scenario here is that the Town Council says this is outside our jurisdiction. The worst-case scenario is that he's excommunicated from Dark River."

Susannah's outrage was written all over her face. "You mean he can never come back? He has a home here. Friends."

Raine looked between us. "Don't borrow trouble just yet. Home can be all sorts of places, or with all sorts of people. If Tanner is anything, he is adaptable." She looked at Nico. "Call the Town Council. May as well get this over with and rip it off like a band-aid. Prolonging it only ever makes it worse."

Nico smirked. "What she means to say is that we need to head home, because she's found two new mates to keep her entertained, and the orgies have been on point."

Raine gave him an unimpressed expression, but I could see the humor dancing in her eyes. There was obviously a lot of love between them, but that wasn't an orgy I'd ever want to be in.

Tanner sighed. "Okay."

"Go to the diner, get your little Pack something to eat, and then meet us at the Town Council building in say... an hour?" Raine said, looking to Nico for confirmation.

"Should be long enough to get a quorum. And if Grim doesn't show, who's gonna be mad about it?" he asked lightly. All the vampires in the room exchanged a loaded look. I was kind of glad I didn't know who Grim was.

Tanner stood, ushering us up and out of the door. Susannah grabbed his hand and clung to it, and I waited for the wash of jealousy from my Beast. It never came. He'd accepted that *his* Omega wanted the vampire, and we'd wanted her for long enough that we'd do anything to make her happy.

Besides, he was fucking nice to look at. He mightn't want to get down like that yet, but maybe one day he would, at least with Quinn. He hadn't seemed to mind getting his dick sucked during the yearning. Maybe it was the draw of the forbidden, or maybe sexuality was a little more fluid than society would have you believe. Maybe he'd just been caught up in the pheromones— which I wouldn't really blame him for. But we needed time to figure these things out.

He walked us across the town square, which was

still lit up. The Manix saw well in the dark, but it was nice to be able to see the possible threats all around.

"Don't worry, I don't think anyone is going to break and attack. As you just heard, the consequences can be pretty shitty, and while you're tasty, no snack is worth expulsion or worse," Tanner teased, slapping me on the back. Susannah huffed at the reminder that he could still be executed.

I felt like a sloth in a village of cheetahs as we stepped up to the door of the diner. It was a weird feeling. We'd always considered ourselves the apex of evolution, but this small town of Dudley Do-Rights was proving that maybe *de*-evolution could fuck us all up if it chose.

The little brass bell above the door tinkled as we walked in, and all conversation stopped, again. I was almost used to it by now.

"Tanner, ye handsome wee bastard! I've missed you. Come here." An elderly woman—no, vampire— bustled over to Tanner, wrapping him in what could only be described as a buxom hug. She squeezed tight, then stepped away. "And who have you got with you today?"

Tanner straightened, looking slightly mussed from the experience. "Merrick and Murphy," he said, pointing to each of us. "And Quinn and Susannah."

"Aye, I heard Raine found the Manix again." Well, not so much Raine, but the end result had been the same, so I didn't correct her. "Take the booth in the back, lad, and I'll grab you the menus." The elderly vampire looked at us. "I'm Beatrice, seeing as this young lout doesn't have the manners the Queen gave him. Don't worry—you'll be safe here. No one is dumb enough to step out of line in my diner." I had a feeling that the last statement was more for everyone else than us.

Tanner herded us toward a booth, and I slid the Omegas in closest to the wall. Murphy and I bracketed them on each side, with Tanner taking the chair at the end.

Beatrice came back over, holding a huge platter of cheese fries and the menus. "You look hungry, so these will tide you over until you choose what you'd like. On the house." She placed the fries in the middle of the table. They were coated in melty cheese, bacon, and chopped shallots. They smelled so good, and my mouth was watering. "Take your time ordering. Just give me a shout when you're ready." She gave Tanner's shoulder one last squeeze and hurried away.

"So, this is Dark River," Murphy mumbled around a mouth full of cheese fries. "I can see the draw."

Tanner shrugged, but I could see the worry in his eyes. "It was a good place to land in an uncertain time of my life."

"This is where you want to stay forever?" Susannah

asked softly, her fingers curling like she wanted to reach for him.

"That was the plan. It's as close to a community as vampirekind has managed."

And we might have ruined that for him. Guilt was a bitch.

24

TANNER

We sat around the diner for an hour before someone was sent down to fetch me to stand before the Town Council. I'd tried to make the Manix stay at the diner, happy that Beatrice would protect them—no one fucked with Beatrice—but that stubborn Pack refused.

"If you don't think we're coming with you to defend you, then I'd worry some kind of crazy Australian brain-eating parasite was living rent-free in your skull," Susannah had muttered, which was both gross and endearing.

This Pack was getting to me. The only parasites worming their way into my body were these guys, right into my heart.

None of that mattered right now, though, because I sat before the full Town Council and held in a groan.

Obviously, it was a slow day, because all five members had shown up—including Grim. His name wasn't actually Grim, that was something Raine and her consorts called him, due to his penchant for wearing a black cowled cape and being tall and skinny. And pasty pale.

Murphy leaned closer to Merrick and whispered, "I get it now."

I gave them a frown. The Town Council weren't like Raine and Nico. They were traditionalists as much as they could be, most of them being old as hell and stuck in the seventeen hundreds with their ideals. That meant these proceedings were done with some kind of pomp and gravitas. Except Nico, who always looked bored, despite being the oldest of them all.

Raine sat in the back row with Lucius and Judge, who were watching the proceedings. The idea of such dangerous vampires—who made my instincts go haywire—sitting behind my Manix made me feel squirrelly, but I ignored it. I trusted Raine and her consorts, mostly.

"So you hold no remorse for the murder of these two men?" Grim asked, and I winced. I couldn't even fake remorse for the death of Wilkie and his Packmate.

"No, sir." I wanted to correct him that they were Manix and not men, but I held my tongue. Talking back wasn't going to change the outcome of this trial, and I knew it. I'd known what the result would be as soon as Grim and Eduardo sat down. Nico and Catherine, the head of the Council, were pragmatists, but the rest? Not so much. They'd have the majority, and I knew the result wouldn't be in my favor.

"If presented with the same scenario, would you do it again?"

I looked Tomas—Grim—dead in the eye. "Without hesitation."

He huffed and looked around at his counterparts. "So be it. I find Tanner McCulloch guilty of breaking the covenants of our community and suggest execution immediately."

"*What?!*"

"That's fucking ridiculous! You *can't!*"

Susannah and Quinn's protests were loud, and I almost smiled at their defense of me. Looking over my shoulder, I gave them what I hoped was a reassuring look. *It'll be okay,* I mouthed, projecting way more confidence in the outcome than I actually felt.

Catherine snorted. "Unlikely, Tomas. We aren't in the business of executing perfectly fine vampires to satisfy your repressed bloodlust. I vote we find him not guilty and let him get back to the business of healing."

"Healing them straight into a hastily dug grave," the other Council woman complained, and they bickered back and forth for a while.

Finally, after another thirty minutes of negotiation, they turned back toward me. The scent of Omega distress was starting to make my skin itch, and I wanted them out of here already.

Catherine spoke, her lips pinched. "Tanner McCulloch, we find you guilty of breaking Dark River's covenant laws. These are sacrosanct and create the very foundation of our society. While the circumstances certainly made your actions warranted, you were acting outside your Convocation given orders —*far* outside—and therefore are not covered by the exemptions that could apply. Therefore, we have no choice but to expel you from Dark River, with a non-reapplication period of two hundred years."

I swallowed, pushing away the feeling of being cast adrift once more. I could be dead, and that was a fate I was glad to escape for the second time in my life. "I understand."

Merrick stood. "This is bullshit. He could've buried that waste of space and never mentioned it again, and you assholes would never have known the difference. You're punishing him for being honest, and that is the most backwards bullshit I've ever heard. He was protecting *Omegas*. You mightn't understand what that means up there on your fucking high horses, but to the Manix, it makes him a hero."

Catherine raised an eyebrow at Merrick, and I moved toward him, placing my body slightly in front of his. "Then I suggest you take your *hero* and leave Dark

River." She gave me a sympathetic look. "You have until dawn to gather your things."

"Thank you, ma'am," I said softly, then turned to the Pack. "Let's go." I needed them out of the room, away from the threat of the most powerful vampires in Dark River. I wasn't sure where this protectiveness had come from, but now wasn't the time to examine it.

I met Raine and Judge outside, though Lucius was gone. Raine looked peeved. "I'm sorry."

I waved her comment away. "I made my own choices. I wasn't lying—I'd do it all over again." I looked at Quinn and Murphy. Remembered how brutalized they'd been. Then glanced at Susannah, imagining the horror of what her future would have been if I hadn't interfered. If I hadn't arrived in time. "Every damn time."

Raine nodded, looking around at the Pack. "Excuse us for a moment," she murmured. I hesitated, then she grabbed my shoulder and pulled me along. "Judge will protect them if they need it. Which they won't." She dragged me further away from the group, and despite her reassurances, I kept them in my eyesight. Raine dropped her voice low. "Even if you aren't a citizen of Dark River anymore, you're still working for me. I'm happy to relieve you of your position if you want to head out and find somewhere new to settle. I'm also happy for you to return to wherever the Manix decides to stay and continue on with your role for as long as you like. The choice is yours, Tanner."

I frowned, my eyes sliding back to the Pack over and over. That was what they were: a Pack. They mightn't have bonded yet, but I had no doubt they would. Merrick and Murphy would protect the Omegas, and eventually, they'd have a bonding ceremony. After that, there'd no longer be a place for me.

When had I become so attached to them? During the yearning? Or before that, when Susannah and Quinn had been so stubborn, so defensive in my office as I patched up their injuries? Maybe right even at the beginning, when Susannah had yelled at me at the Alpha General's mating party? I was heading down a path that was going to end in heartache, but I was unwilling—or unable—to stop it.

I looked back at Raine, clearing my throat. "I'd like to continue on as the town doctor for however long they'll have me, or until they train up someone new. There's a Pack expecting its first litter of cubs with their male Omega, and I think they'd be happier if I was there."

Raine just smiled at me, like she knew I was full of shit. "Certainly, Tanner. I'll pass it by the Alpha General."

I winced. "I know it's a lot to ask, but is there any way we could keep this between us? The whole Alpha-murdering and burying in the woods thing?"

Raine sighed. "No."

Fuck. The Manix wouldn't want me back anyway then. Who'd want a murderer delivering their cubs?

"I'm sorry, Tanner. I'll only tell the Alpha General, though, and if I know the kind of man Courtland is, he'll slap you on the back in thanks and keep you around."

I lowered my head. "I understand."

I could feel the eyes of the Pack on me, and Raine raised her brows. "Interesting fan club you got there. They've certainly changed your scent."

I flushed. "I had to help them through the heat. I haven't had time to de-scent just yet."

Raine's face was contorted into a polite mask of concern, but her eyes were definitely laughing at me. "Very noble of you, Tanner."

I hadn't realized my feet were carrying me back toward the Omegas subconsciously, but soon enough, I was back in front of them. Judge gave me a shithead grin. "We'll let you guys get on with it." The mirth from his face slid away. "Sorry about the shit outcome. It ain't fun, but at least it ain't forever. You never know what'll happen today, tomorrow, or two hundred years from now. You should take happiness where you can, while you can. Then come home to Dark River when you're ready."

His eyes flicked to Susannah, and I knew what he was saying, but my brain rebelled against it. I wasn't ready for that. I doubted I'd *ever* be ready for what he was suggesting. It was obvious to both of them, probably because I was a shit poker player, that I was interested in the Omegas—hell, I was even fond of the Alphas—but they were Manix, and therefore mortal.

And I was not.

It was something that Judge and Raine would have to deal with in their own family, but it wasn't something I was ready to think about or inflict on myself. Shaking my head, I gave him a tight smile I didn't feel. "We should go."

Susannah reached out and gripped my hand, and I looked down at her. Ready or not, they were here, and I wasn't sure my heart was going to give my head a choice.

25

MURPHY

We were back on the road again, hightailing it out of Dark River before sunrise like we were desperados. It had been surprisingly easy for Tanner to pack up his life into a couple of boxes, which he loaded into the back of the SUV.

He seemed... sad. No, resigned. And it was making my Beast mad. I didn't know why, though; he wasn't Pack. He wasn't Manix. He was neither Omega nor Beta. Nothing about him should set off my Beast's instincts, but I still wanted to give him a hug and thrum soothingly for him.

I didn't know which of us would be more weirded out if that happened. I had to face the fact that since the heat, when he drank from me, the status of the good doctor had changed in my eyes. He'd gone from being a peripheral figure in Manix society, to someone important to me. A friend, at least. Maybe even part of the Pack, though it didn't exist just yet.

I looked over at Merrick. I dug into our bond and felt his own contemplative thoughts. I wasn't sure if we were thinking the same thing, but he was definitely thinking about Susannah and Quinn and the Pack we wanted to build.

We were going to swap out drivers and go straight through to Moonburst, Montana, where the rest of the Manix had landed. Tanner was taking the first shift until the sun through the windshield got too bright, and then one of us would take over.

My poor Omegas were exhausted. Quinn's head was on my shoulder, his eyes closed, his plush lips open slightly so I could hear his gentle snores. Susannah had her face buried hard into his hip, inhaling him with every breath. They were so fucking cute, they made my heart grow ten sizes. I wanted them forever.

Finally, the scent of Tanner's emotions got too much for me. "Are you okay, man?"

Both Merrick and I watched his face for answers that wouldn't necessarily come out of his mouth. "I'm fine. This is what I planned on doing anyway, so it makes no difference."

"There's a difference between voluntarily coming to

Moonburst and being ejected from your home," Merrick murmured.

Tanner nodded, but didn't add anything. Only the soft sound of sleeping Omegas broke the silence.

"We owe you," Merrick said eventually. "A debt that can't really be paid because there's nothing I value more than their lives."

Tanner sighed. "I don't expect repayment for doing what's right. I wasn't lying—I'd do it again, even knowing that I'd be kicked out of home, like some delinquent child caught smoking weed in his parent's garage." He shook his head. "It was the right thing to do, and sometimes the right thing has hard consequences. One doesn't negate the other."

Fuck, he was breaking my heart. "We should talk about the Omegas," I said softly to them both.

"We've talked about this, remember?" Tanner replied. "You're going to court them, then in a couple of months' time, the inevitable will happen. You'll bond, because you'd have to be blind and stupid not to see the connection between the four of you."

Merrick tilted his head. "And what about *your* intentions?" Tanner went to protest—you could see it on his face—but Merrick interrupted. "Don't be stupid and tell me you were just doing your job. We aren't fools, Tanner. You want them; I can see it in the longing way you watch them. I *know,* because I've looked at them the very same way for ten Goddess-damned years. I was on the outside, watching someone else touching the Omegas I wanted so badly, it was an ache in my heart. Every time that fucker Wilkie laid a hand on them, it was a lash to my soul."

I leaned forward in my seat, but not so much that Quinn's head shifted from my shoulder. He squirmed, trying to get comfortable, and I lifted my fingers, stroking them through his short hair until he went back to sleep.

"Don't be an idiot. They want you as well. God, sometimes Susannah looks at you like she wants to eat you, not the other way around." I grinned, so Tanner knew I wasn't taking a stab at his species. "Don't let your fear stop you from taking something that's so freely offered."

Tanner was frowning now, his eyes laser-focused on the road in front of him. "And you guys? Because it's not just the Omegas in this Pack, unless you're stepping aside?"

Merrick snorted. "Not in this fucking lifetime." He turned his whole body toward the driver's seat. "I would literally give my left ball in a silk purse to those Omegas if they asked for it. Sharing them with a man who can protect them from any danger that comes their way? Not even a consideration. If you want to be Pack, you won't get any backlash from me."

"Or me. My Beast already seems to consider you his, and he's kinda pissed you're sad, so stop it," I teased, and a small smile curled the vampire's lips. "We've been through a lot in a short time, and that creates bonds in itself. I know you just lost a type of family, but I'd be honored if you'd consider being Pack."

"If Susannah and Quinn agree," Merrick added.

"Of course. I..." Tanner cleared his throat. "I'm honored. It's been a crazy month. Let's give life a bit of time to settle down before you make any life-altering decisions. Maybe in a year or so. I want Susannah and Quinn to feel secure before they're forced to make decisions."

I laughed. "You're funny, Tanner. If Susannah wants you, you won't know what hit you—waiting period be damned."

Merrick laughed along with me. "Pull over. Climb in the back between the Omegas and have the best sleep of your life. You look like you need it. When you wake up, remind me you want to wait a year."

Tanner flipped him the bird, but he pulled over at the next rest stop. Susannah and Quinn woke up with bleary eyes, but soon fell back asleep as we got back on the road. I sat beside Merrick up front, and from the corner of my eye, I could see the small tilt of his smile. More than that, I could feel real happiness coming down our bond. We finally had our Omegas, and we were on the way to the rest of our lives.

What more could we ask for?

. . .

WE PULLED INTO MOONBURST, Montana, just past six in the evening. The sun was still in the sky, but it was starting to dip lower, casting the large, flat prairie in a warm, pink glow. So different from our mountain home.

Merrick had sent through a text to the Alpha General, telling him of our arrival, and he'd directed us straight to his temporary office. Clearly, we were going to get that ass-chewing immediately.

We pulled up in front of a small, wooden building with peeling paint and dozens of plants out the front. This place had a weird vibe, but not as bad as Dark River.

An older woman I didn't recognize, with wild hair that poked out in all directions, appeared in the doorway of the temporary Legion offices. She was followed out by Courtland, who looked like shit. Dark circles sat under his eyes, and his face was pulled down by the weight of the last week. Poor fucker couldn't catch a break.

Spotting us, he lifted his chin, summoning us. Susannah and Quinn were immediately alert, and I could smell their distress. "It'll be okay, Omegas. You did nothing wrong."

Quinn snorted. "Like fuck we didn't, but nothing can be done about it now." He gripped Susannah's hand, and I could see her bitch-mask fall back into place. For as long as I'd known her, she'd hidden behind it, using it as a shield against everything that came at her during her life. The mean kids when we were in grade school, the ones who teased her about being the only Beta in a family of Alphas and Omegas. Then in defense of Raiden, when people tried to use her to get to him. To protect Quinn. To defend her actions. She kept everyone at arm's length with snarling disdain.

I hated to see it on her face now, and no matter how much I wanted to brush it away, I couldn't. Not yet. Soon enough, I'd be her shield, and she could just be the stubborn, loving person I knew she was.

As a united front, we walked into the Alpha General's office. He had a desk and a ratty old couch, and he indicated we should sit. I stood aside so Susannah and Quinn could sit down, and when Courtland caught a whiff of Quinn's scent, his eyebrows rose.

"Well, that's a new development."

My lip curled back in a snarl, and Courtland turned those intense black eyes toward me, staring me down until I was forced to submit. Fucker was powerful, but I'd throw caution to the wind and challenge him right now if it protected Quinn.

"Easy, Murphy. I don't want your Omegas. Now sit the fuck down, because I feel like this is going to be a long story, and I'm already tired." He leaned back in his office chair, pointing to Quinn. "We'll come back to how you magically turned from Beta to Omega later. Now, you better start at the beginning, because when your baggage turned up and you didn't, everyone thought you were dead. Several grief-stricken Alpha brothers is not something I ever want to deal with again."

Susannah winced, but she began. I'd heard this story a couple of times now, and it still made my heart beat faster with fear at how close we'd come to losing them forever. Quinn took over, talking about what Wilkie had planned to do against his will, and how I'd appeared in time to save him.

I was transported to the scene, viscerally reliving the horror of what Wilkie was trying to do. The surge of adrenaline as my Beast rose up to tear and rend, to protect. It was all flashes of red, blood, and pain, but that fear stayed in my chest, even now.

Susannah stood, grabbing my hand and dragging me down to the couch, sitting on my lap, her very presence soothing me from my memories. I snuggled into her hair, breathing her in.

They're safe. They're safe.

I repeated it over and over until the Beast backed down. Luckily—or unluckily—by that point, Quinn had gotten to the yearning part of his story, and my dick got inconveniently hard at those memories. Susannah looked at me with mock disapproval, but her eyes danced with humor. Fuck, I wanted to kiss her. I stared into her eyes for so long that I was lost.

Well, until the Alpha General cleared his throat and dragged me back to the here and now. He was looking at Tanner with sympathy. "I am sorry for the decision made by the Dark River Town Council. Know that you always have a place among the Manix while I'm in power. The loss of those"—he swore long and vehemently in Spanish, before clearing his throat— "uh, wastes of oxygen is not something that will be lamented by many, if any, of the Manix. As far as I'm concerned, their whereabouts will stay between us."

I breathed a sigh of relief. Well, until he turned to Quinn.

"Now, tell me, where did you get the Omega suppressants?" The full weight of his Alpha command banged around the room. Hell, I kinda wanted to know the answer too, so I didn't kick up a stink.

Quinn told a wild tale about a bar and a witch and giving him blood to make these suppressants, and honestly, by the end, my mouth was hanging open. *What in the actual fuck?*

"What did you say his name was?" Courtland asked, but the Omegas shook their heads. Loyal; I'd like that in any other situation than this one. Courtland stood, stretching his body, like he'd been stuck behind his desk too long. "I would like to show you something, and then I'll get the witch lights to direct you to your new home." It wasn't a request, so we all stood and filed out of the room, trepidation burning through my veins.

Moonburst was the opposite of Maxton. Not just in the landscape, which was flat and wide, traveling on for as long as my eyes could follow until the plains melted into the horizon. It wasn't just in the obvious signs that humans had once inhabited the town: train tracks, grain silos, mining equipment that sat abandoned and rusted, a bar, and hastily thrown together houses. No, it was the fact that here, the Manix were out of their element with the witches who walked casually down the street, greeting people happily and handing over bushels of vegetables to wary Manix, like a cat giving a human a dead rabbit. Magic literally hummed through the ground, wrapping up and around us, and it was so casual that it formed part of the landscape. I watched a witch frown at a garden plot, wave her hands, and then the cabbage increased three sizes.

We were out of our element, but it was for the best. Too long we'd stagnated, believing we were the center of the universe. Being out in the world would be good for us as a whole.

We entered another small, wood-paneled building, much like the rest. It was slightly raised, so you had to walk up a few steps—probably to keep it out of the snow—and it had a thick wooden door, faded by age. A shit-ton of plants hung off the sagging gables. I was sensing a trend.

Courtland held the door open, and inside was his second-in-command, Dominic. The Beta wolf shifter got to his feet with a grin. "Tanner! Thought you were dead, brother. Rick. Murph. Sight for sore eyes." He bowed his head low at Susannah, though his wide smile remained. "Omega." He cocked his head a little to the side, one eyebrow raising. "Um, Omegas?"

Courtland huffed. "It's a long story; I'll fill you in later. Grab me the keys to the back?" Dominic nodded, handing him a ring of keys. Courtland walked further into the building. "This was the lock-up when this was a human mining town. The bar is conveniently next door. Not much to hold a Manix, though the witches helped, but it's been adapted for our current purposes. Though, I think it has more to do with this inmate's willingness to play nice than anything else."

We stepped into the holding area, a single walled cell occupying the back corner. We stopped in front of it, confused. But both my Omegas went rigid beside me, and Susannah's gasp echoed around the silence.

"*Jericho?*"

26

SUSANNAH

Of all the things I thought I'd find in Moonburst, Jericho wouldn't have made the list. He looked exactly the same as he had ten years ago, all dark eyes and dark edges, but with a busted nose. My accusing gaze shot to Courtland at the sight of the split lip and the healing cut.

"So, he didn't play nice right from the start. Communication issue. We're over it." The Alpha General had the good grace to look a little ashamed.

"Susannah. Quinn. Fuck, it's good to see you guys alive and well." Jericho's voice was exactly how I remembered it. Dark and deep, a caress across my skin. He had more tattoos now, though. They moved up his arms, and from what I could see, across his chest until they crawled toward his jaw.

I stepped closer to the bars, and Merrick growled. I

threw him an annoyed look, then turned away, purposefully ignoring him. "What are you doing here? Your cabin?"

Jericho shook his head. "Burned. Wind changed and came down the other side of the mountain. I could have stopped it from consuming the place, but it would have looked as suspicious as hell." He shrugged. "Didn't need to stay there anymore anyway."

There was so much about this witch I didn't understand. I'd almost convinced myself that he was a figment of a shared hallucination between Quinn and I, except every month Quinn's suppressant pills had appeared on the edge of Manix territory, like clockwork.

Ah fuck. The pills. I casually looked over at the Alpha General, trying not to seem suspicious. My shock had given everything away. Maybe he hadn't noticed.

A scoffing laugh quickly disabused me of that notion. "I can add very well, Omega, and two and two in this case definitely equals four. Jericho was creating the suppressants for you."

My eyes flicked back to Jericho, and I grabbed the bars. "I swear I didn't tell him your name or anything about you. He just wanted to know why Quinn was suddenly an Omega, and I didn't think it would hurt because you were long gone. I didn't know—"

"It's fine, Susannah. I made the decision to follow

yo—the Manix to Moonburst. It was bound to come out eventually." He looked at Quinn. "I got worried when you stopped picking up your meds. I thought your Alpha might have gone too far." His eyes went cold and flat. "Which one of you is Wilkie?"

There was violence in his tone, an audible challenge that Wilkie definitely would have taken up if he was here. As it was, both Alphas growled. Quinn put a gentle hand on both of them, gripping Murphy's hand and laying a soothing palm on Merrick's spine.

Shaking my head, I looked at the witch I barely knew, but who'd kept all our secrets for a decade anyway. "Wilkie is no longer an issue," I said carefully, but that was all Jericho needed.

His eyebrows raised slightly. "Good."

I sucked in a shaky breath. "Can we get him out of the cell? He doesn't need to be in there."

But the Alpha General wasn't having any of it. "He's in there for a reason, Omega. It isn't because he was selling untested drugs to the Omegas of a dying race either."

Jericho's lip curled. "I wasn't selling them drugs. I was *protecting* them. They were scared and running for their lives. What would you have me do? Send them back to an abusive society? An Alpha General who wouldn't help them? Parents who gave them away, like they were two heads of oxen with a damn plow?"

I could feel Murphy's eyes on my face, but I didn't

look at him or Merrick. Not yet. "Then why is he in there? He isn't a criminal. He saved our lives. He's the reason we weren't bonded to fucking Wilkie."

Jericho's fingers brushed over mine. "Calm, Susannah." But the small touch was too much for Merrick and Murphy. With a growl, Merrick pushed me behind him, snarling in Jericho's direction, and Murphy did the same, his body caging Quinn between his body and the wall.

Tanner was suddenly there, standing between the bars and the two Alphas, who were doing their best impression of territorial dogs fighting over a couple of bones. "Okay, now. Easy. I'd suggest you don't touch the Omegas until we get this all sorted out." He looked expectantly at Courtland. "Is he in here because he's dangerous?"

The Alpha General stared at Jericho. "He snuck into Moonburst. It took three Legion soldiers and two witches to get him in here. At first, we thought he might be a poacher taking the opportunities presented now that the Manix have left Maxton."

"And now?" Quinn asked softly.

"Now we don't know. He's a whole different type of problem."

Fuck, this was so confusing. "Why?"

But it was Tanner who answered, his head tilted as he sucked in a breath. "Because he's a hybrid. Manix and witch."

"Uh, excuse the fuck me—*What?*" Quinn gasped.

Courtland was watching Jericho intently, and the *hybrid* in question stood rigid, like a statue.

Quinn shook off the shock faster than I did. "So what? There are a ton of half-breeds. Naja is a half-breed. What's the difference?"

Tanner was shaking his head. "Not a half-breed. A hybrid."

Finally, my sense of righteousness dug its way through my shock. "I don't give a damn *what* he is, he doesn't need to be in a damn cage. He's not a threat to the Manix, right?"

Jericho stilled, and Courtland growled low under his breath, threatening to bring me to my knees with just the small show of power. But Jericho stood in front of him, looking completely unbothered by the Alpha power of our supreme ruler.

Courtland just continued to stare. "He's under a truth geas constructed by the leader of the Moonburst coven. He's refused to answer that question, no matter how many times I asked. Until we are sure he isn't a threat, he stays in the cell." With that, the Alpha General whirled out of the room.

I looked at the man in front of me. He'd helped us without expecting anything in return. Or had he? I'd given him vials and vials of my blood that night. As had Quinn. Had he worked some kind of voodoo to turn himself into a Frankensteined version of us?

"I can see your brain working overtime over there. I promise that whatever you're thinking is wrong."

I stepped back from the bars. "What I'm thinking is that you lied to me. That night you pretended you didn't know that Manix existed. I was so fucking dumb. Of course you did. You were a witch on the edge of the last Packlands of the damn Manix. Of *course* you knew we existed. You lured us in, and we followed like damn fools," I growled. "'Oh, you're a Manix, so surprising.' *Bullshit.* You lied to us. To me."

"Susannah, it wasn't like that. You really were—"

I cut him off. "I don't want to hear anymore lies, Jericho. If that's even who you are." I turned to Merrick. "I want to leave."

Merrick didn't hesitate, sweeping us out of the room. I ignored Jerico's shouts and pleas, moving out of the room, out of the building and onto the street. A woman was waiting there for us, and she was beautiful.

"You're the late Manix. I'm Electra. We've set up new homes for you. Your Alpha General said you weren't a Pack yet, so we've allocated you three different households until you decide to complete a matebond. Omegas have choices here in Moonburst," she said with a gentle, but firm voice. She opened her hand, and three glowing balls were in her palm. At a single word, they leapt into the air. "Omegas, please follow the yellow sphere. Alphas, the blue." She looked behind me, then plucked the remaining red ball from the air. "I shall give the vampire his guide sphere when he emerges."

"The Omegas need protection. I won't leave them unprotected," Merrick growled.

Electra raised a brow. "Protection from whom? Not from us. The Moonburst coven would never raise a hand against another person, unless it was in the defense of life—their own or others. The only people here to fear are your own kind." She looked at the spheres. "The magic chooses the right home for you, by fate or the will of the Goddess or by your energies." She gave us a soft smile. "Trust the magic."

I shrugged, following along behind the yellow ball as it bobbed ahead of us like a tiny helium balloon on a string. Merrick and Murphy's blue one rolled along beside it, seemingly inseparable. I looked behind me, but Tanner still hadn't come out of the jail. "You don't think they stuffed him in there beside Jericho while we weren't looking, do you?"

Murphy shook his head. "No, Courtland likes Tanner, and he hated Wilkie almost as much as Dominic does. I'd be surprised if he doesn't give Tanner a medal," he said in a soft voice, almost too soft to hear. The walls had ears in a town filled with supernaturals. We couldn't talk about what had transpired with Wilkie, and I was okay with that. I hoped I'd never have to think about him ever again, but that'd definitely be too much to ask.

Quinn reached down and grabbed my hand. "He'll catch up. Don't worry, Zanny."

I narrowed my eyes. "He better, or I'll track him down myself."

We walked in silence, the two glowing orbs still side by side, as I tried to digest what had just happened. Thoughts of vampires and hybrids, and old friends being liars, and even older friends wanting to matebond me—it all left me so fucking exhausted.

The orbs stopped in front of a small, single-story house with an enclosed porch. The yellow orb went up to the door. "I guess this is us."

As I said the words, the blue orb zipped up to a larger, two-story house with a sagging porch. It had light-blue painted cladding that looked newer than a lot of the empty houses we'd passed. On the far side of the yard was a large tree that stretched toward the sky, and a tiny wooden table and bench seats sat beneath it. It was a family home.

Were the orbs playing matchmaker right now?

Murphy laughed. "What's the chance that the red orb leads Tanner straight to the house beside yours?"

The witch's words about fate and the Goddess choosing the magic echoed in my head, and for the first time in a long time, everything felt like it would be okay.

27

JERICHO

I let my head flop onto the cold bars. *Fuck. That could've gone better.* The look of betrayal on Susannah's face hurt more than it should. I couldn't even see .Quinn from where he'd hidden behind the back of one of the Alphas.

You fucked that one up, Bowie said. I looked in the corner where my brother sat, bored. Unseen.

"Well, that went kind of shit for you, don't you think?"

I reared back, my eyes finding the vampire in the darkness, his words echoing Bowie's a little too closely. The vamp had been a surprise, that was for sure. The fact I didn't even realize he hadn't left annoyed me, though. My instincts were going to hell being locked up in this box.

I knew he was here, Bowie said smugly. Of course he did. Dead things spoke to other dead things.

I nodded at the vampire, walking further back into the cell and sitting on the hard bed. I'd been here for three days, waiting for Susannah and Quinn to realize I was here. I'd started off just needing to see that they were okay. But fuck, they weren't the same people they'd once been. Neither was I, but Jesus, Susannah was beautiful now. The fire in her eyes was like warmth in my veins. And Quinn? He'd gotten impossibly better looking. He'd grown into his body, filled out until he was almost too beautiful for a man.

They are alluring, Bowie added, and I resisted the need to turn to face him as he spoke. That wouldn't help my case with the vampire.

I looked back at the monster in question. He had an accent, but I wasn't sure what yet. "You aren't wrong, bloodsucker."

He snorted. "Once upon a time, I would've argued with that label, but not so much now."

I narrowed my eyes on him. "What do you want?"

He shrugged, sliding down the wall until he was sitting on the floor, his back resting against the stone. "Curiosity, I guess. It might have killed the cat, but I'm already dead." He laughed at his own joke, and Bowie laughed along with him. It was undead humor, and the ghost of my deceased twin had a warped sense of humor to start with.

"Let me introduce myself. I'm Tanner McCulloch. Vampire. Doctor. Extremely interested in the wellbeing of the two Omegas you were just eyeing like they were roast lamb on a Sunday." He raised a brow. "This is the part where you share." When I said nothing, he sighed but continued. "I'm not a witch. Or a Manix. In fact, my kind and yours haven't always been friends. But I've known a couple of pretty powerful witches, and I know the feel of the magic on my skin. I can tell that if you wanted to, you could bust out of there. So I want to know who you are, and why you're letting yourself be imprisoned." His smile was genuine, and it was both disarming and alarming, given the fangs.

"Jericho Wheeler."

What, you aren't going to introduce me too? Hi, this is the ghost of my twin brother, Bowie, who I may or may not have murdered in the womb.

I flinched. *I didn't murder you in the damn womb. Not anyone's fault. The Goddess can be cruel sometimes.*

Bowie snorted. *Amen to that, brother.*

"Nice to meet you, Jericho. And the other part?"

I froze, thinking for a moment he meant Bowie. But then I realized he meant why I was letting myself be imprisoned. I shrugged. "It makes them feel better if I'm in here, and besides, where else was I going to sleep?"

The crazy-ass vampire laughed. "Good point. I don't think Quinn really got the gravitas of why being a hybrid was a thing, but they haven't done the studies I have. I want to know how you exist. You aren't half-half anything; you're something completely new. Man, what I would give for an ounce of your blood right now." I stiffened, and he laughed. "For research. Not for tasting." He paused. "Well, maybe for tasting. You smell kinda nice."

"Uh, thank you?" There was no fucking way I was giving him my blood. Hybrid or not, I was still a trained warlock, and I knew better than to give my blood to anyone.

Bowie was laughing hysterically. *I really like this guy.*

"You're welcome." Tanner stretched his legs out in front of him. "It's been a long week, and I need a good bedtime story, so let's get to it. How do you exist?"

Man, this was a fucked up story, and I really didn't want to tell it over and over, but I guess I had to explain it to someone. Bowie frowned, because he hated this story too.

"My ancestors weren't... well liked in the witching community. They were too ruthless, too willing to bend the laws that had guided us for centuries, in their pursuit of more. When their insane ideas started to seep out to the ears of other supernaturals, the greater community had an ultimatum. Excommunicate us, or it would be war. This was a century or two before I was born. Before my mother's time, even."

"Yeah, I get it. A long time ago, in a galaxy far, far away. Continue."

I snorted. He was kind of likable for a bloodsucker. "So, like I was saying, we weren't well liked, so they were more than happy to cast us out in the name of peace." I sighed. "But that just made them more extreme, more bitter, more willing to go to any lengths. So they started coming up with more radical ideas, playing with power that was darker and darker until it was so sullied, it was no longer a gift from the Goddess but a curse.

"Around this time, a girl stumbled into a trap my family had set. She walked into it willingly, but blindly, and she'd never escape. She'd die in that trap a few years later." It was why Quinn and Susannah running around in the woods that night had rattled me so bad —because I knew how bad the things that went bump in the night could really be. "She was a Manix Omega. They weren't quite as rare then as they are now, but they were definitely beginning to thin. Not enough that the Manix as a whole would tear apart the world to find her. No one came for that girl. And the things my family did..." I'd read my great-grandfather's grimoire, and then I'd burned it. That shit was pure evil that deserved to die with him.

Tanner shook his head. "I can imagine."

"You really can't. Anyway, after many unsuccessful attempts, my great-grandfather managed to do what the family had wanted to do all along. He managed to create a being that was both monster and magic. Something that was impervious to the harm that so easily destroyed a witch, while still having full access to the earth's magic."

The vampire frowned. "Normally, one designation or the other reigns supreme. Or if that's not possible, they cancel each other out."

I stood, gripping the bars. He got it. "Exactly. What my ancestor did was manage to merge the soul at conception. He created a whole new beast. He created my mother. Combining part witch essence and part Manix. The Omega he stole died giving birth."

Bowie's face was a hard mask. We'd often wondered if that was the reason why Bowie's body had died in the womb, because of the magic fuckery our ancestor had undertaken. We'd never know, but if I ever found the soul of that fucker, I was going to piss on him.

I continued, because I wanted this story over. "When he tried to, uh, breed with her, his magic was too familiar so their offspring came out witches, with barely any Manix traits, and certainly not the ability to shift. So he did it again. Captured a Manix Alpha, forced a young witch to mate with him, and then fucked with nature once more to create another hybrid offspring. Then he made the two offspring procreate, and voila, you get a perfect genetic hybrid. It was a truly heinous, foul thing to do from beginning to end, but he was a foul and evil man. All my family grimoires said so.

"Fortunately for humanity, once you start kidnapping and doing other terrible shit to Omegas, you also get a pretty fucking pissed off Manix Alpha. One day he forgot to shut the door properly, and my Manix grandfather ripped the head off my crazy old patriarch ancestor. Then he went through and murdered the rest of my witch ancestors. Anyone who'd ever participated died. My parents disappeared with my siblings, and despite being hybrids, lived reasonably happily ever after in hiding from the supernatural world. I am the last of my siblings, born thirty-five years after they escaped. My parents and siblings are all gone now."

What I didn't say was that my mother had died giving birth to me and Bowie's deceased body. Died right there on the operating table. My father hadn't wanted to live without her, so he blew off his head a week later. My oldest sister had raised me, but when she realized I had Bowie's soul with me, she'd abandoned me at sixteen, deciding I could fend for myself. I had, but I'd been so alone ever since. When I looked her up years later, I found she'd died from her own self-inflicted wounds. We were creatures without a Pack, and that drove us all slowly mad.

You've got me, Bowie whispered, and I could feel his sadness like it was my own.

The vampire whistled out air between his perfect white teeth. "Well, that's pretty fucked, mate. Your family tree is more a shrub than an oak, but that's okay, kinda makes you even more Manix. No, not Manix. Gotta give you a name like one of those designer puppies. A Winix? Nah. A Match? Nah, a Mitch. I like it." He laughed at his own joke, and I relaxed. "You don't sound like a maniacal warlock, threatening to go Rasputin on people's asses, so why is the geas preventing you from saying you aren't going to hurt anyone?"

I shrugged. "Because that isn't what they're asking me. They keep saying, 'Are you a threat to any of the Manix?' and I am. I'm a threat to all Manix, as a species."

"Man, I'm sure you have some neat tricks, but I can't see how you could be a threat to a whole species that can Hulk out and tear a car in half."

I looked at the vampire, and raised an eyebrow. "I have no designation."

"Holy Harold Holt in a bathtub..." Understanding lit up his face. "That could be rather problematic. So when the Alpha General does that staring growl thing that kind of makes even me want to shit myself, you feel..."

I shook my head. "Nothing."

"Okay, I see your predicament. But I'm with Susannah on this one—you don't need to be in there.

One sec." He moved out of there quicker than I could follow.

Bowie watched him go with an amused smirk. *I like him. But he wants your Omegas too. Did you see that she was an Omega now as well? What are the chances of you pseudo-bonding with two Omegas?*

I shook my head because it was highly unlikely, unless the Goddess was back fucking with my life again. Bowie and I had decided that's what had happened with those two Manix teens back when I was little more than a teen myself. My Beast had become automatically attached to the first other Manix I'd ever met.

Five minutes later, Tanner walked back in with the Alpha General and the Beta wolf who was doubling as my jailer. Tanner waved a hand in my direction. "Jericho Wheeler, do you intend to cause any physical or emotional harm to any member of this community by your actions?"

I could feel the heavy weight of the truth geas across my shoulders. "No."

"Do you intend to cause purposeful harm, with your actions, to the Manix community or the community of Moonburst?"

"No."

Tanner gave a ta-dah flourish. "And there you have it. A perfectly safe member of the community. He could get a job brushing kittens or helping the elderly across the road."

The Alpha General narrowed his eyes at me. "I still have questions."

I gave him my most disarming expression. "I'm happy to answer them."

He sighed, and lifted his chin at the wolf. The wolf watched me carefully as the cell door unlocked and slid open. I stepped out, feeling suddenly unsure of myself. What the hell did I do now?

The Alpha General looked at Tanner. "He's in your charge. If he fucks up, it's on your head too, and you're already walking a fine line."

The big vampire—who I was beginning to think might be Australian—slapped the Alpha General on the back, like he had a death wish. "Someone once told me it's not the leap of faith that kills you, it's getting stuck in the muck at the bottom and drowning beneath it all." He frowned. "Or maybe that was for bridge jumping?"

Dominic, the wolf, just looked at him like he'd lost it. "Is that meant to be inspiring advice?"

Tanner laughed. "Nah, mate. This is inspiring advice: don't jump off any bridges, and trust your gut when it comes to weird hybrids." He tilted his head at me. "Let's go before they change their mind," he stage-whispered, and I was more than happy to get my ass out of there.

28

QUINN

I slept for a full twenty-four hours wrapped around Susannah. Tanner had ducked his head in the night before, checking on us, but we'd already been out to it. The only reason I even knew he'd been here was a small note that said, *Next door, give me a yell if you need anything, T xo.* The little red glowing orb had indeed put him in the house attached to ours, and I didn't know if it was some divine comedy or fate, but man, it felt good to be sandwiched between Tanner and the Alphas. I'd never slept as easily without the doors being barricaded.

My phone flashed, and I reached over Zanny's sleeping head to grab it.

Good morning, Omegas. We left you a care package on the front step. We have to see the Legion Generals today

for our assignments, but maybe we can do dinner? -
Murphy (and Merrick) xoxoxoxo

Not going to lie, I loved presents. Even when I was a kid, I'd adored someone thinking about me and gifting me something they thought I'd like. Granted, it was usually Zanny, or Merrick and Murphy. Once, Murphy had found a milky white quartz at the bottom of the river when we were ten, and I still had that rock. I loved it so much.

How I hadn't realized I was an Omega earlier was the real mystery.

Untangling myself from Susannah, I wondered if I should wake her up before retrieving the care package. Nah. I'd just bring it in off the porch, and we'd open it together when she woke, like a good Packmate.

On the porch was a sealed box, which I hefted up and into the kitchen, leaving it on the small formica table. I desperately wanted to open it and see what it was inside, but resisted, heading into the shower instead. I rinsed away the light sheen of sweat from the already hot day.

We'd have to head to town and track down our things that had been evacuated from Maxton without us. It would be nice to have some of our stuff for our new place.

Ours.

My heart beat faster at the idea that this tiny cabin

was ours for the foreseeable future. Not Wilkie's, or my parents', or even Susannah's father's. Mine and Zanny's. Whatever happened from here on out would be *our* choice, not made under duress, not forced by fate, fear, or our families. We could just be a pair of Omegas forever, if we wanted.

I thought about how the message from Murphy had made me feel this morning. Okay, so probably not just the two of us forever. But we wouldn't make decisions out of desperation ever again.

We were fucking free.

Getting out of the shower, I wrapped a towel around my waist, and walked out to the kitchen to turn on the coffee pot. I needed caffeination if I was going to face today. When I made it to the tiny kitchen, Zanny was already there, sitting on the countertop and staring at the box.

"What's in the box?" she said by way of greeting, and I walked up to her, unable to resist the urge to kiss her sleep-creased face.

She pulled back, wincing. "I've got morning breath."

I sucked her bottom lip into my mouth. "Don't care. I love you."

Wrapping her long legs around my hips, she pulled me closer. "I love you too. Why are you feeling so mushy this morning?"

Ah, my mate. She was never big on grand displays

of romance, mostly because they made her feel awkward. Sometimes you could tell she'd been raised by males. It didn't matter; I was romantic and affectionate enough for the both of us.

"Why wouldn't I be? I woke up with the woman I love in my arms, without panic, without fear, without worrying if your dad would walk in on us fucking. Life is good." I gave her a hard kiss. "Plus, Murphy and Merrick sent us presents, and you know how much I like gifts."

Zanny rolled her eyes. "Such an Omega. Open the box."

I tried not to bounce with excitement. Ripping off the tape, I pulled out the note on top. "It says, 'To start your nest and your new life. We hope we can be a part of it. Love, Merrick and Murphy' with like ten x's and o's." Zanny laughed, but I kept pulling things out of the box. The first thing was a blanket made of fibers so soft, I immediately lifted it to my cheek. "That's so freaking fluffy."

I passed it to Zanny, and she rubbed her face all over it too. Didn't hurt that it smelled like Alpha either. Next thing that came out of the box was a cooler. Opening it, I found waffles and whipped cream, brownie fingers, strawberries, and chocolate dip, and some kind of chia pudding in a container with berries. It was a feast. I unpacked everything onto the counter and looked over it with amazement.

"So this is what it's meant to be like," Zanny said softly, "to be cherished and cared for?"

I nodded, swallowing down the lump in my throat. It wasn't an insane show of power or wealth. It was the fact that they cared enough to ensure we were fed, even when they couldn't be here. It was the fact that there were no blueberries, because I hated blueberries, and they'd remembered that. It was the fact that they were hopeful, but not pushy.

Lifting a brownie to Zanny's lips, I sighed happily. "They're it for us, aren't they?"

She nodded. "They always have been." She grinned. "Doesn't mean we aren't going to make them work for it, though. Now, grab the chocolate sauce and the whipped cream, because I know just the place I'd like to lick them from." She jumped off the counter and walked toward the bedroom, throwing me a saucy wink.

Fuck, I loved her.

An hour, two orgasms, and actual sustenance later, we left the house. We walked toward the main street in Moonburst, our temporary new home. Or maybe not so temporary, given that so much of Maxton had burned. Though, according to Raiden—who Zanny had called last night—they'd held a town meeting and basically split the Manix in two. Anyone who wanted to head back to Maxton and rebuild would have a new Alpha General, and those who wished to remain would continue to live under Courtland's rule. Raiden said Susannah's father had volunteered to be the temporary new Maxton Alpha General. I couldn't tell how she felt about that, but I wasn't going to push. Not yet. I didn't think she'd want to go back to Maxton, but I'd follow her lead.

The other news Raiden had dropped on us was that Loren—the Alpha General's witch sidekick, who everyone thought had died during the coup—had suddenly reappeared, and he was the reason we'd all ended up in Moonburst.

The town was bordering on dilapidated, but it was also kinda cute. It had a small, beaten-up cafe, and a grocery store. When I looked through the large plate windows, the witches inside smiled. We'd walked past a garage, and the scent in there was one of the guys from the Wiley-Fletcher-Reid Pack—probably Corvin, given he'd been a mechanic for the Legion. It made me wonder if the Legion members would be split too and sent back to Maxton. Would Merrick and Murphy be forced to return because they were unmated males?

My chest hurt at the very idea that might happen. My Beast growled. We wouldn't let that happen.

Susannah looked at me and raised an eyebrow, but I noticed her eyes scanning the people around us, searching for a threat.

"Sorry, I was just thinking," I murmured, slinging an arm over her shoulder.

She frowned. "Didn't seem like happy thoughts."

I waved a hand. "It was nothing." I hadn't realized how attached to those Alphas my Beast had become. I didn't want to unduly influence Zanny, though. She'd bent enough to accommodate me. This time I'd bend for her. "Let's get some coffee first."

I walked into the little cafe, and the old witch with wild hair behind the counter smiled at us broadly. There was another witch writing hurriedly in a journal on the other side of the room, and two other Manix who looked kinda nervous.

"Hello, guests. Welcome to Moonburst. You're new."

I blinked at the woman's booming voice. It was deep and kinda husky for a woman. "We just arrived," Susannah replied, walking up to the counter. "I'm Susannah, and this is my mate, Quinn."

The woman grinned. "I'm Wilbur. Yes, I know it's a man's name. Spent the first seventy years of my life as one. This"—she waved at her boobs—"was all due to an unfortunate transfiguration spell in the seventies. Zero out of ten stars, would not recommend." The witch in the corner snorted, but Wilbur kept looking at us consideringly. "You look like a double-shot latte kinda girl. Sweet and creamy but with a little kick," she —he—said to Susannah, who nodded. Wilbur turned to me. "Oh, and you definitely have a sweet tooth. I bet you're a mocha kind of Omega."

I huffed a laugh. "That would be great."

We chatted with Wilbur while she made the coffees. Apparently, the cafe was new. Well, not new—it had always been here, but closed. The arrival of the Manix had brought it back to life. Apparently, it was the same with a lot of the businesses in Moonburst. The way Wilbur told it, before we arrived, the whole place had almost been dying, just the bare bones of a coven to keep the place alive.

"The Manix arriving is a blessing. Or maybe it was that smooth-talking Loren who was the blessing. Now the town is alive again with life and magic—the way it was supposed to be."

I'd never met the witch Loren, one of the Alpha General's most trusted friends, but I knew that Merrick and Murphy had grieved for him. They'd be glad he was alive.

We stepped out of the cafe and back into the warm summer air. The great plains stretched out in front of us, and that much space made me feel exposed.

Susannah tilted her face to the sun. "I want to go see my father before he goes back to Maxton."

Gah, she was beautiful. "You don't want to go with him?"

She turned to look at me like I'd lost my fucking mind. "Go back to Maxton? Fuck no, Quinn. Goddess.

We'll visit, but that town is the last place I want to return to."

I nodded. "But what if they make Merrick and Murphy go back?"

That made her pause. Yeah, she wanted them too. "No point borrowing what ifs. We'll make sure they stay where they belong—here in Moonburst."

The *with us* remained unsaid.

"You go see your dad, and I'll go get our bags from the Legion offices."

Zanny hesitated. "Are you sure you'll be okay by yourself?"

My heart grew ten times in my chest. Dragging her toward me, I gathered her into my arms and held her tight. "The threat is gone. We're safe," I whispered in her hair, and she nodded against my chest. It would take time for the trauma of the recent past to dull, but eventually, it would be gone. And then we'd truly be free.

29

MERRICK

You didn't have to be a trained Legion soldier to know we were being given the side-eye. No one had outright said anything yet, but it was coming. I knew it was.

"Did you kill him?" A young Legion soldier, Ben, fronted up to me with more audacity than he should possess.

"Who are you referring to, Beta?" Sometimes these young soldiers needed to remember who the fuck they were talking to.

"I'm Alpha!"

Murphy snorted derisively beside me. "I've taken shits that were more Alpha than you, kid. Fuck off."

Yeah, the kid obviously didn't have a lot of brains. He pushed up against Murphy until they were chest to chest. Dominic—who was meant to be running these training drills—just laughed from where he sat on a fence behind us. He knew as well as I did that this kid was about to get his ass kicked. I should stop it, but...

In a flurry of movement, the kid was on the ground, wheezing, with Murphy's boot on his throat. "You aren't Alpha enough to play in the big kids' pool, little '*Alpha*.'" He actually did the finger quote thing. "To answer your question, though, you're going to have to be more specific. I've killed many men, something you should remember." He pushed a massive wave of Alpha power at the kid, who turned his head in instinctual submission, even though it made Murphy's boot scrape across the soft skin of his neck.

Someone behind us piped up. "Wilkie. We want to know if you killed Wilkie and took his Omegas. People are saying you're Omega stealers."

I didn't turn fast enough to see who said it, but I rolled my eyes. "We didn't kill Wilkie, though the fucker deserves it. If I ever see him again, I'll happily plunge my claws into his chest and rip out his damn heart." Little did they know that I had no idea where his heart was. I turned to the group. "If any of you believe that Omegas are possessions that can be 'stolen,' then I hope to the Goddess you die alone. Omegas are a gift. A *treasure*. But they are people with minds and hearts of their own. They choose who they wish to love. Not me. Not you. Not their parents, and not the fucking Alpha General. Got it? Or do I need to beat that point into each and every one of you?"

No one would meet my eyes. Half of them would end up back in Maxton, guarding the borders of our forefathers. Murphy and I would go wherever Susannah and Quinn went.

I walked over to Dominic and climbed onto the rail beside him. On his other side was Loren. Fuck, it was good to see him.

"Little shits. Wouldn't know morals or loyalty if it slapped them in the face," I grumbled at Dominic. "Have you decided how you're gonna split them?"

Dominic shook his head. "Court wants to give them a choice, like everyone else. More than you think will go back to Maxton, just to feel like they have some power again. It's hard to stand in the shadow of an Alpha as strong as Courtland and pretend you're the biggest badass in the world."

Yeah, Courtland was something else. His power was like a thick blanket that smothered you, and if you were a weak Alpha—like the guy still under Murphy's boot—it would be a reality check.

"Murphy," I warned.

With a dramatic sigh, he lifted his boot and leaned down to pull the kid to his feet. He slapped his back. "You're brave, I'll give you that. But you know what happens when you're brave and stupid? You end up dead. Work on that." My mate walked over to me, barely holding back his smirk.

Dominic called out for the others to work on their hand-to-hand combat, and off they went, fighting in the thick heat of the midday sun.

"Fucking little shit," Murphy muttered as he dragged himself up onto the fence with us. "Luckily, I'm in a good mood." He grinned, and I smirked back. We'd gotten a picture this morning from Quinn and Susannah, and it was just a trail of chocolate sauce over the flat plane of Susannah's stomach. Quinn must have taken it from between her thighs, because you could see the underside of her breasts and the sugary stripe of chocolate right down to her belly button. My mouth had ached with the urge to go over there and lick it up myself.

Loren laughed. "You guys do seem to be walking on sunshine over there. A couple of pretty Omegas making you happy?"

Murphy leaned forward. "The kid was right about that. I intend to steal those Omegas and worship them for the rest of my life. We just have to convince them that we aren't like their old Alpha." We fell silent for a bit, just watching the soldiers practice. Finally, Murphy shook his head. "And you, you wiley fuck. I'm so glad you're all right, but I'm going to kick your ass for having us so worried. How'd you survive anyway?"

Loren grinned, sending Murphy a wink. "Luck,

more than anything. I don't know why my portal dropped me here, but I can only imagine it was the will of the Goddess. I was convinced that I was a dead man, and then Electra appeared like a fucking angel." His voice went wistful. "She'd felt the force of my magic within the wards of Moonburst, and rescued me. Hefted me back to town by herself—I've never been so colorfully sworn at in my life, and we used to operate a fucking cartel."

I shook my head. I'd seen the beautiful witch that had Loren tied up in knots. She didn't look like she ever smiled, but she was kind. They'd be a weird match, but they'd work.

"Are you trying to woo her?" Murphy teased.

"Nah, man. She'd rather cut off my balls than have sex with me. Her words, not mine."

I couldn't help but laugh. Yeah, he had his own problems. I jumped down from the fence. "I'm going to grab some lunch, then I need to talk to Courtland. Want to come?"

Murphy shook his head. "Nah, I'm going to watch the recruits suffer a bit more, then I'm going to see if I can track down our Omegas. Make sure they're properly cared for. Check in on Tanner too. I know that the witches aren't the biggest fans of vampires."

Loren shrugged. "We operate with life, and the vamps are the exact opposite of that. They're like black holes for energy. It screws with the balance, but it's nothing personal."

We all had our unfounded prejudices. The Manix feared the Lycanthropes on a cellular level, due to generational trauma. Fortunately, unlike vampires, there were very few Lycans left. I'd met one of the last. He'd been nice, not at all like the boogeymen they'd built them up to be when we were children.

I squeezed Murphy's hand and said goodbye to Loren and Dominic before I made the short walk back to town. Every witch I walked past said hello, and honestly, it was almost creepy how excited they were to see us. Like our own little witchy cult.

"They get a rush of magic whenever any of the Manix walk by. That's why they're so happy."

I whirled in surprise at the voice behind me, unsheathing my claws. The hybrid Jericho stood off to the side, and while the witches were looking at me like I was a rainbow, they looked at him like he was a bear trap waiting to spring.

"Like little hedgewitch junkies."

I purposefully slid my claws back inside my knuckles. "It doesn't take anything from me, and they've given up most of their town to us. A little boost is the least we can do."

Jericho rolled his eyes, stepping up beside me. "We got off on the wrong foot."

I kept my face neutral. I wasn't going to give him

any insights that he didn't tease out on his own. I didn't trust this guy, who by all accounts had been lurking on the edges of Manix territory for a decade, and was worryingly attached to *my* Omegas. "Did we?"

He nodded, and as I kept walking, he continued to keep pace with me. "I know how it looks. But I swear, I mean Susannah and Quinn no harm. I've watched over them for so long that I feel"—he paused, finding the right word—"attached to them, I guess. When the fire ripped through Maxton, I was convinced they were dead. Or that their Alpha had used the opportunity to do something, like finally matebond them."

I halted and turned to face him. "How did you know that they weren't bonded, and that Wilkie was mistreating them? Were you stalking them?"

Jericho tensed, but he met my eyes, no matter how much Alpha dominance I sent his way. "How'd I know? You'd have to be fucking stupid to miss it, and you don't look like a stupid person. I'd see the bruises every time one of them came to pick up the meds. I'd hide in the trees and pray to the Moon Goddess that I didn't see a mate bite somewhere on their bodies every single time."

"Why didn't you tell someone? Anyone? The Alpha General. Their parents. Why didn't you get them out of there if you knew they weren't mated?"

His face folded into its own angry sneer. "Why didn't *you*, asshole? I couldn't step foot onto Manix lands, but you could. You were part of the force that was meant to protect them, and what did you do? Turned a fucking blind eye, just because that asshole had some kind of claim on them. Fuck you and your righteousness. My hands were tied, but you purposefully did nothing."

Guilt washed over me in a wave. It wasn't new. Every time I went to sleep at night, the self-loathing that I'd left them in that situation for so long ate away at me. I was never going to forgive myself. Ever.

Jericho was still chewing me out. "Tell their parents, my ass. You know who *gave* Quinn to that old fuck? How do I know more about their lives than you? And I only spent forty-eight hours with them ten years ago. You don't deserve them."

He was right, again. We didn't.

He continued. "I hope those bastards are as far away from them both as possible, preferably burnt like a side of beef back on the mountain." His tone was vicious, but I knew they weren't. Quinn's parents were still here, and I was going to be paying them a visit real soon.

"I'll take care of it. Stay away from the Omegas," I growled.

I walked away from the hybrid, leaving behind all his jabs and the guilt he was piling onto my shoulders. That guy was going to be a problem; I could feel it in my gut.

As if he knew the direction of my thoughts, he called out behind me. "Hey, Alpha!"

I forced myself to stop and turn.There was an intensity that wasn't there a moment ago, written on every part of his body language.

"I want them too. So learn to share or get the fuck out of the way, because Quinn and Susannah belong with me. I feel it in my soul."

"Over my dead body," I snarled.

The hybrid's face went flat. "So be it."

30

TANNER

I was definitely getting the cold shoulder treatment. Everywhere I walked, witches would cross the street, moving out of my path as if vampirism were the plague. It was kind of annoying, but I forced myself to understand. Witches and vampires weren't normally a good mix. Witches could control a vampire up to a point, especially if they were skilled in necromancy, and vampires didn't enjoy that at all. Obviously. Plus, we were kind of walking magic-suckers, so that didn't endear them to us either.

But I wasn't here for the witches. I was here for the Manix. Right now, Radic was showing me my new medical offices. Fortunately, most of the medical equipment had been removed from town by the Legion Force, so the new examination rooms were well stocked. We had told the general population that I'd been healing injured people when I'd been recalled by Raine in order to explain my absence. No one needed to know I'd been fucking two of their new Omegas in a three-day sexfest, which I still saw behind my eyelids every time I closed them.

"We saved what we could, but if you need anything else, we can order it in. The Moonburst coven has quite a good supply chain out here, and since we aren't hiding in the woods anymore, pretending we don't exist, goods will be easier to obtain," Radic said from the doorway.

I nodded, looking at all the boxes that I'd need to unpack. "Thanks, Rad. Did you manage to save the medical files and journals?" Most of those had been down below the Legion building. There were too many to carry out, and I'd only packed the active patient files.

Rad nodded. "The stone vaults beneath the Legion building survived pretty well. A lot of smoke damage, and a few animals took refuge down there, but otherwise, everything that was below ground is intact. I know that Legion General Joshua is going to enforce that all new houses built are to have a stone cellar installed, just in case. Both for shelter, and to save some possessions so no one has to start again. It's not like the Manix can take out insurance."

Sadness came off Radic in a wave so thick, I could taste it. Most of the Manix had lost almost everything.

They'd have to start again from scratch, and not all of them could afford it.

"The Convocation won't help?" That really didn't sound like Raine, but I knew she had to pass things by all the other Convocation Members too.

"Word on the street is that Raine is job-sharing now with an incubus," Rad whispered, like it was a big secret. "So maybe their votes will help swing things our way, so they'll give us the funds we need to rebuild. It's so damn sad, Tanner. Breaks my heart every day. It's just all gone."

I patted him softly on the back. "I'll call her and see if I can't help with persuading. I'll call Titus too." The Convocation Member for the Vampires actually scared the living shit out of me, but I would do it for these guys. I felt a kind of kinship with the Manix after living among them, even if it had only been for a short amount of time.

"Thanks, Tanner. All right, I'll let you get settled in. Give me a shout if you need a hand putting all this stuff away." At my scoff, he grinned. "Yeah, yeah. You can move at the speed of light, I get it. I pity your girlfriend one day."

Ah, so the Alpha General hadn't told his Packmate that I'd bumped uglies with Susannah and Quinn. I honestly didn't know how I felt about that. I wanted the whole world to know that they wanted me, but I knew it would come with a little backlash too.

I got to work, finding a place for everything and memorizing its location. Knowing where things were could be the difference between life or death, though it was probably less drastic with the Manix. They were pretty resilient.

A knock on my door had me turning, and my breath stuck in my throat. Susannah was there, her smile hesitant. "Can I come in?"

My fangs ached, but I beckoned her closer. "Of course. How do you like my new chop shop?"

She laughed, and it was a deep, sweet sound that made my dick hard. Her scent reached my nose, and I breathed deeply, trying not to remember how her pussy tasted against my tongue, and what she sounded like when she orgasmed.

"Very, uh, rustic. I like it. But can we agree to never call it a chop shop again?" She walked around, running her fingers lightly over the well-worn cupboards and the massage table that was currently doubling as an examination table. I'd get Radic to order a proper stainless steel one that could be sanitized in case of surgery, but this would do right now.

"All right, just for you. Here, take a seat." Unable to help myself, I wrapped my hands around her waist and lifted her onto the table. "What brings you to my neck of the woods? Are you feeling okay?" I hated drawing this line in the sand again, but I needed her to step over it voluntarily and not in the heat of... well, her heat.

"I feel fine. Just wanted to see how you were settling in. Make sure you're feeling good too."

My hand was still on her waist, and I pulled it away slowly. "I'm undead, Omega. I always feel good."

She cocked her head to the side, watching me as I restacked things I'd already stacked. "Did you organize your blood supply?"

My fangs ached again. I was hungry, but I'd taken some blood bags from Dark River's stock when we left, so I should be okay for a while more. "Not yet, but I have a supply for a couple of days, and then I'll get it figured out." I pushed the patient files into a filing cabinet that looked like someone had kicked it at some point. I'd probably need a new one of those too.

"Tanner."

"Mmm?" I said, still reorganizing.

"Look at me."

I sucked in a fortifying breath and straightened. I had a stern word with both my dick and my fangs about behaving, then I turned. God, she was beautiful, though.

"I want you to drink from me."

My mouth dropped open, my fangs hanging out in the breeze. "What?"

"I don't want you to find an alternate blood supply.

I want you to drink from me. Quinn feels the same, so you can rotate between us."

"Susannah, you don't..."

She held up a hand, her face fierce. "Don't tell me I don't know. I saw you drink from Murphy during the heat. I know you make it pleasurable, and I know you have control. Come here."

Jesus, I was powerless to stop myself walking toward her, like she was a siren and not a Manix.

When I was within touching distance, she reached out and dragged me closer, until I was forced to look down at her, and her knees bracketed my hips.

"My Beast goes feral at the thought of your fangs in someone else. That someone else's blood—someone not Pack—is giving you nourishment. The idea of your lips on anyone else's pulse makes me feel wild." She reached her hand up and buried it in the hair above my ear. Gently, she pulled me down until my face was an inch away from her lips, her soft breath fanning over my face. "I want you to kiss me. Drink from me." She pushed up until her teeth grazed over my lip. "Fuck me."

I shuddered, helpless to resist. My mouth smashed down onto hers, and as I pushed my tongue into her mouth, I pressed my body tight to hers until she was forced backwards. Her back pressed flat on my examination table as I pulled her right to the edge. Her thighs wrapped around my hips, her sweet pussy warming my cock. My arms bracketed either side of her head, and I continued to kiss her like I wanted to fuck her. Hard. Mercilessly.

But she wasn't submissive, not this little Omega. Instead, she purposefully scraped her tongue over my sharp fang, cutting it enough that the taste of her blood was passed between our mouths.

My already painfully hard dick got even harder, and I ground it between her thighs. She moaned and curled up against me, seeking friction that I was more than happy to supply. It didn't help that she was in a sweet little summer dress, and the only things between us were a few pieces of fabric and my moral compass.

"Bite me, Tanner."

Fuck the moral compass.

Turning her head to the side, I pushed one hand beneath her panties and slid my fingers through her lips. They were so fucking wet, slippery with that Omega slick that tasted like goddamn ambrosia. She moaned as I softly circled around that hot button, bringing her higher and higher. I had to be inside her when she came. I continued to put pressure on her clit, but slid two fingers downwards, pressing them inside her. She clamped down, and I moaned.

Scraping my fangs up the column of her throat, I nipped at her earlobe. "Are you going to come for me, Susannah? Wet my hand with your slick?" I purred, and like the good little Omega she was, her whole body tensed. As her climax kicked off, I buried my fangs in her throat and pushed all the pleasure-inducing toxins into her bloodstream, heightening her orgasm until she was writhing on my hand.

I wasn't like X; I couldn't make a girl come with just one puncture of my fangs. But I could add to the pleasure she was already feeling. I stroked her through her orgasm until her body went lax, and then I pulled my fingers from her core and my fangs from her neck, licking up any traces of blood.

She lay beneath me, sweaty and panting. "Sweet Goddess," she murmured against my shoulder, wrapping her arms around my chest and holding me tightly to her body. She gripped the back of my head, tugging on my hair until I was forced to move back and look down at her. "No one else but us."

I swallowed hard, because along this route lay eventual heartache. Still, I was helpless to do anything but agree. It was too late for anything but commitment. I was already invested. "No one else."

She kissed me again, softer this time, and I swore I could feel my heartbeat in my dick—it was that hard. "Tanner..." she breathed, rolling against me, and I groaned. My lips brushed across hers again. I wanted to sip from her lips every day for the rest of my—

The door to the clinic burst open, and a sweaty, panicked Manix Alpha stood in the doorway.

Cooper. One of the Alphas from the Wiley-

Fletcher-Reid Pack. His Omega was pregnant. I willed my blood to fly from my dick back up to my brain, jumping away from Susannah like she was on fire.

"Darius is in labor."

Well, that was enough to make my dick behave. Turning, I grabbed the bag I'd packed earlier for this. Darius was really my only long-term patient, and I'd judged that he had to be due really soon. Like a Boy Scout and a serial killer, it always paid to be prepared.

"I'll be right there. Uh, about this..." I looked at Susannah, whose eyes were wide and worried.

Cooper waved a hand, like a vampire fucking one of their precious female Omegas meant nothing. "I couldn't give a fucking shit." His eyes met Susannah's. "Good for you. You deserve this. Now, my Omega is in pain and about to give birth in an extremely dangerous manner, so let's get the fuck out of here." He gave me a slight smile. "Your kinkery can wait."

He gave me quick directions to his house and raced out of there again, saying something about getting Corvin.

I stared down at Susannah, kissing her lips softly. "I've got to go."

She pushed my chest, her eyes smiling as brightly as her lips. "Go deliver some miracle babies."

I kept my panic locked down, going over the notes I'd made in my head. I had this. Time to welcome some Manix into the world.

31

MURPHY

I went to check on Tanner, but I found a flushed and delicious-smelling Susannah instead. Stumbling out of the new medical clinic, she had that freshly fucked expression that was almost universal. *Well, well, well.*

I tried, and probably failed, to hide my grin. "Hello there, Omega. You're looking radiant." Her cheeks flushed even redder, and I resisted the urge to chuckle.

"Hey, Murphy."

I couldn't help myself. I grabbed her arms and pulled her against my body, wrapping my arms around her smaller frame. She felt so damn good against me, and I wanted to bury my face in her neck and breathe her in for hours. "You smell like you've been having fun."

She slapped my arm, looking up at me with a frown. "Don't be gross, Owen Murphy."

Now it was my turn to screw my nose up. "Don't call me Owen. Only my mom calls me Owen, and she's not who I want to be thinking about when I have a beautiful woman in my arms."

She gave me a devilish smirk, and I knew I'd just handed her ammo to tease me with forever. I didn't care, though, because it meant I'd have her forever. I'd hand her all of my weaknesses if it meant I could keep her.

Stepping back, I kept an arm slung over her shoulders. "Where's the good doctor?"

"Darius went into labor. He's delivering cubs."

A longing feeling came over me. Would I one day see this Omega in my arms round with my cubs? Or Quinn, big and laden down with a whole litter, grumpy enough that I would do anything in my power to make him happy? Would Tanner deliver them for us, our children?

"Did he look nervous?"

Susannah laughed, snuggling in closer. "Terrified, but determined. He'll do everything he can to deliver them safely." The surety in her voice made my heart swell. She'd have that much faith in me too, eventually, and I was determined to earn it.

I kissed her temple. "Want to get some lunch with me? Where's your other half anyway?"

She pressed into my side as we walked down the street. I ignored the stares of other Manix. She was mine, and if they wanted to say something about it, I would put them down like that upstart Legion Alpha.

"Tracking down our luggage. I was going to see my father before he left for Maxton, but thought I'd stop in and check Tanner was doing okay."

"And was he doing okay?" I murmured beside her ear. I felt her shiver beneath my hand, and I resisted the urge to push her against the wall of this dilapidated building and fuck her brains out.

"He was doing real well before he left," she said on a purr, and fuck, my dick got hard. This was awkward in public.

"How about we skip lunch, and I eat you instead?" I felt her skin pebble beneath my fingers.

"*Whore!*"

The venomous word made Susannah jerk back, and I growled, my Beast roaring to life. I spun, trying to find the source of the voice. There were at least a dozen other Manix on the street around us, and I snarled.

"Who said that?" No one stepped forward, showing they weren't as fucking stupid as they sounded. "Step forward and say it to my face, you fucking cowards."

Everyone was silent, and no one looked in my direction, but I was still snarling. I was close to shifting and just maiming everyone because they were so fucking weak. Unable to hold back the change, my body transformed and my Alpha blanketed across the street.

"She is *mine!*" My voice was all Beast. "Say it again!" I was growling loudly, and all these fucking sheep Betas looked terrified. As they fucking should, with their flapping jaws but nothing to back it up. "I will fucking gut any person who has the balls to speak to her like that again. And I will eat your fucking heart."

"Like you did to Wilkie?" someone spat, and I whirled. The woman in front of me was Quinn's mother, Gwenda, and I peeled back my lip. Fuck, I couldn't kill my potential mate's mother, right? "You little slut—I knew you'd lead my boy into ruin. Knew it the moment you got your dirty little Beta hooks into him in elementary school."

The pure poison in Susannah's glare told me everything I needed to know about her feelings for Quinn's parents. Guess murder was back on the menu.

"He's not your boy. He's mine now. You have no control over him anymore. You can't palm him off for power. I hope sucking Wilkie's dick was worth it, you heinous old hag."

Quinn's mother lunged for Susannah, but I was there, stepping in between them with a low growl. The woman showed a tiny ounce of sense and backed up. "I know you killed him, you little whore. I'll find proof, and then you'll be dead and gone, and Quinn will be mine to do with as I please once again."

We were gathering quite a crowd, and my Beast was getting harder to control. He saw a threat to his mate and he couldn't let that stand. But the man inside me knew this was a bad situation; aggression would only make it worse.

"Wilkie was a piece of shit Alpha who abused his Pack. When Maxton was burning, he ran away like the coward he was, leaving his Omegas to perish. Your loyalty is in the wrong place, and I suggest that either you fuck off like Wilkie"—I let the violence show in my eyes, and I hoped she saw her death reflected there— "or you shut the hell up and never even breathe in the direction of my Omegas again."

Quinn's mom, Gwenda, curled her lip at me. "Not your Omegas yet. And if I have my way, they never will be." With that, she whirled away, pushing through the crowd of people. At the edge of the crowd was Courtland with Bonnie, one of his Omegas. His eyes flicked to me, and I shrank back to my human form.

Except, I kind of shredded my clothes. Not a big deal for Manix, but the witches squeaked in horror, and one actually covered her eyes.

"Whoops. Sorry." I covered my dick with my hands.

"For Goddess's sake," someone grumbled, and I turned to see the witch Electra. She waved her hands at a small patch of grass until it grew and weaved itself together into something resembling a grass loincloth. She plucked it out and handed it to me, her eyes averted but a smirk on her face. I gave her a nod of thanks as I stepped into my brand new grass skirt.

Bonnie looked apologetically at the witch. "Apologies, we forgot about that small aspect of Manix society. We'll put spare clothing bins around town so there are always clothes in case of accidental shifting. Though it doesn't happen often, except among teens coming into their powers." There was a light censure in Bonnie's tone, and I'll be damned if she didn't manage to make me feel two inches tall. That was Bonnie's superpower. Quiet disapproval.

I lowered my eyes to the ground. "Apologies, Omega. Alpha General." I wasn't really sorry. I'd do it again.

Courtland's expression said he knew exactly how remorseful I really was. "Take your Omega home, Murphy. We'll talk later."

"Yes, sir." I grabbed my stuff from the ground and gripped Susannah's hand, battling the urge to run home, back to our temporary den, back to a place where I could defend her. Shoving my ruined clothes under one arm, I pulled my phone from my pocket and called Merrick.

"Hey?"

"I need you to find Quinn and bring him home. He should be at the temporary Legion offices."

One thing I loved about Merrick is he didn't ask questions first. I heard him start running. "I'll meet you there as soon as I can." He hung up, and I went back to herding Susannah to my place as fast as possible.

"Murphy..." she started, and I just grunted, picking her up in my arms and moving a little faster. "Hey, it's okay," she murmured, holding my face.

I shook my head, but pressed my cheek harder into her hands. "It's not okay. She threatened you. She threatened Quinn."

Susannah rolled her eyes. "She's a bitter old hag, but she isn't a threat to me or Quinn. Not anymore. She's powerless. She's always been powerless. His dad is just a Beta weakling. She's just mad she's not getting her kickback from Wilkie anymore. She'll get over it." Logically, I knew she was probably right. Didn't matter, though. Until this threat had passed, or my Beast had chilled the hell out, I wasn't leaving her alone.

God, I wished I was bonded to her already. I could protect her properly then, and no one would dare to call her names. Susannah didn't try to dissuade me anymore, just hung on until we made it to the house, up the stairs, and into the beginning of the bedroom we'd begun to work on. It would be Merrick's eventually, but we were going to work our way through all six bedrooms of this place. The attic space we would eventually turn into a nest, if we stayed. If the Omegas agreed to be ours to cherish forever.

I placed her under the blankets protectively, then climbed beneath them with her. Wrapping my body around hers, I held her tightly, calming my Beast and my heart rate simultaneously.

When Merrick appeared with a pale-looking Quinn, he took one look at me under the blankets and whispered something to my other Omega. Quinn climbed in on the other side of Susannah, his arms going over her and resting on my hip. Merrick hopped in beside him, and I could finally breathe.

Safe. They were safe.

32

SUSANNAH

The birth of the Wiley-Fletcher-Reid cubs shifted the flow of gossip from Quinn and me onto a topic more pleasant. The birth of a litter of cubs from a male Omega was still a miracle too new not to be the subject on everyone's lips. It gave us a good couple of days reprieve from the judgemental glares of the townspeople.

It also deflected speculation about Jericho, who Tanner had adopted like a stray puppy. Most people just assumed he was part of the Moonburst coven, and the coven just eyed him warily every time they saw him. Not quite as badly as they reacted to Tanner, though they'd thawed to him a little. He really was hard not to love.

I should know.

In comparison, when I saw the witch-Manix

hybrid, I felt an entire gamut of emotions. A flaring of an old crush, gratitude at the only person who'd known and kept our secret for so long, and anger at the man who lied. So damn confusing.

Murphy and Merrick had been wildly overprotective, not going out to work. Instead, they'd been working hard on the house. Their Packhouse. Maybe, one day, our Packhouse too. They didn't put pressure on us, but they asked us for our opinion on a lot of things.

"Susannah, what color is the most calming for an Omega?"

"Quinn, which fabrics are the most comfortable for Omegas to lie on?"

It was always a generic "Omega" and never "Which ones do you like?" Like they were trying not to pressure us, despite the fact they'd been very clear it was us they wanted. Murphy's Beast had made that *very* clear.

They were also wary of Jericho, watching him closely if they saw him in the distance. Quinn didn't seem to have my misgivings, though.

Tanner had invited us over for dinner tonight, and I was desperate to spend more time with him after our little moment in his clinic a few days ago, so I agreed. Merrick and Murphy had insisted on coming too.

Yippee, sounded like it was going to be a very relaxing night. *Not.*

Quinn had stepped into the room and basically

purred at Jericho, who watched us both with heavy, hot eyes. There was no doubt in my mind he was attracted to us. But he was equally as protective as my Alphas.

Tanner hooked an arm around my waist as we stood in the backyard of the duplex. He was grilling meat, and I'd brought a salad. The guys had insisted on bringing the beer and dessert, all picked up from the tiny commissary/general store that had been inundated with enough staples to feed the Roman army.

"That looks a bit wild. Like two swamp rats fighting over a bone."

I snorted. "Colorful imagery." He wasn't wrong, though. Jericho and Merrick were eyeing each other from either side of the yard, especially since Quinn was flirting up a storm with Jericho. "What do you think of him?" I asked.

My blond vampire squeezed me tighter, which made me feel safe, but also kind of freaked me out. If Tanner wanted to, he could squeeze me so tightly that my organs would crush. Relationships were funny like that, where the balance of physical power was skewed so far one way, you had to have faith that one day they wouldn't snap and kill you. That was a new one for me —even as a female Manix, I could probably hold my own against anyone but the most powerful of us. I'd been trained to fight by my father, honed by growing up with Alpha brothers. I could fight.

But against Tanner? I stood no chance.

This must be how human females felt.

"I'm not going to pretend that I know the guy. But he seems all right to me. His story is kind of fucked, but so is mine. So is yours. Doesn't make us bad people." Tanner kissed the side of my head. Aussies were touchy-feely people, I'd come to realize. "I mean, he did go full Sting 'Every Breath You Take' for a decade, watching you guys from afar like a creeper. But I don't think he was doing it in a jack-off-in-the-bushes kind of way. More like a guardian angel who couldn't actually help you."

I stared up at him, wide-eyed. "You're really selling this, you know."

How anyone could not fall for Tanner was beyond me. He was just so pure, so empathetic. Even though I knew very little about his life before he was a vampire.

"Did you leave a wife behind when you got turned by Scuba Steve?"

Tanner shook his head. "Nah, I was a shitty doctor in the slum parts of Sydney. Plus, Australia in the early 1800s was a massive sausage fest. You had convicts or soldiers, and the only women were in chains for fifteen to life. Not much opportunity for romance. It was better that way really— I didn't have anyone who'd cry that I was gone, and the break from my old life was swift and easy. Not everyone is that lucky."

"Only you would call being bitten by a shark lucky."

GRACE MCGINTY

He huffed a laugh. "Well, yeah. But without it, there was a whole world I'd have never known about, right? I would have just continued with my boring life, until I either burned out at thirty, or stuck it out and married some uptight gentleman's daughter and lived until I had thirteen spoiled kids, a dog, and played lawn bowls twice a week to escape them all."

"I'll remember to send Jaws a Christmas card as a thank you," I teased, squeezing his hand. "We better go make peace before it comes to blows."

"You go. I'll finish off dinner." He kissed my head and slapped my ass, sending me off toward the guys like I was a ship on my maiden voyage.

I moved toward Merrick, linking my fingers with his and Murphy's, then dragged them with me to where the other two were talking. Quinn laughed at something Jericho said, and the way the hybrid—or Mitch, as Tanner called him—watched my mate made something in my chest flutter. He gazed at him almost in awe, like all his dreams were coming true or something.

I looked at Quinn like that some nights, when he was asleep and his face was peaceful. He was so fucking beautiful, and everything I'd ever wanted. If I closed my eyes, I could see how our Pack would look, even if it was unorthodox.

When I opened them again, Quinn's eyes were on my face, and I knew—the way anyone who'd spent their entire lives together knew—that we were on the same page. We'd chosen, and while Jericho might be a surprise, I was going to keep an open mind for Quinn.

"It's almost time to eat. If you guys could stop hissing and snarling long enough to aid in good digestion, that would be appreciated. The alternative is that you have a smackdown fight and whoever wins, wins. Then we can all move on with our lives without this dick measuring."

"Can we just measure dicks to decide the winner? Because I think I'm coming out on top," Murphy piped up, and you know what, he was probably right. Murphy was hung like Seabiscuit, even in his human form. Considering I'd seen his dick in his Beast form yesterday and could attest to the fact he was proportionate in all forms, it was an across-the-board wipeout. No wonder the witches had been scandalized. I hoped for Merrick's sake that Murphy was the bottom. Not that I'd ever ask that.

Well, not yet anyway. I'd rather find out for myself.

Jericho raised an eyebrow. "So I heard. Wilbur said you had the biggest cock she'd ever seen, and she once toured with an Ecuadorian football team along the West Coast when she was a man. It's the hot topic of conversation at the Shiny Rock Cafe."

I still couldn't believe that they'd decided on that name for the cafe, but hey, having met Wilbur, it made sense.

Merrick tightened his arm around my waist possessively, still glaring at Jericho. "Sorry, Zanny."

I sighed, because he really wasn't. "Look, let's get this all out in the open, okay? I'm not one for dodging around the point." I grabbed his face, bringing him down to me. "I want you, Merrick. I always have. Nothing and no one is going to change that. One day, we'll be Pack, and it's going to be the most amazing fucking day ever."

He puffed out a quick, relieved sigh. Surely he wasn't worried we'd change our mind, right?

A little voice inside my head told me I was being dumb, because of course they were worried. I'd already broken their hearts once. Changed my mind once. Held them at arm's length.

I kissed his lips softly. "You and Murphy have always been the Alphas for me. For us." He looked up, past my cheek, to Quinn. Whatever he saw made his face soften again. "But I refuse to let an Alpha use his power to control me again, Merrick. Whether that be within the Pack, or who my friends are, or what I can do with my time. I refuse to be a possession again."

"Never," he growled. "I would never try to control you." He hesitated slightly. "But I want you to be Pack, and that means some decisions have to be made as a group, especially something as important as who'll be part of that Pack forever. There's no takebacks, Omega.

We've all seen what happens when Pack members hate each other."

Yeah, we had. Over and over again.

I kissed him once more. "I would never make such a decision without you and Murphy. Neither would Quinn. But you have to trust us, not growl and snarl at every male who steps in our direction." I chewed my lip, keeping my eyes on Merrick for this next part because it felt too raw to say to Jericho. "Something about him calls to me; it always has. I saw him across a fucking bar parking lot and my gut said to go with him. I trusted him when I trusted no one. My Beast trusts him, and more than that, she wants him. But she's fickle, and quite frankly, a little horny. I promise that I'll figure out if it's fate or some kind of weird hybrid magic before I fully explore the feeling, but I need you to trust me on this."

Merrick's jaw flexed, and I could hear him grinding his teeth. "Okay, Omega. I trust you. But just know, if he so much as hurts your feelings, I'm going to tear him to pieces, bit by fucking bit, and then let Tanner eat his heart."

"Duly noted," Jericho said behind me, closer than he'd been before. I could feel his warmth on my skin, feel the soft puff of his breath across my bare shoulders. "I've needed this for so long. I'm like a rejected Pack animal without a Pack. All I've had is the memory of the anchoring feeling in my chest that I got when I met these two a decade ago to keep me sane. I promise, I won't fuck it up."

I believed him, and from the resigned look in Merrick's eye, so did he. He gave a single nod, and I smiled at them. I felt that expression right down in my chest, and I knew this was how it was supposed to be.

Merrick straightened, looking at Jericho. "Let's go. We can talk over beer."

I watched them walk away, feeling right. This was what Omegas were made for: to calm the internal fire inside Alphas.

"You have him by the balls—you know that, right?" Murphy whispered beside me.

Turning, I kissed him softly. "I know. But I promise to take good care of them."

He kissed me hard and quick. "I know you will. Mine too." With that, he slapped my ass and walked up to Quinn, kissing him and moving back into the house.

Pack. This was what it was all about.

33

JERICHO

I was happy. It was a completely foreign feeling that felt a little bit like I'd drank a pop way too fast and gotten a massive gas bubble in my chest. It wasn't indigestion, so happiness was the only other answer.

I was with Quinn and Susannah, having a picnic on the prairie. They'd knocked on my door and asked me if I wanted to come hang with them this morning, and I had been embarrassingly overeager. Not that I'd let it show. I maintained my cool facade, giving them a half-smile and murmuring, "Sure."

I'd walked with them across abandoned train tracks and into the wide expanse of open field on the other side. It was like a sea of grass that swayed in waves. It was truly beautiful. I carried a basket filled with treats, and I could smell the faint scent of Alpha on it. A gift, obviously.

I helped lay down the blanket they were using as a picnic rug, making a mental note to order them a proper one online. They deserved all the good things, and I'd read that Alphas wooed their Omegas with gifts. I needed to up my game if I was going to convince them to let me be Pack, even if I wasn't an Alpha.

Even if I was an abomination instead.

Hey, don't forget about me. Watch who you're calling an abomination. Bowie was walking through the grass around us, making the long strands sway gently.

Quinn flopped down across the blanket as soon as it was spread, starfishing. "God, this is nice." His face was tilted up to the sun, and the way the morning light hit his hair made it look like burnished bronze. I wanted to bury my hands in it, tilt his head to mine and kiss him until he was breathless. The urge was like a physical punch in the chest. I still didn't know how much of my reaction was the Manix side of my nature and how much of it was the man who had been enamored with these brave, stupid teenagers, set to run away to the West Coast even though they'd never been off the mountain.

At first, I'd just wanted to help them because their plight was a little too close to my own family history. But during those two days, while I'd come up with countless tinctures and potions to keep them hidden, to keep Quinn's Omega scent from giving them away, something in my chest had shifted. I taught them the things they'd need to know to survive in the human world. How to blend in. Where to look for jobs that paid cash. Where to find the areas that were cheap and not too dangerous. Where to get help if they needed it. The Convocation buildings where they could run for refuge, or avoid completely, as needed.

Finally, I'd given them cash, driven them to the train station, and set them free. From that point on, after watching them leave, my chest had ached. I'd thought I was having a heart attack at first, but as it persisted, I knew it wasn't. My Beast had been crying for a Pack, yearning for what it didn't know it had been missing. Well, maybe the Beast knew, but the man had been blissfully unaware. Even Bowie had been solemn in those days after they'd left. He mightn't have a Beast, or any real form, but he'd seemed brighter, more corporeal when they were there. Maybe he was feeding off my connection, or maybe he had his own. We couldn't be sure.

Bowie and I had decided later that I'd somehow shadow-bonded with them, being the first of my kind I'd ever met. I hadn't lied to them when I said they were the first Manix I'd ever seen, despite living right outside the Packlands. They didn't come down often, and I was never in a position to get close enough to talk to any of the Betas who did.

Shaking myself from the past, I took the bowl of strawberries Susannah handed to me. She nudged Quinn's hip. "Move over, or I'm going to use you as the table."

"You can use me as the table, the plate, even use my face as a seat if you want." He smirked at her, and it was an intimate expression between lovers. Jealousy flared inside me. I wasn't jealous of either of them, exactly. I wanted them both. But I was jealous of their easy manner. Their sexy teasing. I wanted that with them so fucking bad.

She pinched Quinn's nipple through his shirt, and it made him hiss. "Maybe later, you pervert. Shift over before everything goes bad." Susannah was wearing a big hat to protect her against the sun, and her smile was ethereally beautiful. Had anyone ever been so beautiful?

Fuck, you're such a pussy. I'm glad she can't hear your thoughts like I can, because you're totally blowing that mysterious witch enigma thing you try so hard to cultivate.

Quinn scooted to the edge of the blanket, and Susannah finished unloading all the picnic supplies. Finally, when she was done, she lay down until she was just propped up on her elbows. It pushed her breasts out, and I dragged my gaze away. I wasn't going to be a leering creep. But I wanted nothing more than to strip her naked and kiss every inch of her that the sun touched.

"Jericho?"

I jolted my gaze toward Quinn's knowing smirk. My cheeks flushed, and I cleared my throat. "Sorry, what?"

"I asked what you've been doing for the last ten years. I don't think you've been just sitting around in your cabin waiting for us to need suppressants."

Well, actually... "Not really. Mostly, I did exorcisms."

"What?" They both gasped, and I laughed.

Bowie's chuckle was silent to everyone but me. He was sitting beside Susannah, and he trailed his hand down her hair. She tilted her head back with a sigh, like she could feel his touch. Bowie, who was normally acerbic and kinda bitter, looked completely transfixed.

Who's the pussy now, shithead? I asked silently.

Drawing my eyes away from Susannah and Bowie's incorporeal form, I smiled at Quinn. "Don't worry, most of the time it was just a possum, or rats that had chewed through already old wiring. So I guess you could say I was in pest control and electrical work too." Best paid pest controller ever. "I get maybe one or two real exorcisms a year."

Most exorcisms were just really confused ghosts. Usually, Bowie gently led them toward the light, and it was a job well done. I'd once asked Bowie if he ever wanted to go with them, and he'd just looked at me sadly and said I was his light. Which was both sweet and so fucking tragic.

Quinn raised his hand. "I have several follow-up questions, starting with, what the actual fuck?"

I lay back on the blanket beside them and chuckled. This was nice. So damn perfect I knew I'd been missing this forever. "Call it an old family skill. We've always been gifted with necromancy and soul work. It's why the witching community didn't like us."

Bowie snorted. *Understatement.*

"Didn't like you?" Susannah looked offended on our behalf, which was sweet. When was the last time anyone had defended me just because?

Tanner?

Good point. Twice in two weeks must be a new record. But I also realized that Tanner had kept my deep, dark family secret from the Omegas, which made me respect the vampire more.

"The family deserved their disrespect," I soothed. "They were terrible people."

I plucked a strawberry from the bowl and moved it to Quinn's mouth. Would he let me feed him from my hand? Even I knew the connotations of that, the silent etiquette.

He wrapped his lips around the strawberry and sank his teeth into it softly, never taking his eyes from mine. He was eating from my hand, and it meant something. His expression told me it meant something. I tried to push down my excitement.

They didn't know about the abomination of my

family story, and part of me didn't want to tell them either. Didn't want to risk it forever altering how they looked at me, like the sins of my ancestors still painted my skin. That was how most of the witching community still saw me.

But I also couldn't pursue something more with them while these big secrets sat between us. I couldn't get more invested with them and then have them reject me. I looked over at Bowie. *Reject us.*

Because it wasn't just me who'd be hurt by that. It was Bowie too, though he'd never admit it.

Swallowing back the fear, I flopped down onto my back and stared at the sky too. It was beautiful out here today. The moonstones buried deep in the earth of Moonburst made Bowie stronger. Everything was right. I just had to have faith in these two, like they'd had in me all those years ago.

"Before we go any further, there are some things you should know about my family. About me." I looked at Bowie where he sat by Susannah's shoulder. He gave me a reassuring thumbs up, and I launched into the whole sordid story.

I watched as their faces clouded over with confusion and horror, and although I was a few generations removed from it, I was still tainted by my ancestors' actions. I told them about my great-grandfather, about his crimes against the Manix. I told them about my parents, who had such long lives that I had six siblings that spanned six decades before my mother died. About how my oldest sister had raised me and hated me all at once.

"How could you hate a small, defenseless baby?"

I flicked a look at Bowie. His face was locked down to an expressionless mask.

Do it.

Sighing, I closed my eyes slowly. This was it. Make or break. Because no matter how badly the Beast wanted them—needed them, even—nothing would come between Bowie and I.

"She died giving birth to me and my twin. He'd died in the womb, and the strain of birthing us both killed her." Susannah lifted her hand to cover her mouth, and Quinn reached out to cover her other hand.

"Susannah's mother died the same way. Not birthing twins, but birthing Susannah's baby brother. It's one of the few ways a Manix can die of natural causes. Susannah raised Raiden, her Omega brother, too."

"And I never hated him for a second. Maybe I resented him a little when I was a teen, but he was my baby by then. I would never have made him feel unwanted."

I smiled softly, because I knew that about her already. She was too kind beneath that mask of stubbornness to be anything but loving to her flesh and blood.

Not all siblings were like that.

I steeled my spine. "There's one more thing." Susannah's eyes were big and understanding, and I could feel Quinn's gaze on my face. "My twin's soul didn't really pass over, and now his ghost is kind of attached to me. Fuck, this didn't sound as insane in my head." I lifted my chin at Bowie, who was still beside Susannah. "He's sitting right there. He says hello."

Don't put words in my mouth, asshole, Bowie grumped, but I could see his worry.

Quinn sat up. "That's a kind of fucked up thing to joke about, Jericho."

I sighed. "Trust me, it's no joke." I looked at Bowie. "You're going to have to prove it."

He reached over, moving his body along Quinn's until his incorporeal lips hovered over Quinn's plump ones. Then he kissed him softly, and Quinn's eyes went wide. "Holy fuck!"

34

QUINN

I thought Jericho was being an asshole—an insensitive one, considering what I'd just shared about Susannah's own mother—but the feel of lips brushing across mine had me freezing. There was no mistaking the feel of a kiss, even if it wasn't like any kiss I'd had before. It was the promise of a kiss, like a cool breeze on overheated skin. I almost wanted to kiss him back, but I wasn't even sure how you'd do that.

I scrambled backwards until I was on my feet. "Holy fuck." I paced around the grass. "Shit. Fuck. You weren't joking?"

I could see the wariness in Jericho's eyes, like he was waiting for me to spit on him or something. His scent smelled almost burned, and my Omega whined. We were hurting his feelings.

My eyes shot to Susannah, who looked concerned

and a little skeptical. "Does he have a name?" I asked softly.

Jericho's lips curled into a small smile. "I call him dickhead most of the time. But his name is Bowie."

Tilting her head to the side, she breathed the name. "Bowie."

Jericho looked at the spot between us and nodded. "He wants to know if he can touch you, to prove he's there."

Susannah, my beautiful, empathetic mate, merely nodded. There was no fear in her, and she tilted her head to the side, waiting for the unknown. Her lips parted a little as she moved her face closer to an unseen thing, and if I stared hard enough, I could almost see the indentation of fingers on the soft skin of her cheek. She sucked in a shocked breath, and I desperately wished I could see what it was doing. He. It was a person. A soul.

Kind of.

Bowie must have said something to Jericho, because his eyes were laughing. Well, now I wanted to know what he said too.

"It must drive Bowie crazy not to be seen or heard."

"Honestly, he has the worst sense of humor, so the world might be a better place for it." Jericho chuckled, and I didn't know if it was at his own joke or something the ghost of his twin said. My head shook in amazement.

"How?" Susannah asked. "I mean... his touch just feels real, if a little softer. *Your* touch, I mean," she said, looking at the empty space beside her.

Jericho shrugged. "I think that has more to do with you guys than him being a ghost. Touching other Manix makes him more corporeal, at least for a moment. I don't know the whys or hows really, but I think it's because the Manix have so much magical energy. It's why the Moonburst coven doesn't mind you being here. You're fuelling their withering magic. Plus, the moonstone vein that runs under the town helps him focus too. It's almost the perfect recipe to make him a real boy..." he joked, but I could see the sadness in his eyes for the brother who was just a shadow.

It made me so fucking sad for both of them.

"Don't be sad, Omega," Jericho said, his voice almost a growling whine. "Bowie said he's used to it now, and it has given him more freedom to—no, I'm not repeating that. They'll think you're a pervert." He rolled his eyes. "He said it gives him more opportunities to live outside the social niceties."

Yeah, I bet that's what he said.

I raised an eyebrow, and Jericho sighed. "Fine. He said he likes to sit in your company, even if you don't know he's there. Last night, he sat on the sofa beside you and pretended you were a Pack. He said he excused himself when you started getting naked, no matter how tempting it was to stay and watch."

My skin flushed at the thought of a set of eyes watching me make love to Susannah, and while that should horrify or creep me out, the idea of a voyeuristic entity watching me eat out my mate made me feel kind of hot.

Susannah's cheeks were pink. "Just squeeze my hand or do something to tell me you're there, and you're welcome to join us anytime..." Her eyes went wide. "To watch TV, I mean. Or just hang out. Not, you know, uh..."

Jericho started laughing, and Zanny buried her face in her hands. I was laughing too, because I loved seeing her like this. It reminded me of the girl she'd once been, before living in Wilkie's Pack burned all the innocence right out of her. Maybe being here in Moonburst, with the men we wanted to make our Pack, would set that old Zanny free from where she'd hidden behind an impenetrable wall.

"He'll take you up on that," Jericho said, a wicked grin curling his face.

I shook my head. "This isn't going to work for us." I wouldn't have thought it possible an hour ago, but I can almost smell the hurt of a ghost in the air. It smelled bitter. Flat. "Not Bowie himself—Susannah's right, he's more than welcome to join us." I gave a wink, because I was honestly enjoying the idea of a little voyeurism. "I meant the fact that Bowie can't communicate with us directly. That's what needs to be fixed. Is there a way we can make him more corporeal? To us, at least?"

Jericho frowned. "You want to make him a poltergeist?"

"I want to be able to have my own conversation with him. He's a part of you, but he's his own person too, right? Maybe it's just me, but I would definitely struggle with having all my words passed through someone else first. Even if it's just touches, or enough corporeality to write on the windows, or something."

Jericho shook his head. "I've never had enough juice to make him physical. Maybe with prolonged time in Moonburst, and with you, he might store enough magic to be heard at least? Maybe to be felt. I'm not sure what it would take for him to be seen."

Susannah was chewing her lip, like she always did when she was about to say something controversial. "If being in our presence has made him stronger, what would a bond do?"

My eyes went wide. Okay, controversial it was.

Jericho looked like she'd sucker-punched him. "He can't bond with you. He doesn't have the physicality needed to create a bond. No teeth to bite with."

Oh, I saw where Susannah was going with this. She cast a quick look at me, but still continued. Stubborn woman. "But if we bonded to you, would it feed down to Bowie?"

Goddess. What she was suggesting was crazy, but it

might work. I didn't know shit about magic and the metaphysical world. But I did know that a Pack shared its strength sometimes, especially in moments of heightened emotions. It was part of the bond.

Jericho looked blindsided, his eyes going to that empty place which I now knew must have held Bowie. "I mean, maybe? Not for a long time, but maybe for short lengths of time. An hour or two? Otherwise, it would be too big of a drain on your magic and mine."

I grinned. "But if we were in a Pack, with a couple of real nice Alphas, in a town filled with magical rocks... Who knows? Would that make a difference?"

"I don't know. I just don't know."

I could almost feel the desperation coming off Bowie now. I'd thought that scent, like sweet oranges, was part of Jericho's complex earthy scent, but I was beginning to think maybe it was Bowie all along.

Susannah nodded, her eyes alight with the same knowledge as mine. It wasn't something we often talked about, and hell, it wasn't the only factor, but the Beast knew within five minutes of meeting someone that they wanted them to be a mate. It was the human side of us that needed convincing—that higher reasoning where we'd delve into things other than the raw, primal urges of the Beast. Were they a good person? Were they selfish or cruel or did they have a drinking problem or, or, or? The decision of the human was as important as the decision of the Beast, which was why we were taking shit slowly with the Alphas and Tanner.

But the Beast, both mine and Zanny's, had decided on Jericho a long time ago. We needed to get to know the man he was now, rather than the hero we'd put on a pedestal so many years ago. But the Beast was still a hundred percent convinced that this Manix right here, he was one for us.

And if he came with a ghostly add-on, well, hopefully that was just a bonus. But it was hard to get to know a man if you couldn't speak to him.

"We should approach the Moonburst coven. Maybe they'll help? Wilbur seems open to trying some weird-ass things, obviously." How Wilbur had gone from a man to a seventy-year-old woman was still a mystery to me.

Jericho was still staring between us, his face neutral but his eyes shiny with hope. "You'd do that for us?"

I leaned forward and squeezed his arm, holding back my growl at the tingling attraction that raced between us. "I'm not sure if we made this clear when we dragged you out here, but we like you. One day, if everything goes well, we'd like you to be Pack." My eyes flicked to the empty space. "Including Bowie. We mightn't know much about him, but we want to. That means we have to find a solution so he can at least speak to us, if nothing else."

The hope in Jericho's eyes, behind the bruises of

past hurts, made me even more resolute. The urge to soothe his pain was an Omega response, but I didn't care. If this was what I was made for, then I'd step up to my calling and finally appreciate my designation as more than a curse that I had to hide.

The silence was heavy out here in the wide, open space, but finally, Susannah clapped her hands. "As far as I'm concerned, that's settled. We'll track down Wilbur or Electra when we get back to town and see if they can help." She smiled, and just like every time, I fell a little more in love with her. I slid my eyes to Jericho, and he was looking at her with a similar awestruck expression.

Yeah, man. That first fall was always the hardest.

35

MERRICK

Everything should have been going well, but it wasn't.

No, that was a lie. Everything with our burgeoning little Pack was going fine. After Susannah basically told me to cut the crap or lose the chance she'd given us, I'd made a concerted effort to rein in the Alpha instincts that screamed Jericho was wrong, and get to know him. And I kinda liked the angry little fucker.

It wasn't even the fact that the number of dead-but-not-really members of our budding Pack had increased by one. I hadn't seen that one coming.

No, it was the town that was the problem. Someone had started a smear campaign against us, and it didn't take a genius to figure out who. But whatever they were saying was working, because people who'd once been friends were now looking at me with distaste. Worse, they were actively jeering at Susannah and Quinn, and I hated it.

I wanted to tear the tongues from every person who said anything remotely bad to them. I wanted to pound the face of everyone who so much as frowned in their direction. It was riling up my Beast, and soon it would explode into violence, and I'd deserve the reputation people were saddling me with.

I ground my molars when two Manix who'd been friends with my parents for decades spat the word, "Disgrace," as they walked past me.

"Easy," Murphy said under his breath, and I tried to shake out my clenched fists. "We just gotta get home. Our Omegas are waiting for us, and they're worth all this."

He was right, but fuck me, I wanted to wreck some people. We hurried along the streets, and I was glad when we turned into the quieter streets. The town was small and flat, so you could get wherever you needed without an ATV. It was actually nice.

The street we were on held most of the community gardens, and there were small clusters of witches tending to them. More than that, there were a few of the younger Manix there learning from them. Probably a class from the makeshift school they were running out of the community hall down near the railway tracks. Seeing the two groups together eased some of the anger still smoldering in my chest.

The older Manix might struggle with the change, and I honestly hoped that the closed-minded old bastards went back to Maxton. It could be the place they all retired to be among their closed-minded buddies. Moonburst was an opportunity, and I wasn't going to let anyone run me or my Pack out of here, no matter how unconventional we were.

A young witch—Ruffles? Rufus? Rufio?—raced up to us. "Merrick!"

I wanted his name. Murphy came through for me, like always. "Hey, Rafferty. How's things?" Damn, I'd been close.

"Raspberries. We just harvested some, and I thought you may want to hand-deliver them?" He produced a soft mesh bag. Inside were the fattest raspberries I'd ever seen.

"Holy crap, Raff. Those things are basically small apples!"

Rafferty laughed and flushed. "It's all the extra energy from the Manix. We're having record crops."

I raised an eyebrow. "You trying to woo my Omega with your big berries, Rafferty?" I was joking, of course, but the young witch's eyes got real wide and a little scared.

"No, Alpha. I mean, sir. I mean, Merrick. I'm gay! And I have a boyfriend!"

"I have two Omegas." I couldn't help myself.

Rafferty blanched more, and Murphy slapped the back of my head. "He's just teasing you, Raff. Don't even worry about him. Zanny will appreciate these so much, thank you." Murphy gave me a pointed look.

"Thank you, Rafferty. I promise we aren't that territorial. You should bring your boyfriend over to our Packhouse soon and have a beer with us, as a thank you for the berries."

Rafferty nodded vigorously, but I had a feeling he'd never be coming around. I kinda felt bad now.

We said our quick goodbyes, and then hurried back to our brand new Packhouse. I couldn't wait until I opened the front door and Quinn greeted me. Or Susannah. Hell, maybe I'd be a stay-at-home Alpha and take care of our cubs one day. I wanted Susannah and Quinn to do whatever the hell they wanted to do with their lives. Did I even know what their dreams and hopes were? What kind of Alpha was I?

Skipping our place, we went next door to knock on the Omegas' door. I needed them now, to soothe the prickly feelings growing in my chest before it turned to violence.

Susannah opened the door, wearing nothing but a pair of cut-off shorts and a white tank. Her hair was down, and her freckles were prominent. *Fuck.* Maybe my Beast was still too riled for this.

"Omega," I rumbled, stepping into the room. "Zanny." I was embarrassed that her name was almost a plea on my lips. I reached out and grabbed her hips. "Can I kiss you?"

"I insist on it, Alpha," she purred back, and something inside me, something that was barbed and cracked, healed at her words. I kissed her hard, trying to convey how much she meant to me with just my lips and tongue. I lifted her until her lips were level with mine, and she wrapped those glorious legs around my waist.

She tasted so fucking good, like mint and ripe cherries, and I walked her further into her tiny little house. "I've dreamed about this for years. That you'd just want me. Not during the heat. That I'd just be able to come home to you every night and you'd climb into my arms and I'd kiss you like you were my world."

She moaned and caught my lips again. I could hear Murphy's amused voice behind me. "We also brought raspberries."

I could scent Quinn's arousal, so I knew he was here somewhere too. But I couldn't drag myself from Susannah to look. Especially not when she gripped the back of my hair. "Fuck me, Alpha."

Goddess, I was gone for this woman. I kept going back to her bedroom, because the things I wanted to do to her needed a large, soft surface. I wanted her so wet, she'd soak the blankets.

Susannah and Quinn's bedroom was as close to a

nest as you could get, without being one. The curtains were thick enough to block out the light, and they had soft ambient lamps spread around, bathing the room in a soft glow.

Setting her onto her feet, I started to unwrap her like the gift she was. She reached out, tugging at my shirt until it slipped over my head, then her nimble fingers were going to work on my jeans. I pushed her back on the bed, taking my time kissing every inch of her body that I could reach. I sucked her pretty little nipples into my mouth, one at a time, and I didn't even growl when another body came down beside me.

I looked over at Quinn, floppy dark hair framing his face as he grinned around her breast, biting down gently on the mate mark marring the underside. I hadn't noticed it before, but now I wanted to lick it. I wanted to create its partner on her other breast even more.

I didn't stop; even as someone kissed down my spine, I moved further down Susannah's body. The scent of her slick curled up in my senses, making me lightheaded. I wanted to eat her pussy for days. Months.

Growling against her hip bone, I flopped onto my back, grabbing her hips and dragging her onto my torso. "Ride my face."

Zanny grinned down at me. She wasn't shy, not my Omega. She shuffled up my chest, leaving her slick cooling on my abs, until she was poised over my face. Gripping her thighs, I pulled her down and ate her. Her juices were all I needed to sustain me forever.

"God, you look beautiful, my Omega, riding our Alpha's face. Grind down, baby, take what you want from him. Do you think you can pleasure your mate while you're riding Rick's face?" Susannah moaned, and I sucked her clit just to double down on her pleasure. Murphy wasn't done, though. "Do you want his cock in your mouth, swallowing him down, while you take what you want from your Alpha?"

"Yes," Zanny hissed, shifting forward, and I growled like she was taking away my toy. Pulling her tightly back down to my face, I heard Murphy chuckle as Quinn's moan echoed around the room.

"That's it, my Omegas. You're so fucking beautiful together. God, the amount of time I've jerked off to this very image," Murphy groaned. Quinn let out a whine, and I wanted to know what Murphy was doing to get him to make that noise. "That's it, Q. Feel how slick you are for me already. Are you going to take your Alpha's knot today? Are you going to let me fill you full of cubs?"

He couldn't really. Quinn and Susannah hadn't fucked today, and it was unlikely for an Omega male to get pregnant outside of the yearning. Unlikely, but not impossible.

Quinn's hissed, "Yes," was more visceral than audible, and I could feel his thrusts into Zanny's mouth, making her jerk against me. I wanted to be inside her. I wanted to be inside them both right now.

First things first—my Omega had to come. Pulling her tighter against my face, I bumped her clit with my nose on every grind until she was panting around Quinn's dick.

"Oh fuck," Quinn grunted. "I'm coming."

And like the synchronized pair they were, Susannah came all over my face in one squirting gush, falling off me with shaky legs. I sucked in the air I'd been deprived of, licking my lips.

This was going to be wild.

36

MURPHY

Seeing my mate's face shiny with our Omega's release set something primal off inside me. Zanny and Q were kissing, and it was fucking beautiful, but I also wanted to taste. Crawling toward Merrick, I ran my tongue up and over his cheeks, licking off all the slick I could before capturing his lips.

"Are you ready for this, mate?" I growled, and he gripped the back of my head, his kiss an attack on my senses. Pulling back, I laughed. "I'm going to take that as a yes."

Zanny's release had almost sent him into a rut, so now was the perfect time to drive him completely crazy.

"On your hands and knees, Omegas. You can kiss while you present for your Alphas." Man, I was enjoying how responsive they were to my dirty mouth. I couldn't talk through sex when I was making love to Merrick. It was always a fight, a race to see who could get the other off first, or the most amount of times.

The way Quinn's pupils blew wide when I told him what I wanted to do with my dirty Omegas—well, that was a fucking heady experience.

Both of them whined, but did as they were asked, and I rewarded them with a soft kiss. I leaned over, captured Zanny's lips, then turned and caught Quinn's lips. Zanny let out another whine, a pitiful, needy sound, and I laughed.

We weren't the only ones playing fast and loose with our hormones, apparently. I stroked my hand down Quinn's back, and Merrick gripped Zanny's hips tightly, his thumb rubbing soothing circles on her back.

"Are you ready for me, Susannah? Fuck, I love you so goddamn much. I want to be yours and Quinn's forever."

"Yes," she breathed. "Please, Alpha."

He had a weakness for her begging, and he pushed inside her hard and quick, filling her up with one hard stroke. They both moaned, making my dick throb. Quinn whined, and I smirked. "Don't worry, Q. We're going to go a little slower, but I promise it's going to feel so good. You were made to take my knot, baby. You were made to be mine, just like I was made to be yours. My heart. My soul. My knot. All yours."

With those words, I pushed inside him, watching him stretch obscenely around my dick. It was above average size, and I never usually got to be top, happy to be fucked by Rick. But this heady sensation of my Omega gripping my cock was going to make me pass out.

"Yes," I hissed. "That's it. You're such a good Omega, Q. So perfect. I want to fuck you every day. Want my cum leaking out of you as you walk through town, so everyone knows that you're mine, and that I fucking love you so damn much." Pulling back out, I moved in again, and Quinn's moans turned into breathless pants. "Are you okay, Quinn?" Fuck, we should have talked safe words.

"Yes! *Fuck me*, Alpha." His words were a desperate plea, and who was I to say no to our dirty Omega?

I fucked him harder, and his hands gripped Zanny's, like they were both holding on for dear life. It was fucking bliss. It was like I was home, and this was how it was meant to be forever: my mates, all together, in one huge pile of sweat-soaked skin. If I could figure out a way to maneuver us so we could all fuck at once, I'd probably die happy.

Those were the goals. Soon.

Quinn's tight muscles gripped me harder, and all

coherent thought left me. The sound of slapping bodies and moans was so fucking loud, I wondered if Tanner could hear it from the clinic. My knot swelled, and I knew this was it.

"I'm going to knot you now, Quinn. Is that what you want?" He'd never had a knot outside the yearning, which by all intents and purposes was a wild experience where your body was in control and every other thought was on the backburner. I wanted him to consciously choose me now, choose to be knotted to me. Tied to me. Loved by me.

Quinn's forehead fell to the mattress. "Fuck, it's too good. Please, Murphy. Alpha," he gasped, and that was it for me.

Slamming my cock home, I felt him lock around me, and my knot ballooned as I pumped my cum inside him. We both collapsed onto the bed in time to see Merrick's fingers flick across Zanny's clit as he locked inside her. She screamed so loud as she came, I was worried she'd be hoarse, or that the Legion would burst in, thinking she was being murdered.

I lay panting on the bed, the two Omegas sticky and sated between Merrick and me. It felt so perfect. So right. Knotted in my Omega, keeping my release inside him, was the most amazing fucking sensation I'd ever felt. All sex would pale against this moment.

I hugged Quinn close and reached over to hold the

hand of a pink-cheeked Susannah. "Love you," she murmured, and I grinned.

"Love you too, Zanny. Can't wait until you're mine forever."

Merrick stroked his fingers up and down Quinn's arm soothingly, his eyes closing. He always fell asleep after sex. Such a typical guy. We'd be knotted in the Omegas for a little longer, and I kind of wanted to stay here forever. I wondered if I could convince them to turn this little orgy into a full-week bacchanalian sexfest.

The smile wouldn't leave my face as my eyes closed too, completely wrung out, and in the happiest place on earth.

A KNOCK on the door woke me with a start, and I grinned down at the still limp Omegas. We'd fucked them hard, and if they weren't walking funny for the next day or so, I was going to have to up my game. My knot had fallen from Quinn at some point while we slept.

Stretching, I grabbed my sweats from the floor. "I'll get it. Probably Tanner and his super senses picking up on the fact we were having a great time without him."

Susannah scooted out after me. "I need to pee and clean up," she said, grabbing my shirt off the ground and pulling it over her head. I watched as an obscene amount of Merrick's release dribbled down her thighs. Fucking delicious.

I walked down the hall to the front door, my nose twitching at the smell of Alphas at the door. I'd honestly expected Tanner, because there was no way anyone with hearing like his could have missed the sound of Susannah screaming our names, even from three blocks away. Maybe it was the Legion coming to check we hadn't been murdering her with our dicks.

I wrenched open the door and was immediately met with the business end of a cattle prod. My muscles seized, and I fell to the side. My body convulsed as 9,000 volts of electricity contracted my muscles painfully.

"Stay down, Murphy," a Legion soldier said as another one held the cattle prod to my chest a little longer. I couldn't even look up to see who they were.

"What the *fuck* is going on?" Susannah screeched, and then Legion soldiers were in front of her.

"Susannah Wilkie, you're under arrest on suspicion of murdering your previous Pack Alpha, Alduous Wilkie."

Fuck.

They dragged her out while one held the prod to my chest, burning my skin. Merrick roared out of the bedroom, and the guy lifted his gun and shot him.

"No!"

"It's just a tranq, sir," the soldier said flatly. "Here's one for you too. Sorry." Then he shot me in the neck, and darkness crept in around the edges of my vision.

"Quinn," I breathed. "Zanny."

Then nothingness.

37

SUSANNAH

I was pushed into the back of an SUV, and lucky we weren't too picky about nudity, because I wasn't wearing any underwear and was fairly sure some of my Alpha's cum was still leaking out between my thighs.

I hoped these fuckers choked on the scent of it.

"What's going on? I didn't murder anyone, and that fucker wasn't my Pack Alpha."

The Legion soldier in the front gave me a look of disapproval. "You'll have time to plead your case."

"Did the Alpha General approve this?"

The guy in the front shrugged. Was his name Ben? "Doesn't matter. The Alpha General put this process into place, so it applies to his special little people as well as the rest of us. Besides, he has no interest in finding out who Wilkie's killer is."

Well, that was a no, obviously, since Courtland was well aware of who'd killed Wilkie and why he was dead.

"The asshole probably isn't even dead. He probably ran away like the piece of shit he was."

The driver slammed on the brakes, and I was flung forward onto the car's floorboards. "Sorry. Rabbit ran across the road," he said, his lip curled in a sneering smirk.

I forgot how much I hated Alphas sometimes. I couldn't help but see Murphy, lying on the floor, his body twitching as they'd basically electrocuted him to keep him down.

"I want to see my father!" I yelled as they dragged me from the car into the temporary jail. They snapped cuffs around my wrists, and I growled at them.

"Stops you from shifting," the first soldier told me. "Sorry, Legion General Joshua is currently in Maxton, so Daddy dearest won't be able to bail your entitled ass out."

I realized that there was no one manning the prison—no Dominic, not anyone—which meant that they'd premeditated this. They'd made sure there wasn't anyone around to kick up a stink until it was too late. My blood ran cold.

That heinous old bitch.

As they tossed me into the cell, slamming the doors

shut, I hissed at them. "Do I at least get to know who made these accusations?"

"No."

Then they both walked out. I reassured myself that they didn't have anything, because I hadn't killed Wilkie. But I didn't want them to look too closely either, because I'd rather they didn't execute Tanner.

As if I'd summoned him by my thoughts alone, there was a ruckus in the reception area. "You will let me through."

"Sorry, no visitors."

"I heard you grievously injured an Omega on her way into the cell. Are you denying her the right to medical care?" His voice was scarily low.

"Is she sucking your cock too?" the soldier asked, and I didn't have to be out there to feel the sudden shift in the air. There was cold violence in his tone.

I quickly moved to the sharp edge of a bed spring and scraped my arm along it with force, until blood welled on the surface.

Tanner wasn't dumb, obviously. "I smell blood. Either you will move, or I will forcibly remove you, as per my orders from the Alpha General and the Convocation. Do you think whoever's giving you orders is prepared to go against the Convocation? Against Titus Flett himself?"

Showing the first sign of brains they had today, they let Tanner past. Everyone was scared of the Flett brothers; it didn't matter what flavor of supernatural you were.

Tanner strode toward my cell at a pace that was human slow, showing the Manix soldiers his back, a definite *fuck you* move. "Omega, are you injured?" His tone was soft, and I was so glad we hadn't told anyone of our relationship yet.

I let him see how pissed I was in my eyes, and then I turned on what I liked to consider the Omega waterworks. I burst into tears so hearty, I could have won an Oscar. "They were so rough, and I cut myself as they dragged me from the car, and they hurt my Alphas, and..."

"Hush, Omega. I will check on your Alphas after I make sure you're okay. Can I see your wrist? I'll see if I can do anything to help... stem the bleeding." I held out my self-inflicted wound that was barely more than a scratch. "I will personally talk to the Alpha General about your treatment."

I huffed out a breath. It would have to do. The dumb-fuck soldier had been right; these were the new Alpha General's rules, and he couldn't shirk them any more than we could.

"Is there anything else I can do to ensure your comfort?" Tanner's voice was professional and even, but his eyes promised death to whoever put me in here.

"I'm okay," I whispered back. "Thank you, Tanner."

"I'll come back and check your wound tomorrow, if this ridiculousness isn't over by then." His voice was hard, and when he turned back to the soldiers, they flinched away.

Yeah, safe move, fuckers. Tanner was a nice guy with a definite cinnamon roll center, but he was still a walking death machine.

When he left, I'd never felt more alone. I moved back to the hard bed. If I breathed deeply, I could smell Jericho in the sheets. I tried not to think about what else could be living in that bedding, instead taking the comfort where I could.

Eventually, the soldiers left and I let go of the emotions I'd been holding onto tightly, curling myself into a ball and crying until I fell asleep.

IT WAS dark outside the tiny window when I woke. It was too small for anyone to climb out of, and too high up to use for the view unless I stood on the bed. Standing on the bed end, I could barely see the first break of dawn across the plains, painting the sky and the grass pink. I'd been in here for twelve hours then. The longest twelve hours of my life.

"Susannah?"

A voice beside my ear shocked the shit out of me. I fell forward, my arms windmilling like I could fight gravity, but I was going to land on my face for sure.

Instead, I landed on something hard, but not concrete-hard, hovering a few inches from the floor. "What the actual fuck?" I hissed to nothing.

At least, until nothing chuckled back. "Sorry. There's no way to politely make yourself known if you don't have a visible form."

"*Bowie?*" I squeaked. I patted the nothingness beneath me. "Is that you?"

"Yep. Sorry, I didn't know if I had enough effect on the physical world to catch you. Using myself as an air mattress seemed like the best bet."

I sat up, and he groaned. Shit, was I hurting him? How could you hurt someone who didn't have a body? I wiggled, trying to climb off him, but two hands came up to stop me.

"Fuck. This is what that feels like? No wonder Jericho spent the better half of our teen years jacking off."

I was sitting on his ghost dick. As if just thinking about it made me more aware of the fact that it was a body underneath me and not air, I could feel the hard press of what could only be one of two things: a dick or a bottle of Dr Pepper.

I scooted off him, climbing back to sit on the bed. "How are you here?"

The bed sank a little beside me. "Quinn and Jericho decided that you needed support in here, someone to give you answers and act as a go-between, because they won't let them in. Quinn can feel your sadness and your anger. He's..." I knew what he was, because the bond worked both ways. "So they went and woke Electra from her bed, explained who we were, who our great-grandfather was, just really laid it all out there. She still decided to help us, which, not gonna lie, was a bit of a surprise. I'm not really any more real than I was, but I'm strong enough that you can feel me and hear me, and that's more than I could ever ask for."

"But how?"

How was he away from Jericho?

How could I hear him, but even better, feel him?

A hand brushed down my arm. "Over there, beneath the window? There's a small chunk of moon-stone. It's acting as a talisman and an amplifier. I don't know. I never trained as a witch. I just lead confused souls to the Pearly Gates—that's it. Jericho is the witch in the family."

I walked over to the window, looking for the stone he was talking about. I sifted beneath the bed, and there it was, the cloudy blue rock that was bringing Bowie to life. Kind of. Picking it up, I felt a jolt of the magic, and the presence of Bowie got stronger.

I couldn't believe it. I wanted to feel him. Jericho had said they were identical, so in my mind's eye, I knew what he looked like. But I still really wanted to touch him, feel his features beneath my fingers. Breathe him in.

"Can I?" I lifted my hand, and I felt his hand wrap around my wrist. A cheek touched my palm, and I stroked downward, feeling his sharp jaw with smooth skin, none of Jericho's dark stubble. My thumb went further over to tug at a soft pillow of a lower lip, and he nipped it with his teeth, making me squeak. The feel of his body wasn't what I would call average. Less physical and more like a resistance of air. It was hard to describe, but the fact I could feel his tongue flick against my skin was blowing my mind.

"Wow," I breathed. "It's really nice to meet you finally, Bowie."

"Say my name again?" he whispered, his voice rough.

"Bowie."

He let out a shuddering breath that puffed over my face, telling me how close he really was to me. "I've been invisible for so long. You have no idea how this feels." He cleared his throat. "Fuck, she's beautiful, her lips parted so I can kiss her or maybe put my di—"

I cleared my throat. "You realize your thoughts are out loud now, right?"

The presence of Bowie leapt off the bed beside me, and he groaned. "Fuck. I'm sorry. Shit. This is going to take some getting used to. Is it too late to go back to being invisible?"

I laughed. I couldn't help it. I laughed until tears streamed down my face, flopping back onto the hard bed. I laughed until a different Legion soldier came to check on me. "Are you okay, Omega?"

I wiped my arm across my eyes. "Sure. I'm sorry. It's been a hard twenty-four hours. I like to talk to myself to calm down. You know, meditation and manifestation and all that stuff. Sorry if I woke you."

The soldier—who seemed familiar but I didn't know his name—just nodded, his eyes soft. "Let me know if there's anything I can do for you."

"You could let me out?"

He gave me a pained expression. "Anything but that."

He walked away, and I lay back down on the blankets. "Bowie?"

"Yeah?"

"Do ghosts spoon?"

A chuckle echoed around the room. I couldn't tell where he was, but I knew he was here. His warm scent filled the space around me, like an orange grove in summer. "We sure do. Well, this one does, at least." His voice was warm and fluid, washing over me like a weighted blanket.

I curled up on my side, and then a hard body was behind mine, pressed along my back, knees tucked up behind mine. An arm was slung over my waist and lips pressed to the base of my neck, making me feel better than I had since I got thrown into this hellhole.

"You won't be here much longer, Susannah. They're

going to get you out, even if they have to raze the whole town to do it," he whispered softly against my neck.

My body relaxed. "Bowie?"

"Mmm?"

"I'm glad you're here."

"Me too, Omega. Me too."

38

TANNER

"This is fucking insane. *Do something*," I barked at the Alpha General, but he just raised an eyebrow. I guess he wasn't used to people telling him what to do.

"I am doing something, vampire, and you better watch your tone."

I stepped closer to his desk. "Or fucking what?"

Courtland narrowed his eyes at me. "I understand that you're worried right now, so I'm going to let the fucking challenge in your eyes slide. But if you don't back the hell up, I'm going to expel you from *my goddamn town!*" He growled the last bit, and the Alpha command of it brushed over my skin like tiny needles.

I sucked in a few deep breaths, stepping back. "I'm sorry, mate."

The Alpha General shook his head. "I understand, Tanner. I get being riled up by fear for your Packmate. I promise you, I'm working on it. I put these laws in place to stop the Manix from being a lawless Wild West—where might equaled right—so I can't outright overrule it. I could have squashed the idea before it started, but they purposefully went around me."

I growled again, a sound worthy of a beast, and resisted the urge to put my fist through the cheap particleboard walls. This was stupid. She hadn't done it, and Courtland knew she hadn't.

"What evidence do they have?" I stepped forward and lowered my voice. "If I admit guilt, what would happen?"

"You'd be forced to leave, and I'd be forced to petition the Convocation for grievances, all that bullshit." He shook his head. "Don't hastily throw away the possibilities of your future. Susannah didn't kill Wilkie, so they have no proof."

"What do they have then?"

"Errol."

I stumbled back, shocked. Why would the Beta we set free give evidence that Susannah had killed Wilkie? He'd been there. He knew full well who'd ripped out Wilkie's heart. It didn't make sense.

Sensing my confusion, he shrugged. "Look, I don't understand either, but we'll let this all play out, and then if we have to, we'll take more drastic action. I think Gwenda is grasping at straws, and I want to know why. There's something more going on here, other than loyalty to an Alpha who had no loyalties himself. I want to know what it is."

Quinn's mother, Gwenda, was number one on my fucking hit list.

"All the while, my girlfriend rots inside a prison cell."

Courtland's nostrils flared, like his patience was waning. Fuck his patience. "I promise she's not uncomfortable, Tanner. As soon as I found out about all this bullshit, I had either Dominic or a trusted Legion soldier in there at all times. The Shiny Rock Cafe is taking her three hot meals a day, and we've given her so much Omega-approved bedding that she'll be able to turn the whole place into a nest." His eyes softened. "Man, do you think Bonnie, of all people, would let me get away with making that cell anything but a hundred percent comfortable for your Omega? It's basically a waterfall shower head away from being a resort hotel room."

I huffed, and he stood, coming around the desk. "It'll be all done soon. Radic has reported that there are some ill feelings among the population regarding Wilkie's whereabouts, and suspicion about Merrick and Murphy ostensibly swooping in to steal his Omegas. We both know how wrong that is, but maybe it'll be beneficial to the future of your Pack for all this shit to be aired out."

He was probably right. You'd have to be blind not to see the way the town looked at them. It would only get worse when they realized Jericho and I were a part of their budding Pack.

And Bowie. Fuck, how was I going to explain Bowie?

"Uh, so if Dominic is guarding Susannah, tell him not to worry if it appears like she's talking to herself. She isn't losing it."

Courtland cocked his head to the side. "The Legion guards have reported she was talking to someone. We assumed it was one of you outside the cell window keeping her company, so we didn't interfere."

Well, it kind of was, I guess. But they weren't outside.

"Uh, kinda. Hey, did you ever see that movie from the nineties with Patrick Swayze and Demi Moore, and they did that thing with the pottery wheel?"

"What?"

I shook my head. One problem at a time. "Never mind. I'll explain after all this shit is over." I was exhausted. I needed to feed, and hug Susannah, and tear and rend anyone who was trying to hurt her. But tearing and rending was what had gotten us into this situation in the first place. "I'm heading back to the clinic. If you come to any decisions—"

"You'll be the first to know. Or Merrick and Murphy. They've been on my ass as much as you have. Trust me, I want this whole circus over with as fast as possible too."

I believed him, but I still wasn't going to make it easy. I grunted goodbye and left the temporary Legion building. There was a bite in the air, autumn hitting us hard and fast, though I didn't really feel it. My core body temperature was much lower than the Manix who were donning long sleeves and sweaters.

Angry words drifted just inside my range of hearing, and I stopped on the sidewalk, not apologizing to the people who had to walk around me.

"Why are you fucking doing this? Why can't you just let me be happy?"

I knew that voice, knew that pain. Quinn.

"You forget yourself, boy," a barbed voice responded, and I found myself moving toward the conversation.

"It's over. Wilkie is gone, and it had nothing to do with Susannah! I'm mated. I've found my own Alphas. You need to fucking *stop*." He hissed in pain, and that was all I needed to start running.

I was between two small buildings before whoever hurt Quinn could take another breath. Still, I stopped just out of sight, waiting. His parents were with him, and they had him backed up against the wall. Quinn was staring pure hatred at them.

His father, a Beta, stepped forward. "Weak. How could you keep being an Omega from us? The money we could have gotten for you if we'd known. Maybe we could have given you to a Pack that wasn't Wilkie's, but you were too selfish to think of anyone but yourself." He spat the words like acid.

I knew Quinn's parents had promised him to Wilkie, but I had no idea it was for money. Like Quinn, I'd always thought it was for influence and power. Quinn looked like he'd been slapped. "You sold me like a prized horse?"

His mother curled her lip, baring her teeth. "Probably could have gotten better money for a horse. The whole family could have been rich if you hadn't hidden your Omega status, but that's the way you've always been. So hung up on everything that Beta bitch said, and I have no doubt it was her fucking idea to run when you were a teenager, and hide your designation from your Alpha. Hell, I bet she's the reason you remained unbonded too," she snarled. "I can see the truth on your face. Well, guess what? Your little girlfriend is going to fucking rot in prison, if she isn't executed. The Manix believe in an eye for an eye, boy, and you bet I'm going to fucking make sure that I get an Omega for an Omega."

"Fuck you!" Quinn shouted, and his father lifted his hand again.

I rushed in front of him, holding the Beta's wrist

gently like he was a naughty toddler. "I'd stop. I will not allow you to hit this Omega." He still strained against my hold, like he would have a chance to break free. I gave him a look of pity. "I could snap your wrist with the tiniest bit of pressure. Sometimes I don't know my own strength. I'd strongly suggest, as a doctor, that you stop struggling." My voice was cool and professional, but my eyes must have said something else, because the man blanched.

"You misunderstand, Doctor. I was just going to stroke his hair. He's my baby, after all."

I nodded, like I could relate at all with this piece of shit. "Indeed. Unfortunately, it is time for the Omega's check-up, so I'm going to have to insist he comes with me. Have a great evening." I hustled Quinn away, resisting the urge to pick him up and run with him all the way back home. Instead, I took him to the clinic a half a block over.

I breathed a sigh of relief that there was no one there waiting for me, and moved him gently through the front door, slamming it closed behind us. Locking it, I pushed him into my office, then closed that door too.

Finally, now I was sure he was safe, I gripped his shoulders as I inspected him for injuries. He looked up at me with eyes that were too wide, his complexion pale, and I realized his fingers were shaking where they clung to my shirt. I folded him up in my arms and held him tightly against me. His warm body slowly thawed my cooler one, and I ignored the ache in my fangs at the pounding of his heart.

"I'm so sorry, Quinn. Sorry that they didn't see that your true worth has no dollar value." I kissed the top of his head, trying to give him the reassurance Susannah would give him if she was here. "Susannah knows your worth. We all do. I won't let them hurt you again."

He shook his head from side to side, not unburying his face from my neck, though. "They haven't had the ability to hurt me in so long, but they still managed to get at me through Susannah. I hate them so much."

I ran my fingers through his hair, gently scraping my nails on his scalp until he purred softly. "I hate them too. Want me to eat them? They'd probably taste rotten, but anything tastes good with enough tomato sauce."

He laughed softly as he pressed away from my chest. "Thank you, Tanner."

I stroked my fingers across the frown creases in his forehead. I wasn't sure what came over me, but I leaned forward and kissed him. It wasn't deep or passionate, barely a brush of my lips, but when he sighed contentedly, my lips curled. Something in my chest settled at the small sound of happiness.

"You never have to thank me, my Omega. I want you to be happy, and I intend to make that happen, despite your cunt parents and the rest of this town. I'm not just in this Pack for Susannah. You're mine too. "

His eyes got shiny, and he nodded, leaning his forehead back onto my chest. I hugged him, whispering promises I fully intended to keep forever.

39

JERICHO

I felt like a person in a sensory deprivation tank. Without the constant presence of Bowie at my side—and in my head—the world was too quiet. Too still. Too lonely. I missed him like I'd miss a limb. Sure, he wasn't always beside me before, but we'd never been separated for long stretches of time.

On the other hand, as his brother, I was so happy that he'd get to experience a little bit of life without it filtering through me first. I was happy that Susannah had someone with her as she entered her third day in lock-up, since they were still gathering the "witness" from wherever he was holed up.

Merrick and Murphy were alternating between extreme rage and hopelessness, but had thrown themselves into fixing up what I referred to as the Pack-house. I couldn't soothe them, not really. The only person who even eased their anger and guilt a little was Quinn, and he was a mess.

Tanner had told me about Quinn's parents and their threats, and I'd made a mental note to get Bowie to sneak into their house and fuck with them. Go full sleep-paralysis demon every night when they tried to rest.

With a slight shift in the energy around me, Bowie appeared, scaring the ever-loving shit out of me. "Fuck!"

It's been, like, two days, and already you're used to being without me? I'm crushed, brother.

Something inside me relaxed at the sound of his voice in my head. "I'm not used to you being so fucking sneaky, asshole." I wanted to hug him. "How's Susannah?"

The smirk on Bowie's face dropped. *She's comfortable, but she misses her Pack. She gets more desolate every day.*

"Having you there doesn't help?"

He shrugged. *It does. But it's not the same as a warm body around you, you know?* His head flopped back, and he stared at the ceiling. *I'm not sure if my balls can explode, seeing as they don't exist, but the ache I feel when I hold her body to mine is torture. I've never felt anything like it.*

I snorted. "Welcome to the dick-swinging world, brother. Doesn't it feel good?"

Indescribable. The pure bliss on his face made all the loneliness worth it. He was so happy, happier than I'd ever seen him. He shook himself from his thoughts. *Any advancements on getting her out?*

I let out a low growl. "They're dragging their feet, or dragging this witness back slowly, but they promise it'll be done by the end of the week. Tomorrow isn't soon enough for me."

And Quinn?

Another sigh wracked my body. "He feels guilty, and he misses her. He wants her back."

When she gets out, I want to be a part of their Pack. We should make our move. Bond them. Pledge ourselves. Whatever the Manix term is for a group orgy where they're tied to us forever.

A smirk curled my face, because like always, we were on the same wavelength. "It's not just them, though. It's Merrick and Murphy. It's Tanner. We'd be tying ourselves to them all."

The more the merrier. I want this, Jericho. More than I've wanted anything, except to be alive. I want to be able to touch her, and kiss him, anytime I want. I like the Alphas. I really like Tanner. I want this, he repeated.

"Okay, okay. I'm with you on this. How do we make it happen?"

Bowie held my eyes. *We make our intentions clear, first to the Alphas, and then to the Omegas. Because as much as I hate it, if they have to choose between us or Merrick and Murphy, we won't come out on top.*

I nodded, but surprisingly, I wasn't jealous. They'd known Merrick and Murphy for years, since they were children. They had a wealth of memories and feelings that had accrued over their lives. It wasn't a competition, but if it was, Bowie was correct—we'd lose.

I picked up the secondary talisman Electra had given us, which was sitting in the fruit bowl on the kitchen counter. I unwrapped it from its velvet bag, imbued with a dampener to contain the magic inside.

I can't believe you're keeping the magical equivalent of my body in among the stone fruits.

"At least I won't lose it there." I really needed to make some sort of pendant out of it, so it could be worn and protected. For now, I just stuffed it in my pocket. "Let's go."

The Alphas were out behind the back of the house, cutting wood and constructing something that looked like a sex swing, but probably wasn't. Merrick was sawing, his powerful body bent over the workhorse, and his jeans were snug over his butt and thighs. He was sexy as hell.

"They are really fucking hot, though, right? I mean, look at that ass. I bet he can crack walnuts with that."

Merrick stood up, looking over at me, an amused expression on his face.

"Bowie, the rock means everyone can hear your

inside voice *on the fucking outside*," I hissed, but I was the only one who could see Bowie's look of horror.

Murphy's eyes danced with mirth as he stood and stretched his muscles, showing a peek of his flat abdominals. "Bowie's here?"

I nodded. Bowie cleared his throat, walking over to squeeze their arms, the sign we'd decided on to let everyone know he was in the room. "Hey."

Merrick's eyebrows climbed his forehead. "Holy shit, you're so much stronger now. Those shiny rocks actually do something."

I laughed. Such a Manix response to magic. "Yeah, they do. I don't have enough juice to power the moonstones and make him visible, but you can touch and hear him. Two out of five senses isn't bad."

Merrick was looking around where Bowie was. Kind of. "How's Zanny?"

Bowie's sigh shifted the hair on his forehead. That was new. Normally, his incorporeal form stayed the same, no matter what he did. *Interesting.*

"Sad. That's kind of what I wanted to talk to you about. We want to be a Pack. *I* want to be a Pack. And I also want to make her feel better any way I can, including..." He trailed off, like he couldn't find the right words.

"Including with your ghost dick?" Murphy supplied, and Bowie flushed.

"Yeah, basically."

"Why are you here? We have no say over Susannah or who she shares her body with. She'll be the first to tell you that."

I smiled, because no one told Susannah to do a damn thing. "But you're the Alphas. This will be your Pack eventually. It would be your name after mine, under the Manix traditions. We want you to accept us. I know that we're problematic." I was a designationless hybrid and Bowie was a ghost; problematic was a little of an understatement.

They were silent for a moment, looking at each other, and then at us.

"Follow up questions, and remember, we'll know if you're lying," Murphy said, holding up a finger. "A T. Rex is rampaging through Moonburst."

I screwed up my face. "What?"

He raised his finger. "Shh, listen. A T. Rex is rampaging through Moonburst. Sitting in the middle of the railway tracks is Quinn, hog-tied, looking like a sexy dinosaur snack. Beside him is a million dollars in a briefcase, covered in steaks. The T. Rex is almost there, and you have to choose which one to save. Which do you choose?"

Bowie snorted. "Easy. Quinn. Every damn time."

"Second follow-up question: same scenario, except you have to choose between Susannah and four cubs. Not our cubs, just random ones."

I frowned. "What kind of fucked up question is

that?" I looked at Bowie and sighed. *Fuck.* "The cubs. Susannah would flay me alive if I chose her over saving the cubs."

Merrick nodded. "Last question. You have a chance to give a body to Bowie forever. One that's impervious to disease or injury, basically like a Manix. But you have to torture one of our Omegas to get it. They wouldn't die, but it would be painful. In the end, Bowie gets a body and the Omegas heal completely. What do you choose?"

Fuck these guys.

But Bowie didn't hesitate. "I would never hurt the Omegas for my own benefit. Never. I'd rather be a ghost forever, unseen by anyone but Jericho, than hurt anyone in our Pack."

Murphy grinned. "Welcome to Pack Merrick-Murphy. We're going to have to start going by our given names," he said to Merrick, screwing up his nose.

"August and Owen?"

Murphy shuddered. "Let's take our Omegas' surnames. If we're going to say fuck you to tradition, we may as well say fuck you in the biggest way possible. The Calathean-Jack Pack." He looked me dead in the eye. "If the Omegas accept you, we will too. But everything we do is for them, so if their decision even so much as wavers, our answer changes. Got it?"

Bowie was nodding, but only I could see it, so I echoed his agreement. "We agree."

Murphy walked over and slapped my arm. "Welcome to the Pack, man. Now, Bowie, go and make our Omega feel better by any means necessary."

Bowie's face flushed, and he popped out of the yard, the suck of the magic keeping him here going with him.

Merrick looked around. "He's gone?"

I let out a short laugh. "Yeah, he doesn't mess around." I studied the lumber lying around. "Uh, so what are you guys making?"

"A sex swing."

40

BOWIE

I didn't really disappear the way you'd think. Really, I just moved super quickly. Before, I couldn't move away from Jericho. Not far, anyway. Now, I could move between those talisman stones at the speed of light. The only person who would be able to see me is Tanner—you know, if I had a body to see.

I appeared back in the cell, and Susannah lifted her head. "Bowie?"

I climbed onto the bed beside her, kissing her forehead. She had tears on her cheeks, making me feel like shit for leaving her. "Yeah, baby. I'm here. I'm sorry for leaving you."

She rubbed her tears away with angry hands. "I'm sorry for being such a wimp. I'm stronger than this normally. Damn Omega hormones."

I stroked my fingers through her hair, which was growing lank and unwashed. "I know you are, sweetheart. But everyone's entitled to their weakness, especially you. Especially right now." I wrapped my arms around her, holding her tight to my body, uncaring how it would look to anyone outside these walls. I kissed her cheeks and the tear tracks that marred them with lines. I entwined her fingers with mine, and did my best to encapsulate her whole body with my own.

When I kissed the hollow behind her ear, she moaned softly. "Bowie," she breathed, and this was it. My moment. A way I could make her feel better.

"Would you like me to soothe you, Omega? Do you want me to help you find a little bit of pleasure in this shitty situation?" I stroked my hands down her sides, resting my palms on her ribcage, just below her breasts. My thumbs brushed the undersides, but I wouldn't go any further, not unless she said so.

She didn't say the words, but she put her hands over mine and lifted them up, until they cupped her breasts. I held in the groan that wanted to push past my lips, instead brushing my thumbs over her nipples.

"Climb under the blankets, baby. Burrow down into this nest and let me make you feel good?" I wasn't sure why I phrased it as a question, but I was out of my depth here. I was going on instinct.

Susannah let out a shuddering sigh, but she did it. She actually did it. She piled all the blankets on top of her until she was huddled under three or four feather comforters. She was probably going to cook, but hopefully if anyone walked in, this would be enough to hide us from prying eyes.

She was in a pair of tights—the Alpha General's Omega had brought her some clothes—and I peeled them down her thighs. Pushing my shoulders between them, I wished I could breathe her in. Instead, I bit down on the fleshy part of her thighs with a sigh. I wanted to live here forever. I mean, it wasn't like I needed to breathe?

When my tongue slid up her slit, she squirmed and moaned. "Shh, baby. You have to be quiet. We wouldn't want anyone coming back here to check on you."

She picked up a fluffy pillow and covered her face with it, and I took that as my cue to try and make her scream. Pouring my energy into my tongue, I stroked it up and down her slit, flicking repeatedly over her clit in a gentle stroke, finding a rhythm that seemed to make her mewl. Squeezing her thigh, I moved my hand up until I was stroking my incorporeal fingers through her folds. Fuck, this felt so amazing. It was the ghost of a sensation—ha, get it?—but it was more than I'd ever felt in my life. I slid one finger inside her, then two.

"More, Bowie," she breathed, grinding against my face, so I added another finger. Her pussy seemed to suck it in, fluttering around it, stretching to accommodate the new width. It was fucking magic.

Her slick ran down my hand, dripping onto the bed. I curled my fingers, and she gripped my head. I was kind of glad she couldn't see me at that moment, because I was smiling so wide that I must've looked like a fool.

"More... I need a knot."

Uh, I didn't think I had one of those. I looked down at my hand, my fingers disappearing inside her. *I wonder if I could...* Testing the waters, I make my hand a little less corporeal. *Huh, that works.* Folding my hand like some kind of origami swan, I pushed a semi-corporeal hand inside her, and she gasped.

"Is this okay?" I asked, trying to keep the panic out of my voice. Fuck, I should have definitely asked before I put my whole hand inside her like she was a puppet.

"So full," she breathed, and I swore. I was hurting her. I tried to remove my hand, but she reached down and gripped my wrist with inhuman strength. "Don't stop. It's so good," she groaned, pressing the pillow further into her mouth. So I didn't stop. Inch by inch, I gave my hand back its corporeality, until she stretched fuller and fuller, and fuck, it was something else.

She writhed and thrashed, muttering my name over and over again as I twisted my fist inside her, stroking her with my fingers, until she locked down on my wrist so hard, I was glad I didn't have bones. Pressing her pillow to her face, she screamed her release, and I swear, I came right along with her. She was heaving in air, and slowly, I removed my hand, which was so damn obscene. I loved it.

Her fingers released from my wrist, and I wished she'd been able to mark me. Maybe one day. I climbed up the bed, curling my body protectively around hers.

"Bowie," she breathed languidly.

I let her feel my smile as I pressed my lips to the back of her neck. "I know."

"Thank you."

"You never have to thank me for anything. My heart is yours." But she'd already drifted off to sleep.

HOURS LATER, still wrapped around Susannah, I heard someone open the solid door to the cell. Releasing her, I stepped into the corner so I could watch who it was. I was relieved when I saw Dominic.

"Susannah?" he called, and Susannah crawled her way out of the blankets. Dominic's nose twitched, and I realized he could probably smell her release. Shaking his head, a frown came back over his face. "Omega? They've arrived with the witness. Errol is here. Your trial is about to begin."

As if she could feel where I was in the room, she

looked at me in the corner, her eyes wide with fear. I wanted to tell her that it didn't matter; there was no way I was going to let anything happen to her. I'd burn this fucking town down first.

41

SUSANNAH

Dominic walked beside me as I moved toward the warehouse acting as the town hall while the real town hall was being used as the school. Soon they'd have to convert some of the existing buildings to be functional, but at this point, we were all just trying to catch our breath. Some of us more than others.

"Did you call Quinn? My Alphas?" Bowie walked on my other side, the brush of his hand the only reason I knew he was there.

Dominic nodded. "As soon as they rolled into town." His feet slowed. "Look, Omega. There was no love lost between me and your old Alpha. So I'm going to close my eyes for ten seconds, and if you run and I can't find you, what a shame." The sarcasm in his last words was thick. "I don't know how they'll spin your...

circumstances, but if you don't want to risk it, I'm happy to say you outran me."

I gave him a soft smile. "Thank you, Dominic. But I really am innocent, I promise."

Dominic huffed, starting to walk again. "Fine. But I wouldn't have blamed you. Wilkie was a fucking asshole."

"Absolute fact," I murmured, but that was the last of our conversation as we stepped into the warehouse. There were about forty people sitting in chairs haphazardly scattered around, including my guys. My Pack. Quinn looked terrible, and I desperately wanted to go to him. Merrick had him tucked under his arm, pressed between him and Murphy. Tanner sat in front of them, Jericho at his side.

I wanted to run to them. Kiss them. A sob welled up in my throat, but I swallowed it down. Bowie's fingers squeezed mine, and I held him tightly.

Quinn's parents were there, as well as a few more of Wilkie's cronies. But overwhelmingly, it looked like people were here for me. Raiden and his Pack, including Naja, next to my brothers and their mates. My father, though he was sitting with my brothers and not up the front where he would normally be. He looked livid as he stared at Quinn's parents, like he was one second away from making them prostrate themselves on the ground at my feet.

Dominic pulled back a chair, waving for me to take

it. I gave him a tight nod and sat down. Sitting in front of us was the Alpha General, Legion General Theodore, Wilbur, who was the leader of the Moonburst coven, and Electra. I hadn't even considered the witches would have a role in my trial, but it made sense. We were a combined community now. Everyone got a vote.

Courtland heaved a sigh. "Let's get this underway, shall we? These proceedings have been dragged out enough. Gwenda Jack, you accuse Susannah Calathean of murdering her Alpha. As you know, such allegations can lead to the death penalty, so I'm sure you have foolproof evidence of your allegations?"

He knew she didn't. There was no fucking proof.

"Of course, Alpha General." Gwenda stood, grabbing a wrapped package. Walking up to the long table, she opened the package and tipped the contents in front of the judges. A plastic bag slipped out, and inside it was a charred and rotting hand. Even through the sealed bag, I could smell the decomposing flesh, and I gagged. Courtland seemed unperturbed, though Wilbur looked like she wanted to hurl. It was disgusting.

"It's a severed hand."

"Yes, Alpha General. Wilkie's severed hand."

Courtland raised an eyebrow. "How can you be sure?"

She turned the bag over, and I knew what she was

about to show him. The fucking family monogram he'd made up and had tattooed on himself. Courtland's lips thinned, but he gave a tight nod.

The Legion General beside him curled his nose. "Your evidence of Wilkie's demise is accepted, Beta Gwenda. However, the flesh around the wrists looks torn, like a wild animal may have done it. Where was it found? What evidence do you have that this was foul play? Wilkie was living in the woods for several weeks before the fire."

"It was found in the woods outside of Maxton, Legion General. I have a witness, sir."

The Legion General nodded. "Bring him out."

Electra cleared her throat. "Before we go on with that, Wilbur and I would like to hear from the accused about the nature of the deceased? After all, you all know the history, but we don't."

Electra looked fierce and regal. I wondered if it was too late to want to be her when I grew up.

Courtland inclined his head. "Of course." His dark eyes flicked to me. "Susannah, could you please give us a brief summary of your relationship with Alduous Wilkie?"

Sucking in a deep breath, I tried not to look at Gwenda, in case my rage flared. "My mate, Quinn, was promised to Wilkie when we were teenagers, but his parents—"

Wilbur interrupted. "I thought Omegas were

allowed to choose their own Packs?"

"They are, but Quinn was late presenting. Everyone thought he was a Beta. In those days, Betas were afforded a lot less respect than they are under the rule of the new Alpha General." Wilbur nodded, indicating I should continue. "We were part of his Pack for nearly a decade, but we were never bonded. Wilkie developed erectile dysfunction and therefore couldn't complete the matebond properly, especially with Quinn, who was an Omega."

"How could he not know Quinn was an Omega?" the Legion General asked.

I chewed the inside of my cheek. "We acquired a suppressant from the black market in California." Close enough. "Anyway, we lived in his Pack for a decade. He was abusive, emotionally and physically. Every time we tried to run, he beat us. Or Green would, his second-in-command. He bonded us to his Beta, Errol, so he'd know where we were if we actually made it out. He'd drag us back for punishment, and every time, he got more and more unhinged. He threatened to kill our families as a way to keep us in line. Said that he'd ensure my brother's cubs had 'accidents' or that he'd bond Raiden as an Omega. He threatened Quinn's sisters.

"Eventually, we decided it was safer to stay. He left us alone, as long as he could parade us around every now and then, so people thought he had us on a tight leash and that we loved him. So no one would know he hadn't been able to bond us with his floppy dick."

"You were a Beta. He shouldn't need his, uh, penis to bond you," Legion General Theodore muttered, and I shrugged.

"He did need my agreement, though, and I never gave it. No matter how much he threatened, how much he hurt me, I couldn't tie myself to him. He tried to bond Quinn, but with his Omega designation, it never took."

Electra's steely silver eyes flashed like knives in the moonlight. "I'm getting a picture here. Tell us about the last time you saw Wilkie."

My tongue wet my dry lips. "It was the day of the fire. He realized Quinn was an Omega, and it was too much. He wanted the Omega pair. We fought, and he got Quinn on the ground. He tried to..." I cleared my throat. "He tried to..."

Courtland's eyes grew soft. "I think we know what he tried to do, Omega."

"I knew we were fighting for our lives. Errol stood on the sidelines, wanting no part of what was about to happen. But Joseph, the other Pack Beta, tried to hold me back. I got free and got a couple of lucky hits in. My father trained me like I was going to be an Alpha soldier instead of a female Beta." I gave my dad a tremulous smile. "We got away, and ran until we found Merrick. With him and Murphy, we escaped the fire before the town went up in flames, but it was close. That's it."

The Legion General watched my face with a frown. "And why were you so slow to get back here?"

I flushed. "The stress sent Quinn into yearning. We were holed up near the border, riding out my heat and Quinn's yearning with Merrick and Murphy. It was a long one, because it had been repressed for so long."

"Do you have proof of this?" the General asked my Alphas. Murphy nodded, his face grim. These were all lies with enough truth thrown in to make them sound real. I hoped no one would look too hard.

Electra stared at me, and I wondered if she could tell I was lying. She gave a short nod. "Thank you, Susannah." She looked at Gwenda, her eyes hardening. "You can bring out your witness now."

I was holding my breath when Errol stepped in the side door. He looked good. He looked younger, the lines and sadness dragging down his face now gone. I'd always thought of Errol as old, but I realized it was circumstance aging him, not time. He didn't look at me as he walked to a second chair on the opposite side of the room.

"Beta Errol Wilkie, it's good to see you alive and well," Courtland greeted, and I think he was actually glad Errol was looking so good too.

"Thank you, Alpha General."

"Where have you been?"

"Boise, sir."

"By yourself? You haven't felt the urge to return to your Betas?" Theodore asked.

Errol shook his head. "No, Legion General. It was a weak bond to start with, as neither side really wanted it. We'd spent so many years blocking it, that I think it might have just fallen away."

I blinked, but he was right. The place where Errol's bond should've been was blank. I hadn't even looked for him there—that was how unused to being connected to the man I was.

"When was the last time you saw the accused?" Courtland asked.

Finally, Errol turned to me, meeting my eyes. *Fuck, fuck, fuck.*

"When they were running away from Wilkie. He wanted to bond them against their will. It was messed up."

"And how would you describe your old Alpha?"

"He was a sociopathic piece of shit, Alpha General," Errol snarled, and Quinn's parents gasped. "He believed he could just take whatever he wanted. Me, the Betas—I mean, Omegas. They were Betas when we were Pack," he said, with a small laugh to himself.

"When was the last time you saw Alduous Wilkie, Beta Errol?" the Legion General asked.

"When he and Joseph were fighting, after the Omegas escaped. He blamed Joseph for not being able to hold onto Susannah, and therefore them escaping. Joseph was a prick, and he mouthed back. I wanted nothing to do with it, so while they were fighting, I took our SUV and left them there."

"You left your Alpha and Packmates in the middle of a forest fire?"

Errol's lip curled. "Wilkie was like a cockroach. If he wanted to survive, he would."

"Was?" Wilbur asked. "You think he's dead?"

Errol frowned. "I know he's dead. I can't feel our bond anymore. Plus, I can smell his hand from over here. I'm not an expert, but I don't think you can survive having your hand mauled off like that."

"And your Packmate..." Electra looked down at her notes. "Joseph? Can you feel his bond?"

Errol shook his head. "I was never bonded to Joseph. Wilkie didn't want us to be attached to each other. Just to him. Like minions. Slaves."

"Do you think Joseph is still alive?"

Errol shrugged. "Probably. If he got a lucky shot in, he would have run. He was really good with knives," Errol said in a soft voice, which made me think we'd been wrong about Joseph being the least psychopathic. He lifted his shirt, showing slices across the skin of his chest. "Joseph's work."

Courtland ground his teeth. "I see. In your opinion, could the Omega Susannah have killed Wilkie or Joseph?"

Errol shook his head. "No. If she could have, she would have done it when Wilkie first bought them."

Electra's eyes flashed. "Bought?"

Errol nodded, his cold gaze going to Quinn's parents. "Gwenda and David Jack sold Quinn to our Pack when he was sixteen, for sixty thousand dollars, and another ten grand a year on the proviso that they never took him back and would turn a blind eye to what went on in the Pack. They upheld their end of the bargain," he spat.

Courtland's eyes flashed to me. "Is this true?"

I nodded. "We didn't know it at the time, but Quinn's parents admitted it two days ago, when Quinn confronted them."

"Selling your offspring was illegal, even back then." He waved at a Legion soldier, thankfully not the one who'd taken me to jail. "Take them into custody. We'll deal with that on a separate day." He ignored the protests of Quinn's parents as he looked at me, and Bowie's fingers tightened around my own. "Time for a judgment. I find Susannah Calathean not guilty."

Electra was next, her expression disgusted. "Also not guilty." The look she slid at Quinn's parents promised she wouldn't be so lenient with them.

Wilbur was next. "Not guilty, of course. Hell, even if she had murdered him, I'd call it self-defense and sleep soundly tonight."

I looked at Legion General Theodore. "Not guilty.

You're free to go."

An embarrassing, choked sob passed my lips as I stood, running toward my Pack. Quinn climbed over Murphy to make it to me first, and I wrapped my arms and legs around him. I'd never let him go again. Merrick and Murphy bracketed us both in their arms, kissing my cheeks and saying soft things I couldn't really hear. When my feet reached the floor again, I looked over at Tanner and Jericho, standing off to the side.

Fuck it.

Striding over, I hurdled a row of chairs, knowing Tanner would catch me. He'd always catch me. Not disappointing me, he caught me mid-air, dragging me safely against his body. Wrapping my arms around his neck, I kissed him hard. It was a possessive claim, and I hoped everyone here knew. He was mine.

A hand tugged at mine, and I looked over at Jericho, who seemed unsure what to do. I made the decision for him, using that hand to pull him closer until his lips collided with mine. Life was short, and I no longer cared what people thought. I'd leave this town so fucking fast if it meant I could be free and happy with them.

Someone cleared their throat, but there was definitely amusement in the sound. "Take it back to your nest, Omega. This is a court of law."

I looked over at Dominic and smiled. "You got it."

42

QUINN

We slept in one huge pile for two days. I wasn't more than three feet from Susannah the whole time. We piled into Merrick and Murphy's house, and without the stress of her looming execution, I could appreciate how hard they'd thrown themselves into making this place perfect. I had no doubt they'd used their anger and worry to fuel themselves. As a result, this place was a dream.

They'd furnished the house in all the colors we'd suggested, and it was bright and open. They'd knocked out a few walls—definitely the work of some pent-up aggression—and now the whole bottom floor was open plan.

It was there we'd pulled all the mattresses, blankets, and pillows we could find in the house, and camped out until the whole thing seemed like a night-mare in the past.

On the third day, Radic came around and told us that they'd found my parents guilty of trafficking and had exiled them from both Manix communities. They'd packed their bags and left, and the witches had reset the boundaries to expel them, making sure it would be quite painful if they ever returned. I hoped they tried at least once, so they could get a taste of the pain they'd inflicted on Susannah and I. But more than that, more than my wish for revenge, I wished that I never had to see them again.

Radic said he was checking in with all my siblings, making sure they were mated of their own free will and not because my parents were getting kickbacks. I had been younger than my siblings by a decade. I didn't even know most of them, because they'd gone off to their own Packs before I was six.

With everything sorted, we were kind of in a stasis. We'd been through too much to casually go back to courting, but we were still somewhat strangers.

I was in the kitchen, making some kind of pasta from scratch with Jericho. He was hesitant still, like he didn't know where he fit. Even Bowie seemed to be closer to Susannah than Jericho; having spent so much time with her in her cell, they'd bonded over the trauma.

Jericho was on the outside looking in, and that

made me sad. My Omega couldn't stand the thought. He mightn't know how to soothe him, because Jericho wasn't an Alpha or a Beta, but he was ours, and we'd make him happy.

"Now we wrap it and let it rest," he said softly, covered in flour and fingers sticky with dough.

"For how long?" I asked, my brain whirling as a plan formed. We were the same height, and I gazed into his dark eyes.

"Thirty minutes. Two hours, max."

"Two hours? That's good. Plenty of time." I grabbed his hand, uncaring that it was sticky, and dragged him into the living room. Tanner was curled around Susannah, who was holding the joined hands of Merrick and Murphy as they watched some nineties movie that Tanner had insisted on.

"That's not how it happens at all," Bowie complained, and I thought he might be on the couch.

Tanner hushed him. "This is a classic. Just appreciate the beauty of Patrick Swayze shirtless."

Murphy laughed at the big blond vampire. "I thought you didn't 'swing that way,'" he teased.

Tanner looked up at me, his eyes dancing. "Apparently, sometimes I can be swayed."

I grinned down at him. We hadn't had sex, not yet, but Tanner showed his love in other ways. He held me close, kissed me, murmured terribly dirty things he wanted to see me do with Susannah. He protected me.

Defended me. I wouldn't even care if our relationship never progressed beyond that, because I had enough dick to get by, but you could never have enough love.

I cleared my throat. "If I could interrupt? The pasta needs to rest for two hours."

Merrick frowned at me, his eyes drifting to Jericho as if he had the answers. The man beside me just shrugged. "Uh, that's good, Omega?"

"Just enough time to bond as a Pack so we can keep you all forever."

Someone gasped, like they were in a centenarian book club and I'd just suggested they read a smutty alien romance.

"Now?" Susannah asked, but she didn't seem concerned.

I nodded. "No time like the present, and I don't want anyone to go another day without knowing how I feel about them." I looked at Jericho. "All of you."

Susannah sat up. "Well, I'm in. If you'll have us."

Murphy was shaking his head, but I didn't think he meant no. More like he couldn't believe what he was hearing. "Don't you want the gifts and the ceremony and all that?"

"You deserve all that and more," Merrick added.

I leaned forward, meeting both their eyes. It was hard with Alphas, typically a sign of aggression, but between Alphas and Omegas it was a sign that you trusted them with your safety. That you knew they'd care for you. That you loved them. "I want you all more than I want any ceremony. And I don't want to waste any more time," I purred.

As if the sound of my purr snapped them out of their trance, they all reacted. Murphy looked at Merrick. "The nest?"

The other Alpha nodded, and then he was there, kissing me. I pulled back with a gasp. "You made a nest and didn't show us?"

He kissed down my throat, scraping his teeth across the muscles in a way that made me shiver with need. "It isn't ready, but I wouldn't want to make you mine anywhere else." He danced me backwards until I was pressed up against the wall, then he leaned down, hoisting me over his shoulder. I let out a shout and smacked his tight ass, but he just emitted a low growl that made my dick harder as I hung on for the ride.

At the top of the stairs, he pushed open the double doors that led to the attic. With a flourish, he lowered me down onto a well-cushioned floor. I looked around and gasped.

Merrick grinned at my amazed expression. "We haven't installed the sex swing yet, but it just needs to be sanded and painted, so we'll get it done in the next week or so."

I blinked at the insanity of my life. Sex swings and nests this week, yet the week before had been executions and fear. I was going to get whiplash from the craziness of it all.

Susannah was laid down beside me, and she looked around with wide, awed eyes. "It's so beautiful." And it was. The pitched roof created the perfect level of comfort, like a large burrow. An arched window and two skylights that showed the stars provided light—or they would in the daylight—but the place was also lit up with strings of soft fairy lights. Omegas loved fairy lights.

Fluffy pillows and cushions filled up most of the room, along with this big, round, soft pod thing. In the corner, there were other weird-shaped pieces of foam, and I got the feeling they were used for sex positions too.

It was amazing.

I looked between my two Manix Alphas. "I love it."

Murphy grinned. "Jericho provided the lighting. Those little twinkle lights are fuelled by magic, sustained by sexual energy. We'll have to come and make love in your nest at least once a week."

I gave him a lopsided smirk. "Sounds like a hard-ship." I looked past him to Tanner and Jericho, the former leaning against the doorframe, looking relaxed, while the latter looked kind of nervous. "Come into my nest, mates."

Tanner grinned, stripping off his clothes as he teetered over the soft mattresses. This place was made for crawling sexily, not walking. Though I did enjoy watching his dick swing as he wobbled.

"Has anyone ever told you that you sound like a pirate when you call us mates?" he teased, kissing my cheeks softly.

I snorted, hugging him to my body. "Says the Australian. Pot meet kettle."

He kissed me, and I relished in the soft embrace. It was love, that was for sure. He climbed over me and kissed Susannah too. "I can't bond with you, not in the Manix sense, but just know that I fucking love the absolute shit out of you both, and I will love you until you're old and gray. I can't think of any Pack, any *people* I'd love more than you. Now, I'll let you get to the bitey part of tonight's entertainment. Always my favorite," he laughed with a flash of fangs.

He started to crawl away, but Susannah gripped his forearm. "If you weren't going to make love to me, then why did you get naked?" she asked.

He gave her a grin. "Obviously for the ambience."

I couldn't help the laugh that burst out of me. God, I loved him too. So damn much. I couldn't hear what Merrick whispered in his ear, but then it didn't really matter, because my Alpha was crawling toward me, his lips kissing the inside of my ankle, then up to my knee. He peeled me out of my clothes quickly, until I was naked and gasping.

"I swear I'll love and cherish you forever, Omega.

But first, I'm going to suck your cock." He made good on his words a moment later, wrapping his fist around my cock and squeezing it with the perfect amount of pressure to make me buck in his fist. I pushed between his lips, and he sucked me down like a champion. I swear, Merrick had no gag reflex.

Soon enough, I was getting close, my fingers scraping along his skull as I jerked helplessly. "Rick, I'm so close."

He pulled off my dick, and I whined, but not for long, because he was pushing back my thighs and lining himself up with my ass. "I love you," he whispered in my ear, pushing inside me in one hard stroke, my slick giving him all the lubrication he needed to get past the tight ring of muscle. We both moaned, and he rested his forehead on mine. "So. Fucking. Much."

He thrust in and out of me, his strokes powerful, until I was a mess. "Merrick, *please.*"

He grunted, and I could feel his knot swelling at my entrance. He kissed down my face, down my throat until his teeth grazed that sensitive curve of my neck. "Are you ready to be mine forever, Omega?"

"Yes, Alpha."

That was all it took, and he locked inside me, knot swelling. He sucked the skin of my neck hard, then bit down, the scent of my blood filling the air, until the sting was replaced by pleasure. He lapped at the wound, that tentative connection, and when he pulled back, I turned my head and bit him on the pec. Our bond snapped into place like it was always meant to be there, and I came and came, my whispers incoherent odes of love.

Merrick collapsed on my chest, rolling us to the side. "Feels so right," he grunted. "The way it was meant to be."

I kissed his chin. "We have forever now."

43

JERICHO

I stood beside Bowie and watched as the Alpha Manix took our Omegas as mates, one by one. I didn't even know if I could form a matebond, but I was going to fucking try. I'd spent an hour pulling my dick gently, now achingly hard, but only wanting to come in one place: with my Omegas.

The Alphas were exhausted, lying curled around our Omegas, all of them with small smiles on their faces. It was right, the four of them, and it felt like the way it was always supposed to be. Like a fait accompli.

But I was here to be a bump in fate's plan. Had been since my birth. The lost boys who were never meant to be.

As if she could feel my gaze on her, Susannah peeled open one eye. The smile she gave me was so sweet, I'd flip fate the finger to have her. "What are you doing, Jericho?"

"Just rubbing my dick, sweet thing."

She gave me a mock growl. "That's my job." She crooked a finger at me. "Come here."

It was impossible to resist her. I might not be a slave to the whims of the Alpha Manix in this town, but if this sassy little Omega so much as looked in my direction, I'd follow her to the very gates of Hell. I crawled onto the bed, and Merrick rolled out of the way, Quinn making a space for me between him and Susannah. Pressed between the two of them was like being immersed in a wave of pleasure.

Susannah gripped my chin. "Do you still want this, Jericho? Do you want to be bonded to Quinn and me, forever? There's no takebacks. No divorce. You're ours forever and we're yours."

I kissed her lips. "I've been yours since the moment I found you in the back of my truck. I'll never be anyone else's."

They both grinned at me. "Good. You have to accept the bond, and we do too. But first..." Susannah shifted her leg over my body until she was straddling my hips. "First, I'm going to make love to you, Jericho Wheeler. And then I'm going to mark you as mine."

This wasn't the first time I'd been inside Susannah, but it was no less nerve-wracking. I was worried I'd fuck it all up somehow, like I wouldn't be enough for the Omegas. I didn't have a knot. I was just me.

But as Susannah slid down on my cock, I realized it didn't matter if I had a knot. It didn't matter to these two amazing beings if we were the undead. Recluses or rejects. Literally without a body, they wanted and accepted us forever.

I gripped her hips and thrust up, and she moaned. Quinn's hand was there, pushing me to the side, shifting the angle and baring my back to him. His hand slid down my spine to squeeze my ass. "Can I?"

"Fuck yes," I growled, still rolling my hips, thrusting hard into Susannah. I had her spread wide, her knees in my hands as I watched my cock slide in and out of her tight pussy. God, I could die like this.

Someone tossed Quinn the lube, and he poured a generous amount on his hand, rubbing it between my ass cheeks. His finger rimmed my hole, and I grunted with pleasure. When he breached the tight ring of muscle, my grunt turned into a moan.

"We're going to fuck you together, and then we're going to bite you together. This is where you belong, Jericho. Between us. Beside us." He slid in another finger, scissoring them inside me, prepping me. I'd never actually had a guy fuck me before, but I wasn't opposed, obviously. This seemed like the right time to try.

I wasn't prepared for how good his finger stroking

inside my ass would feel. "Holy fucking hell," I groaned, as a full-body shudder of pleasure ripped through me. Fuck, I was going to have to hurry things up with Susannah. Otherwise, I was going to embarrass myself before I could finish her off. I leaned forward and sucked one of her nipples between my lips, the angle shifting my ass more toward Quinn. He seemed to take that as an invitation because he lined up his dick, pressing it against my hole.

He paused. "Still okay?" he asked, and I groaned.

"Yes." It sounded strangled, and he probably needed more reassurance, but I was struggling to formulate words right now. Instead, I pushed back on him, and he took me at my word. Sliding inside me, he moaned.

"Goddess, this feels so good. I have to top more often."

Murphy let out a dirty chuckle from the other side of the bed. "I volunteer as tribute."

The idea of this Omega fucking his Alpha was wild. But Murphy was soon forgotten as Quinn started to move, and I was done for. Biting her nipple softly and grinding hard against her clit, I felt Susannah coming around me and not a moment too soon. I groaned, my thrusts wild as I unloaded rope after rope of cum inside her. Her mouth came down over my left pec, and she bit down hard, marking me as hers. At the same time, Quinn bit the back of my neck, putting his own bondmark on my body. The feel of the connection spread through my body like warmth on a cold day, like an empty place inside me was being filled up.

Susannah gripped my jaw again, tilting her head to the side. "Bite me, Jericho. Make me yours too."

I obliged, biting down on the offered skin until I pierced her flesh. The bond snapped into place, a world of color when it had only been a sketch of black and white a minute ago. I wanted that with Quinn, and I wanted it right now.

An arm appeared, and I bit the soft, fleshy part of Quinn's relaxed forearm, making the Omega moan with pleasure, and maybe a little pain. He came inside me, filling me up like I was the Omega and he was the Alpha.

His bond sat next to Susannah's, and it was just perfection. It was like my world made sense now, and everything was how it was supposed to be. All the pain, all the hardship, all the loneliness led up to this moment.

"Argh! Jesus fucking Christ, you scared the shit out of me!" Tanner yelled, glaring at the person beside him.

No, not a person. Bowie. Bowie was there, more solid than I'd ever seen him. Could they all see him now too?

"Can you...?"

Susannah laughed. "Bowie!" She looked over her

shoulder at me. "It fucking worked. It worked!" She was crying, beckoning Bowie toward her. He lay down beside our Omega, his body pressed along hers. He was still slightly opaque, but Susannah could see his smile, see his blushes. See the way his eyes drifted down her body in awe.

"It worked, sweetheart. This Pack is a miracle."

I'd never agreed with my twin more. The Pack was a miracle, but more than that, these two Omegas were *everything.* I kissed them one more time, settling into the warmth of their bodies as Merrick and Murphy bracketed them, and then Tanner lay down with his head resting between Susannah's thighs. This felt so fucking right.

Pheromones filled the room, and my dick got hard again. "Better go and get your pasta ready, babe, because the yearning is coming."

Oh shit.

EPILOGUE

MURPHY

One year later

I stood behind Quinn, my hands under his protruding stomach, helping to take just a little of the pressure off his abdomen for a moment while we were all forced to stand in the crisp spring sunshine. My Omega sighed with momentary relief, and I smiled into his hair. I loved him so much. I loved our cubs already, even though they were still a few weeks away from making an appearance.

We'd definitely bitten off more than we could chew, but the week after we'd bonded had been one long sexfest when Quinn's yearning kicked off again, and honestly, I wasn't surprised that it had resulted in cubs. We'd been careful, but we'd all gotten a little carried away.

I looked over at Susannah, who was also pregnant. That had been a real surprise. Susannah's birth control had succumbed to the pressure of our new Pack life a few months later. It was a shock, but once we'd all come to terms with it, the preparations had begun. A bedroom was converted to a nursery, and we'd hand-made all the cribs. Though Quinn wanted the exact number of cubs to be a surprise, Tanner had pulled me aside and suggested I make a few more.

We were so screwed, but in the best possible way. What was the real surprise though was the fact that Susannah was carrying twins. They'd be born a few months later—which I was extremely grateful for— since the gestation period for male Omegas was a lot shorter.

I looked over at Jericho, who was holding her hand, Bowie on her other side, and I wondered if it was because the babies were going to be tiny hybrids. Twins definitely ran in that line.

Jericho and Bowie had taken the pregnancies the hardest, and given their history, the way their own mother—and Bowie himself—had died, I understood. But Tanner had stepped up, reassuring them every step of the way that the babies and the Omegas were okay. It helped that he had access to all the good imaging equipment, because Jericho and Bowie insisted that they be checked every three days.

I understood their trauma. We all did. We all had

our unhealed wounds, ones that would mend slowly or not at all. I'd protect the delicate, injured parts of their souls with my own. That's what being a Pack was about. I sent a reassuring zip to Jericho down the bond, and he looked over at me, his face a soft glow of happiness.

Finally, the event was starting. We all stood in the newly constructed, purpose-built Moonburst Legion headquarters. We'd bulldozed what must have once been the office building of the mining production here and dug down into the vein of moonstone in the earth, with the help of the witches. They'd mined out a lot of the stone, but the whole place buzzed with magic still.

There were offices for the administration staff, the Moonburst Legion Generals, and the other white-collar workers whose jobs it was to keep the town of around one thousand Manix and two dozen witches going.

Courtland walked onto the stage, his shoulders finally relaxed. We'd sorted out the two towns now, splitting the remaining Manix into two town Packs: the Moonburst and the Maxton Packs. Susannah's father had gone back to Maxton to rebuild, and be the Alpha General of that town until a new one could be elected, with a good portion of the old-school Manix going with him. Ancestral grounds had a lot of lure, especially to the old-timers who hadn't quite been able to adapt to the new situation we found ourselves in—or the new neighbors. But what remained was a real community of Manix, who didn't want to hide in the mountains anymore, and who wanted to live.

"Moonburst Pack. I'm happy to have everyone here today to finally lay down our foundation stone, not just for this building, but for our whole community. It has been a tough twelve months for the Manix, filled with changes and sadness, but this building, and those sitting inside it, are proof that we are a strong and courageous people. This stone will provide the starting block for a new era of Manix, one out of the shadows and taking up our place in the supernatural community. An era where we let old prejudices like fear and hate go, and move forward as changed people for the next generation. Where we live in harmony with other supernaturals, but especially with the Moonburst coven, who opened their homes and their hearts to us without question. We will always owe this coven a debt of gratitude which we can never repay.

"As you all know, we've held elections to decide on the new Legion Generals, and for the first time, it was open to all designations. As such, I'm pleased to announce the two Legion Generals for the Moonburst Pack. Miller St. Andrew and August Merrick."

Our tiny Pack hooted and hollered for Merrick as he took the stage, still a little shell-shocked that the town would nominate him and then vote him in as a Legion General. I wasn't surprised. I'd known and loved that man my entire life; I couldn't think of anyone else I'd rather have in charge of the welfare of the town and all the people inside it.

Miller St. Andrew was a surprise, though. He was a Beta who'd been in charge of investments under the old Alpha General. He was apparently a Robin Hood figure to the poorer Beta families in Maxton, skimming the profits from the old Alpha General's coffers and giving it to the families in need.

If there was any more proof needed that there'd been a divide between the two sides of Maxton, that was it. The Beta Manix—who made up such a huge amount of the town—had been there, struggling, and I'd missed it completely, caught up in my life as a good little Legion soldier.

Finally, the ceremony portion of events wound down, and I found a chair for my Omega. Quinn collapsed into it with a sigh. "I swear to the Goddess, they're doing backflips in there." Bowie appeared at his side, leaning down to kiss him on the head. The appearing from thin air thing had taken a little getting used to, but I was no longer surprised.

"Do you want me to talk to them?" he asked Quinn, his fingers scraping through Quinn's hair.

Our Omega tilted his head back and purred. "Yes please. Just tell them to stop kicking me in the bladder —that would be nice."

My poor Omegas. Bowie squatted down until he

was right in front of Quinn's bulging midsection. Placing two hands on either side of Quinn's stomach, he gave it a soft smile. "Come on, little ones. Take a nap so your papa can have a break and not pee himself in public."

I snorted a laugh, and Quinn gave Bowie a glare. Susannah waddled over, flopping onto the chair beside Quinn's. She looped her fingers through his, and he sighed again. "Are you doing the stomach-whispering thing? Because your children are giving me indigestion."

Jericho leaned over and kissed them both. "I'll go and get you something to eat." He moved away to where there were huge trestle tables of food at the back of the room in the Legion building designated for the town meetings.

Tanner came over and kissed both Quinn and Susannah, before moving off to talk to a family whose cub had broken his arm falling out of a tree. Most Manix had taken to the idea of Tanner being part of our Pack easily, though there'd been a little distrust and a little resistance to interspecies Packs. When the remaining Manix split, I was happy when the most vocal dissidents left. It would take time for change to occur back in Maxton, but at least those who wanted to escape had somewhere to go now.

I rubbed a hand in soft circles on Quinn's stomach. Everything had worked out for the best, though it was hard to comprehend the suffering we'd all had to endure to get to this ending, especially my Omegas. I'd have done anything to keep that from them. But they were the people they were now because of it. I loved them so much, my heart felt like it was going to explode out of my chest, like in one of those eighties horror movies Tanner sometimes made us watch.

Despite all that, our cubs would grow up in a community that would be better than the one their parents had endured. One without the injustices. One without the gross divide between the designations, where they could be whoever and whatever they wanted to be.

Sometimes, the results were worth the hardships. And this happiness? I'd do it all over again for just a taste of this.

Merrick finally made his way to us and kissed each of us on the cheek, cupping his hands to the two rounded bellies of our Omegas. He looked at me, his brows lowered over those ethereal blue eyes. "Everything okay?"

"Always, when I'm with my Pack."

ABOUT THE AUTHOR

Grace McGinty is eclectic. She has worked as a chocolatier, a librarian, a forensic accountant and finally a writer. Like her professional career, the genres she writes are also eclectic. She writes romance, reverse harem romance, fantasy, contemporary young adult and new adult books.

She lives in rural Australia with her crazy family, an entire menagerie of pets, and will one day be crushed by the giant piles of books that litter every room.

Head over to www.gracemcginty.com and join my mailing list for sneak previews into what she is working on and to stay up-to-date with new releases and giveaways!

ACKNOWLEDGMENTS

Cyclone Gabrielle hit land halfway through the editing of this book, devastating New Zealand (Aotearoa). My editor, Raewyn, was caught up in that devastation. And even through that, she thought of this book and you all, and for that I am eternally grateful. Raewyn, you're the best and you are irreplaceable!

But this stressful time really made me appreciate the wider indie community; the authors who reached out with options, the editors who put their hand up for last minute editing (thank you, Josie and Lin, I really appreciate it) and the readers who took time out of their days to speed beta read this book (Vera, Amy Jo, Caitlyn and Julia, you're all amazing!)

This book was a group effort, and wouldn't be on your kindles without the people mentioned above! So thank you!

INTERCONNECTED SERIES LIST AND SUGGESTED READING ORDER
ALL SERIES CAN BE READ STANDALONE

Hell's Redemption Trilogy

A deal between omnipotent forces puts a dying woman in the path of the Seven Deadly Sins. The only way she can save herself is to save them all.

Damnation MC Duet

What do you do when the Angels are the demons and the Four Horsemen are your protectors?

The Azar Nazemi Trilogy

Azar just wanted to hide from the supernatural world, helping humans with her djinn fire powers. However, when the two worlds collide in the deadliest way possible, only Azar can help save them all.

Dark River Days Series

What happens when you wake up Undead in a town filled with reformed Vampires and your murderer is a citizen who is willing to kill you permanently to keep you from talking?

Black Mountain Mates

Years ago, a knock at her window sent Isla running from her home and the boys she loved. But they never gave up on finding her, and when they do, they are never going to let her go again.

Eden Academy Series

Welcome to Eden. A safe haven for the preternatural, for the lost and for the hunted. An Academy where young supes can learn who they are and grow into their powers safely. Well... almost safely.

Shadow Bred Series

The Manix have been hiding for a century, and now they were nearly extinct. Their female Omegas were all but a myth, and even female Betas were rare. That is until an impossible scent on the wind gives the entire species hope.

NEWLY UNDEAD IN DARK RIVER

I woke to a rat scuttling across my chest, its tiny nose twitching as it paused to stare at me before scurrying off. Damn, I was hungry.

The fact that my initial reaction to a rat was hunger and not disgust was the first sign that something was very, very wrong. The second clue was that I was lying in a drainpipe in the middle of the night. Although it was hard to concentrate on anything but the hunger clawing at my stomach, I could hear the nocturnal animals shuffling around in the silence and smell the stale water that now soaked my clothes.

I tried to sit up and banged my head on the slimy concrete. Groaning, I rolled over and crawled my way out into the open. My body felt like I'd climbed Everest. Twice. I couldn't see my backpack anywhere. Panic began to fill my chest. Everything was in that pack. But it was pitch black, the moon not even visible behind the clouds. I became acutely aware that I was standing in the middle of the wilderness, at night, alone. I was a serial killer's wet dream right now.

I stared down the road, looking for the oncoming lights of a car or truck or something. Maybe I could hitch a ride into the nearest town. It was probably hitchhiking that had put me in this predicament to start with. My mom was going to be pissed that I'd been so irresponsible.

I felt dazed like I'd been tranquilized, but I patted down my clothing with sluggish movements. Nothing was torn, and all my clothes were still on. I didn't feel violated in any way. My brain was cloudy, and I tried to sift through the fog to remember why I was lying in a ditch, outside of...

I looked up at the road sign. *Welcome to Dark River.* Where the hell was Dark River?

Hunger tore at my belly again, a burning ache so painful I moaned into the darkness like a wounded animal. First, I needed to eat something. Maybe then I'd be able to work out what the hell was going on.

I stumbled down the side of the road, and I could see the muted glow of the town lights once I was over the small rise.

Electricity surged up through my chest, and the edges of my vision dimmed. The last thing I felt when my body buckled was the rough gravel scraping my cheek.

I snapped back to consciousness all at once, like when you dream you're falling. My head felt too full, and panic was beginning to mingle with the overwhelming hunger.

I was now in town, beneath the striped awning of Bert and Beatrice's Old Fashioned Diner. How the fuck did I get here? Everything was completely blank as if someone had plucked the memory from my brain like a bad apple. A clock tower sat in the middle of town, proclaiming it to be almost midnight.

I pushed through the glass door, and a little bell tinkled above my head. The place was filled to the brim, which was unusual seeing how it was basically the middle of the night.

Every set of eyes turned to look at me, and the old guy behind the counter dropped the soda glass he was drying, the smashing sound shooting pain into my skull. I must've really looked like hell. An elderly woman bustled out of the swinging doors, which probably led to the kitchen.

"What's goin' on out..." she trailed off when she saw me standing in the doorway. She nudged the old man out of the way.

"Lass, are you feelin' alright? Bertie, get the girl a drink. The house special," she said slowly, her accent a thick Scottish brogue. "Tilda, call the Sheriff, please. Get him down here, quick smart." She was rounding the counter now. "Here, Lass, take a seat."

I obediently took the stool she indicated. She had a no-nonsense, matronly tone that soothed my panicked nerves.

"I lost my money and my passport." My voice sounded so weak that I hardly recognized it as my own.

The elderly lady just patted my shoulder.

"Not to worry, Sweet. It's on the house."

I could hear the sound of Tilda murmuring quietly into the phone down the other end of the diner.

"Yes Sheriff, just stumbled in the door. Looking like death, if you know what I mean."

The old man, Bertie I guess, slid a cardboard milk-shake cup in front of me, complete with red and white straw. It smelled so good that I fell on it like a half-starved animal. When I'd sucked down the last drop, I looked up, embarrassed.

"Sorry. I was really hungry." Bertie just took away my empty cup and put a fresh one in front of me.

"Don't worry about it, Darlin'. Have another one." I was struggling to concentrate on her words. I found it hard to concentrate on anything but the milkshake in front of me.

The bell over the door tinkled, and everyone's eyes shifted in that direction again, even mine. A tall man in a chocolate brown uniform walked into the place, and everyone started talking at once. The cacophony after the complete absence of noise was hell on my eardrums. I pushed my palms over my ears to try and muffle some of the sounds.

"Quiet!" The guy was obviously the Sheriff, judging by the way that everyone's flapping jaws snapped shut with almost perfect synchronization. Silence again. The man strode over, his every movement elegant, to where I was sitting and gaping in his direction.

The man was hot. Like, spontaneous combustion, three-alarm, call in the National Guard, hot. He had sandy brown hair and deep green eyes. The uniform hugged his muscular body. He was so attractive it made my teeth hurt. Literally.

"Ma'am, my name is Sheriff Walker Walton. Do you need some help?" His deep voice was gentle, almost as if he didn't want to startle me.

"I don't know how I got here," I whispered. It was all a blank.

I'd been backpacking my way through Canada with my friends, but they had gone home last week, while I continued to travel up through Alberta by myself. I'd missed my bus to Yukon, so had decided to hitchhike my way through the last stretch to the border of British Columbia. After all, what's life without a little adventure? I'd been picked up by a family with teenage sons, but they'd let me off near Grande Prairie. I'd walked down the highway a bit more, and then poof, everything else was blank.

"Do you remember your name?" the Sheriff asked in the same soft voice.

"Mika McKellan. From Boston."

"That's good, Mika. I'd like you to come down to the station with me, so we can get this all sorted out. The town doctor will meet us there, just to check you over."

I nodded absently, and followed Sheriff Walton out of the diner, clutching my cardboard cup to my chest like a lifebuoy. He walked me over to the squad car, and let me sit in the passenger seat, instead of the back.

We drove in silence around the block, and I took the town in. It was actually quite beautiful. Not the cemetery stillness of most small towns after dark. Fairy lights were strung around the town square, and people milled about. The lights were on in all the shops, and small clumps of people were talking to each other on well-lit sidewalks.

"Is there a festival going on or something?" I asked Sheriff Walton.

"Or something," he replied, letting silence fill the car.

Within a minute, we'd pulled up in front of a skinny brick building. There were shiny bars on the windows, and a Police sign hanging over the front lawn.

Sheriff Walton moved around the front of the car and opened the passenger door. I heaved myself out of the seat. Moving wasn't as painful as it had been when I first woke up, but I still felt sluggish.

A plain woman with sparkling eyes met us at the front door. She looked me over and then sent a pointed expression to Sheriff Walton.

"Mika, this is Doctor Alice Sommer. I'm gonna get the Doc to check you for any signs of, uh, injury."

He held open the door of the station for me, and I gave him a polite smile.

"Let's go into the conference room. We need to have a chat after the Doc has looked you over. I'll be out here doing some paperwork."

He opened the door to an interrogation room. No windows, just a metal table with two chairs. Conference room, my ass.

"Thanks, Walker. I'll give you a shout when we're done," the doctor said softly.

The door closed with a click. The doctor sat a leather doctor's bag on the metal table. "Have a seat, Miss McKellan."

"Mika."

"Okay, Mika it is. But you have to call me Alice. Now, let me have a look at you." She shone one of those penlights in my eyes, and I let out a little squeal.

"Ouch."

"Hmm, light sensitivity. You have a little bruising

on your throat too." She got out a measuring instrument and measured the width of the bruise. "Anything else feel off to you?"

"Except for the starving feeling, the aching muscles, the weird blank spots and the passing out?" My sarcasm was obnoxious, but I couldn't seem to help it. "Other than all that, I'm as healthy as a horse."

The doctor clicked her tongue and wrote down the measurements. "Walker, can you get the cooler from the backseat of my car and come in here please?" She barely raised her voice, but the Sheriff must have heard because the front door of the station slammed.

"Don't worry, Mika. Your symptoms should lessen in a few days."

"Lessen?"

But the Sheriff was striding into the room, cooler in hand. Damn, he was fast.

"It's confirmed, Walker. Though let's face it, it was obvious to everyone as soon as she walked through the door of the diner. You can smell it just as well as I can."

The Sheriff ran a hand down his face and sighed. "I know, but I didn't want to believe it. I didn't want to think someone we know could have done this."

What the hell were they talking about? I sniffed my armpit stealthily. I didn't think I smelled that bad, considering I'd been sleeping in a ditch. My nose twitched. A tangy metallic smell was coming from the cooler. A smell that was so familiar, but I couldn't quite put my finger on what it was.

"You know, I'm still in the room. Do you think someone could take me out to the ditch and see if I can find my wallet and my backpack? Everything I have is in that pack."

"Ditch?"

"The one I woke up in. Under the welcome sign."

The Sheriff's eyebrows knitted together, and I could basically see the cogs turning. "Sure. We'll go take a look out there first thing tomorrow night."

"Why can't we go in the morning?"

Alice laid a hand on my arm and rested her butt on the table. She was looking down at me sympathetically. In my experience, that was never a good sign.

"Mika, we have something to tell you. This is going to sound outrageous and frightening, but I want you to know that we're here for you."

My heart started to race. Something in the back of my mind screamed that in a minute, nothing was ever going to be the same.

"Did my pet goldfish die? Are you two getting a divorce?" I deflected awkward situations with sarcasm. My therapist and I were working through it back home.

It was the Sheriff that answered. "No. Well, maybe, I don't know. I've never seen your pet goldfish, but I understand they die quite frequently." Walker ran his hand through his hair, and my hands itched to follow suit. "Look, Mika, I know this is going to sound strange, but it's our opinion that last night, you, well uh, you died."

I laughed. Maybe I'd stumbled into one of those reality TV shows. The producer was going to jump out any minute and make me sign a media release and a Non-Disclosure Agreement.

But the door never opened, and the two people opposite me never cracked a smile. "In case you guys didn't notice, I'm sitting right here, conversing with you. I haven't seen many dead people in my life, but I went to Great-Aunt Milly's funeral when I was twelve, and she didn't talk back to me from the coffin."

Alice gripped my hand. There was something off-putting about a doctor holding your hand like you were about to get really bad news.

"What Walker is trying to say, Mika"—they kept saying my name over and over like I'd suddenly forgotten it—"is that you are the undead. We believe you have been turned into a vampire. I should say, we *know* you've been turned into a vampire. It's the *how* that we don't understand yet."

I blinked. And then blinked again. They were actually serious. They thought I was a vampire. I'd definitely stumbled onto a TV set. It sounded like something the SyFy channel would come up with. But my heart was thudding, and I felt like I was going to throw up. It was like my body knew they weren't kidding, and it was just waiting for my mind to catch up.

"A vampire?"

Walker nodded sympathetically. "The hunger, the light sensitivity, even the blank spots, are all symptoms of the Turning."

"And you guys know this because..." No, this couldn't be right. My mind rebelled.

"Because we are vampires. The whole town is populated by vampires."

I stared at them dumbly, expecting something, I wasn't sure what. For them to turn into bats, or broodingly sparkle in the overhead fluorescent lights. But nothing happened. They just looked like ordinary people. Not overly pale, their eyes weren't glowing red, they didn't have crooked, needle-like teeth. Nothing.

Alice had mocha-colored skin and smooth blond hair that went all the way down her back. She wasn't extraordinarily attractive by any means. She was pleasant and professional; exactly what you'd want in a physician. Okay, so Walker was hot, but from what I remembered of the diner, it wasn't like I'd stepped onto the stage at Milan Fashion Week or anything out of the ordinary.

"Do you have any questions?" Walker asked. Uh, yeah, I had a few. Like could he pinch me so I would wake the hell up from this bad acid trip?

"So, I'm a vampire, and you're a vampire. And she's a vampire." He nodded. "Do you, I mean I, have fangs?"

Walker bared his teeth, and there, gleaming white against his pink lips, were two pointed fangs. They were actually quite sharp, and I wondered how he didn't cut his mouth up with them. I looked at Alice, and she too was baring her fangs, which weren't quite as long as Walker's and sat in her mouth with more ease. I eased my tongue over my own canines and found they'd elongated. I cut my tongue on them, and the blood dripped into my mouth.

Blood.

Hunger clawed at my stomach like a ravenous beast. Suddenly, I understood what the smell coming from the cooler was.

"Please." It was a half yell, half sob, as I dived for the cooler. Walker was around the table in a flash, his arms like iron bands around my body.

"Calm down. Alice is going to get you something to eat right now." As he said it, the Doc was getting a blood bag out of the cooler, like the ones you saw in hospitals. She unscrewed the cap on the tube and handed it to me.

Walker released me from his hold, and I closed off the part of my mind that was grossed out at the thought of drinking blood, and let my body take over. I sucked that baby like it was my first cocktail on spring break in Cabo. All that was missing was the little umbrella and the frat boys trying to convince me to come to a snow party.

All too soon, the bag was empty. "I want some more." My voice wasn't weak anymore, but it sounded slurred like I was drunk. Alice shook her head.

"With the two you had at the diner, and now this one, you've had enough. If you gorge yourself, you'll be vomiting for the rest of the night. I'll come see you tomorrow and we'll discuss how everything works. For the remainder of the night, you need to rest." She picked up the cooler and her doctor's bag. "Are you taking her to your place?" she asked Walker.

He nodded. "I'll find somewhere more permanent for her to live tomorrow." He walked the doctor out, leaving me alone in the windowless room.

The shock settled over me like a numbing cloak. My mind spun as I tried to process, well, everything. I placed my hand on my chest, and felt my heart slowly beating in there. Somehow, that made me feel better. I may have been dead, but my heart was still beating. The illogicality of that statement was something I'd deal with another day.

Walker was suddenly back, and his warm hand was on my shoulder. "There are a lot of things we have to discuss. We can do it here, or back at my place. I know that sounds almost creepy, but I promise you'll be safe." He shifted from foot to foot, almost uncomfortably. "You are new to this world, and I wouldn't feel right about leaving you on your own. There are rules, life or death rules that you need to know. But, if you'd like, we could do it somewhere a bit more comfortable."

I nodded absently, every warning my mother uttered about going home with strange men now defunct. What was the worst that could happen? I was already dead. Plus the guy was the Sheriff of a vampire town. If I couldn't trust him, who could a girl, err vampire, trust?

We hopped back into the squad car. I looked at the town through the window in a new light. I really studied the people, their inhuman grace, the fact that there were no children around. A guy stood on the pavement waiting to cross the road, and then magically was on the other side. I didn't even see him move in front of the car.

"Did that guy just teleport? Can we do that?" The thought was exciting. To just close my eyes and picture anywhere I wanted to be in the world, it would be amazing. Such freedom!

"I'm afraid not. He just moved really fast. As your vampirism settles into your body, you'll see him move as slow as a human. We can all move that quickly."

I was disappointed, though moving at super-speed was still pretty cool. "If we can move that fast, why the hell are we driving? Wouldn't we be wherever we are going almost instantly? Unless your house is in Alaska."

"Two reasons. Firstly, I didn't want to freak you out, plus you'll need a bit of time to get used to moving at that speed. Secondly, I enjoy the slower pace that a vehicle has to offer. Just because you can go at break-neck speed, doesn't mean you should." He sounded like my dad teaching me to drive. Thoughts of my parents made me feel homesick.

"I need to call my parents and tell them I'm okay. Sort of."

Walker looked uncomfortable. "If you want, but just wait until tomorrow. Give everything you'll learn tonight time to process first."

He pulled up in front of a cute little whitewashed cottage, with a wrap-around porch and a perfectly manicured hedge. I looked at the man in the driver's seat and then back at the house. I saw him as the log cabin type of guy, not the gingerbread vibe that this place had going on.

I followed Walker up to the front door. I don't know when I started to think of him as Walker instead of Sheriff Walton, but it was probably around my third dirty fantasy.

When we walked in, the space had a bit more of a masculine feel. Leather couches, a big-screen TV, and a scarred wooden coffee table occupied the living room. A large breakfast bar separated the living area from the kitchen, with three old diner stools tucked under the overhang.

Walker went over to the kitchen counter and poured two glasses of scotch into crystal tumblers.

"I can still drink?"

"Sure. You won't get drunk, but sometimes it's nice just to indulge in the nostalgia. You can also eat and go out in the sun. Though I wouldn't suggest going out in the daytime just yet. The increased sensitivity to light makes daylight extremely painful. It's something to work up to over time. Please, have a seat."

I walked over to the big scarred leather armchair. There was a burgundy throw rug over the arm, and I pulled it over my lap, even though I wasn't cold. The softness of the mohair was amazing. I could see the intricate pattern of the weave, the tiny flyaway fibers on each of the strands of wool. It was like my sight had become microscopic.

Walker handed me my drink and sat across from me, his elbows on his knees.

"I know this has been a lot to take in, but you have some serious decisions to make, Mika. This is a whole new world, with all new rules. Especially Dark River. We aren't your average community, as you know."

"Because everyone is the undead."

"Right, because we're all vampires. But it's not just that. Even within our own race, Dark River is rather unique. I'll explain the rules, and then it's up to you if you stay or you go. We can't keep you here against your will."

Well, that sounded ominous.

"Rule number one, there is absolutely no drinking from humans. Blood is delivered and distributed around the town by the Town Council, and no one goes hungry. The penalty is banishment from Dark River, forever."

That didn't sound so bad. It's not like I wanted to go around munching on people, giving them the hickeys from hell. I nodded for him to continue.

"Rule number two, you can never, ever, turn a human. The Town Council has decreed that the penalty for disobeying this rule is death. Because, in our eyes, turning a human is essentially murder." He looked at me imploringly. "This is what has happened to you, Mika. Someone has murdered you, and it's my job to find out who and bring them to justice. You are young, beautiful, and full of life. You should have had the opportunity to do everything you wanted to do. The opportunity to have children, get married, grow old with a loved one, live out in the light. You deserve retribution." His eyes lit up, and I don't mean sparkled with fervor, I mean literally started to glow.

"Uh, Walker, what's going on with your eyes?"

"Sorry. I didn't mean to freak you out. That sometimes happens when I get worked up. Plus I need to feed."

He walked over to the fridge and pulled out a bag of O positive. I knew it was O positive because there was a huge sticker on the side. He poured it into his tumbler on top of his Scotch. Ew.

He sat back down in front of me.

"Okay, the third rule is usually the most problematic for new vampires who want to join our community. You must cut all ties with your old life, both for our safety and the safety of the people from before. You wouldn't know this yet, but being around humans is..." —he let out a shaky sigh—"an overwhelming temptation. Especially when you are only just learning to control your new body."

I collapsed back on the couch. I'd have to cut ties with my family? Never see my mom smile again, or hear my dad tell a lame joke? Never watch my youngest brother graduate high school? Tears welled in my eyes as my death sunk in. My mind was in the denial stage of grief, apparently. I mean, I felt fine now that I'd drank that blood bag. Maybe I could go home and become a goth or something. I lived alone in my apartment, so I could keep the blood hidden.

"I know what you're thinking. Really, I do. But think about it. You will never look older than you do today. You will live hundreds, if not thousands of years. If you go home, you'll watch your parents die, and your siblings, and their children, and then their children's children. Trust me when I say that it is a soul-shattering experience to watch everyone you have ever loved wither and die." The level of pain in his eyes told me that he knew from experience.

I couldn't decide this now; I needed time to think it over.

"What if I choose to leave?"

Walker bit his lip, his fangs pressing into his full lower lip. "If you choose to leave, then you are subject to the rules of the Vampire Nation. No telling humans what you are, or revealing your nature in a way that could bring vampires as a whole into the limelight. If you feed on humans, you must do it in a way that they do not suspect your true nature. Which basically means that unless you have the ability to wipe memories—which some vampires do—you'll have to kill them and dispose of their bodies discreetly. If you break these rules, Enforcers will come, and you will die. Trust me when I say that Vampire Nation always finds out if you break the rules."

Well, okay then.

Walker's shaggy hair slipped over his eyes, and he combed it back with his fingers. The move made his shirt pull taut against his chest, and a completely different kind of hunger overtook me. The need to lean over and rip open his shirt was almost impossible to resist.

Walker's eyes met mine, and whatever he saw in them made him look nervous all of a sudden. He stood quickly and took a step away.

"Okay, I'll let you think it over. The guest room is the second door on the left, and the bathroom is right next door. Make yourself at home. If you need anything, just give me a yell." With that, Sheriff Walker Walton hot-footed it out of the room, faster than my eyes could follow.